# MONEY NEVER SLEEPS

Fancy Jones, bestselling crime writer, has discovered that someone is trying to kill her . . . When she is invited to lecture at a writers' conference in the Derbyshire Dales, she leaps at the chance to leave London and hopefully escape the threat of her assassin. But events turn sour when a body is found floating in a lake at the conference venue, and bizarre things start happening to Fancy. Suspicion falls on the other delegates — but has her stalker followed her . . . ?

# SPEC IAL ... TO READERS

## THE ULVERSCROFT FOUNDATION
### (registered UK charity number 264873)

w established in 1972 to provide funds for
rese , diagnosis and treatment of eye diseases.
 amples of major projects funded by
the Ulverscroft Foundation are:-

* Children's Eye Unit at Moorfields Eye
  pital, London
* Ulverscroft Children's Eye Unit at Great
  ond Street Hospital for Sick Children
* ding research into eye diseases and
  ment at the Department of Ophthalmology,
  ersity of Leicester
  Ulverscroft Vision Research Group,
  tute of Child Health
* operating theatres at the Western
  thalmic Hospital, London
* Chair of Ophthalmology at the Royal
  tralian College of Ophthalmologists

You help further the work of the Foundation
 naking a donation or leaving a legacy.
E contribution is gratefully received. If you
w like to help support the Foundation or
 e further information, please contact:

## T ULVERSCROFT FOUNDATION
### The Green, Bradgate Road, Anstey
### Leicester LE7 7FU, England
### Tel: (0116) 236 4325

### website: www.foundation.ulverscroft.com

Stella Whitelaw began her writing career as a cub reporter and rose to become the first female chief reporter in London. She writes short stories for national women's magazines and has won many competitions, including the Art of Writing, judged by Sheridan Morley, for the *London Magazine*. Stella was awarded an MBE in 2001 for services to journalism. She lives in Surrey.

You can visit her website at:
www.stellawhitelaw.co.uk

STELLA WHITELAW

---◆---

# MONEY NEVER SLEEPS

*Complete and Unabridged*

# ULVERSCROFT
*Leicester*

First published in Great Britain in 2013 by
Robert Hale Limited
London


First Large Print Edition
published 2013
by arrangement with
Robert Hale Limited
London

A catalogue record for this book is available
from the British Library.

ISBN 978–1–4448–1787–4

This book is printed on acid-free paper

STELLA WHITELAW

# MONEY NEVER SLEEPS

*Complete and Unabridged*

# ULVERSCROFT
*Leicester*

First published in Great Britain in 2013 by
Robert Hale Limited
London


First Large Print Edition
published 2013
by arrangement with
Robert Hale Limited
London

A catalogue record for this book is available
from the British Library.

ISBN 978–1–4448–1787–4

Published by
F. A. Thorpe (Publishing)
Anstey, Leicestershire

Set by Words & Graphics Ltd.
Anstey, Leicestershire
Printed and bound in Great Britain by
T. J. International Ltd., Padstow, Cornwall

This book is printed on acid-free paper

To all my good writing friends that I have met at different conferences over many years. Thank you for all the fun, the advice and, of course, the parties.

# Prologue

The idea for the Pink Pen Detective came to Fancy in a dream. She had been tossing themes about for her new book for days, more lightweight than the caber but just as unwieldy.

Then she had this dream about a pink pen, the content of which slipped away from her like mist swirling on a foggy morning.

She looked up 'pink' and 'pen' in her *Ten Thousand Dreams Explained* manual and discovered that to dream about a pen meant inspired writing, which was too good to be true. To dream about the colour pink was unrecorded. This was a little disturbing. Was she the first person to ever dream in pink?

Red meant vigour, vitality and power. White meant spiritual innocence and wisdom. Since Fancy didn't want to spend any more time on research about her dream, she decided the Pink Pen detective would combine all these attributes.

As she knew most of her readers thought her heroines were based on herself, it was necessary that the Pink Pen Detective should be as different as possible. Fancy made her

1

heroine short, fair, slightly overweight, with an allergy to cats and a passion for grand opera. This was the complete opposite to Fancy.

On duty the Pink Pen Detective would be addressed as 'ma'am' as befitted her rank. Off duty, as befitted being short, fair and vulnerable, she was usually addressed as 'Missus! Give us yer phone and yer bag!' This was before she punched them in the guts with a tightly gripped bunch of car keys.

# 1

'How much?' she asked.

'Four quid to a nice young lady like you,' said the stall-holder. His stall was piled high with reject and job-lot stationery. Envelopes, Post-it-notes, A4 copying paper, biros, erasers, cartridge ink, jiffy bags. The stock of some retail shop that had gone bankrupt in these uncertain times.

'That's a lot,' she said.

'There's a gross in that box,' he argued.

'But how do I know that they all work?'

He grunted, getting tired of the argument. He'd been up since six, was cold and tired. He thrust the rose-painted box at her. 'Try them,' he said.

It was in her genes. A doctor once told her that she had ink instead of blood in her veins. She still had time to hit that red carpet, to follow in J K Rowling's footsteps. She had already cast her books. Except she did not write about child wizards and dragons; she wrote about money and crime. People killing each other.

Fancy took out a handful of the pink pens and scribbled on a scrap of paper.

Four worked and two didn't. But she loved the pens. They were all a delicate shade of pink, like the inside of a shell. They made the standard biro look like something from a Mumbai slum.

'Three,' she said.

'Three fifty,' he said, seeing her weaken.

'Okay.' She found the money and put the lid back on the box. She reckoned she had enough pens to last the rest of her life, assuming she lived a good few more years. If the accidents stopped happening, that is. She put them out of her mind.

Fancy stood still to savour the moment. It was ten minutes past eight on a summer's morning with a clear blue sky, and only the vaguest errant cloud, somewhere very high. She was at a car boot sale. Rows of stalls with householders selling off their unwanted items on makeshift tables. Piles of outgrown children's clothes lay on the grass. Toys tumbled in boxes. Worn books were stacked in brutal piles. There were a few trade stalls selling soap, detergents, dog bones, plants, fruit and vegetables. She could not look at the bones. They were disgusting.

She came to rural car boot sales out of curiosity, mostly people-watching, gleaning ideas. Once she spotted one of her own books in a fifty pence box and offered to sign it for the astonished stallholder.

'If you say you wrote it, then I'd better read it,' said the woman, taking the book back. 'I could always sell it off next time. For a pound.'

Fancy had to smile. Books were disposable; so were pens. She used a lot of pens. She was a writer. And someone, out there, was trying to kill her.

* * *

Her writing name was Francine Burne Jones. Francine was a derivation of Frances. Her younger brother had never been able to pronounce the 'r' sound in her name. He got as far as Fancy, and gave up. Fancy never minded. She never minded anything. She was one of those easy-going people who never took offence. Life was too short.

Far too short, apparently. Her obsession with time had logged all the moments when the accidents happened. Yet some of them might not have happened, or were only about to happen and never did. How could she know what had not happened?

The first time had been in London, at Victoria Station, the Circle line on the Underground. It was the wrong time to travel. There had been a crush of people behind her, which surged forward as the train whistled into the station with a rush of hot air. Fancy had felt a distinct hard thrust in the middle of her back.

She staggered, then felt a sharp pull on her sleeve.

'Hold on, missus,' said a young student traveller, hauling her back. 'Don't be in such a hurry. There are others who want to get on.'

'It wasn't me. It was the crowd behind,' she said, trembling, as the automatic doors opened. The youth helped her board. She was shaking and white-faced, her feet not obeying her commands. The time was exactly 5.01 p.m.

'Are you all right?'

'I don't know. It felt like someone pushed me in the back.'

'No manners these days,' he grinned.

Then there had been the No. 11 bus incident. Fancy had been to Somerset House to check some facts in their archives. She was the last person to board the bus, waiting by the driver for the crowd to move down. A rucksack came flying through the air at speed. It nearly threw her off her feet and into the milling traffic of the Strand. She caught hold of the door rail. A fellow passenger grabbed her arm as her feet struggled for balance.

'Blimey,' he said. 'That was a close one. You

could have been killed. Where did that come from?' The rucksack was lying in the middle of the road, being crushed and smashed by vans, taxis and another red double-decker bus. It was 12.16 p.m. by the clock outside one of the stores.

Fancy was trembling. She didn't relish being crushed by the red double-decker trundling behind.

'Never saw it coming,' said Fancy, gripping his arm tightly. The wind was blowing through her high-pinned knot, the side wings of dark hair whipping across her face. She would get off at the next stop. She wanted to get off and run.

She disappeared into the crowds milling around in Villiers Street. She needed something to steady her nerves. A strong black coffee. She slid into a café and took a stool with her back to the wall. She didn't want to risk being pushed in the back or hit by another flying rucksack. She had two black coffees, back to back.

There was nowhere to run when someone threw a missile through her bedroom window and showered the bed with glass fragments. She awoke with shock. The night air and street lights lit the room in an eerie yellow. Fancy hardly dared to move. Shards of glass had pierced her pillow like miniature javelins.

The rose-patterned duvet was a sea of coloured glass. She moved gingerly, hoping there was nothing sharp on the floor.

Her slippers were tucked under the bed and had escaped the shower, so her bare feet had some protection as she switched on the bedside lamp and carefully stood up. A tinkle of glass fell around her like a chandelier disintegrating.

It said 2.46 brightly on her digital clock. The second figure clicked on relentlessly. She needed a cup of tea before she swept this lot up. No good calling the police. The perpetrator would be long gone, unless he was planning to break a lot more windows. There was no one outside. She could hear nothing, only a plaintive owl a long way away, probably delivering a letter to Harry Potter.

'Oh my God, what a mess,' she said, shaking.

Fancy pulled on a towelling robe and tied the sash tightly. Both back and front doors were firmly locked, bolted and chained. An old lady had owned the church lodge before her and had had every protection installed apart from a moat and a couple of guard dogs.

The attack might not have been directed at her personally, thought Fancy, trying to be rational as she switched on the electric kettle in the tiny tiled kitchen. It could have been directed at the building itself. Relics of religion got to some individuals. People were always amused by her address.

'And where do you live?' an interviewer would ask. Usually a Sunday magazine reporter who hadn't done his homework.

'I live in a church,' she'd reply.

'Are you a nun, then?'

'It's part of a converted Victorian church. What's left of the original church is only a very small section. They started to demolish the building after it had been empty and derelict for years. A developer came along and turned what was left into two lodges. I have the smaller one. Just room to swing a computer.'

Fancy had rescued two pews, which were now set alongside two walls in the sitting room. The plan had been to arrange throw cushions and sit on the pews. But gradually books took over and rejected manuscripts and current work. Piles of unread magazines leaned against the end armrests. The cushions ended up on the floor.

Her desk faced the window, one of the original church windows. The lower half had been replaced with clear glass but the top was a cacophony of angels, blowing long-stemmed trumpets. Fancy loved the angels with their flowing hair and feathery wings. She hoped they were looking after her.

If she looked long enough, she always imagined, one of them would wink. But they never did. At least, not when she was looking.

So it was not unexpected if some lout, staggering home after seven pints washed down with vodka and lime, took offence at the religious relic standing off the street. There was a low brick perimeter wall there that anyone could leap over.

Her bedroom also had a narrow church window. Some haloed saint tending lambs and little children who gazed up at him in adoration. The colours were vibrant when it caught the sun. It was shattered now.

Fancy spent the rest of the night curled up on her squashy sofa with a blanket, having decided to clear up in the morning before starting work. She was dismayed to find not a stone or a brick, but a huge lump of concrete on the bedroom floor. Head-crunching size. Injury size. She might have had more than a nasty headache.

She sat in her kitchen, thinking about the three accidents. Not exactly accidents because she had not been hurt, only frightened. They were happenings, really. She wondered if she ought to tell someone. Her publisher would be amused.

'It's your imagination,' he'd say. 'You're thinking up another plot.'

Her kitchen was small but modern. The fitments were teak, space-saving, not an inch wasted. She even had corner cupboards with swinging shelves. There was no colour scheme. Nowhere to paint. The floor was black and white tiles, vaguely ecclesiastical. She always made sure there was a pot of some flowering plant on the worktop. She ought to grow herbs. Parsley would be useful.

But a lump of concrete was a lump of concrete. She knew she should report the incident but she was running out of time. By late afternoon she had to be in Derbyshire at the Northcote Writers' Conference. It was a tedious four-hour drive up the M1 after leaving the M25. Not a pleasant journey if the motorway was crowded with huge container lorries or had ground to a standstill because some car had overheated in the middle lane and caused a solid tailback.

She was booked as an evening guest speaker at the conference and to run the crime-writing course, which was four one-hour lectures spread over four days. Her lecture notes and PowerPoint presentation were all ready. It was the first time she had run such a course and Fancy was nervous and apprehensive. She wondered if she had enough material or if the delegates would be interested and amused. She wanted it to be fun as well as informative.

Boredom would have them walking out in droves, yawning and ready to put caustic comments in their feedback forms. She guessed that Northcote would have a popular bar and the website featured spacious, flower-filled gardens in which to chat and drink. They would both be a magnet to the writers.

Clothes were the last thing on her mind. She threw in a variety of items, not knowing what was expected. Posh or casual? It might be cold and wet or hot and humid. She had to be prepared for any Derbyshire weather. She had a feeling there would be parties. Writers in groups always held parties. They were a gregarious lot, chatting and laughing. She hoped they would make her welcome. Shy was Fancy's middle name. Not really. Her middle name was Burne.

What shoes? Black pumps for day; plain slip-ons; gold for evening. And trainers for walking. At least she was organized in the shoe department.

And the pink pens. She took a good supply of pink pens. She knew from experience that her pink pens melted away. Writers collected them as souvenirs, thinking that perhaps her publishing success would brush off on them if they used one of her pink pens. Perhaps it did.

Fancy wrote crime, both fiction and non-fiction. She also edited a mystery magazine called *Macabre Mysteries* whose circulation was thriving. It was her baby. The logo was a double M made of entwined snakes. Pretty creepy. Fancy had not dared to argue with the artist who designed the logo and the front page.

*MM* began as a quarterly, became bi-monthly and now it was monthly. Waterstones, W H Smith and railway stations all stocked it. The problem was getting enough material of the high quality that Fancy insisted on. She was encouraging retired police officers to write articles about cold cases from the past.

'I want real stories,' she told them through their own house magazine. 'People want to read about real people, real crimes, real police work.'

Fancy paid above the going rate. She was not one of those editors who tried to get away with paying as little as possible. Writers had to eat, pay vets' bills, buy petrol. She was the one who went short, drove a vintage 1970 Vanden Plas car that was held together with rust and duct tape, bought the best vintage clothes from charity shops. She had a sharp eye for Jacques Vert shirts. They had style.

There was time to report the incident at the local police station. The building was still of the old-style, which was miraculous in these days of closures.

'Yes, miss? Can I help you?' asked the duty sergeant from behind a high desk. The colour scheme was the usual cream and glutinous dark green. There were a few uncomfortable-looking, hard grey metal chairs pushed against the walls.

'Someone threw a missile through my bedroom window last night and showered me with glass,' said Fancy.

'Did you see who it was, miss?'

'No, I couldn't. They ran off. It was dark.'

'You should have phoned us. Dialled 999.'

'What could you do? He would have been miles away before you arrived.'

'Our officers know what to look for.'

'DNA? Fingerprints? Footprints?'

'What time was this, miss?'

'02.46 exactly.'

'You know the time exactly?'

'I always know the time exactly. It's an unfortunate habit.'

'And what was the missile?' The desk sergeant was writing furiously in the incident book. 'It's evidence.'

Fancy tried to lift a heavy plastic bag onto the counter. 'Here's your evidence. A lump of concrete wrapped in bubble-wrap. Not touched by my human hand. It's all yours. I'm off now to face the motorway.'

The officer looked at his computer screen and switched to the traffic channel. 'Big hold-up on the M1, miss. Two-mile tailback. Take a sandwich.'

'Thanks for the tip.'

'And get that window boarded up. Lot of opportunists around.'

'I have.'

Fancy did not have time to buy a sandwich. There were a couple of bottles of water in the car and a packet of digestive biscuits. They were for an emergency. She hoped the tailback would not turn into an emergency. She had enough on her mind. If she let the conference down, her publishing name would be mud.

★　★　★

Northcote was set in glorious Derbyshire countryside, its vast expanse of green hills dotted with copses and dense forest. Spectacular limestone gorges cutting through history. The residential conference centre was situated in the heart of the Dales.

15

It had once been the sprawling home of a prosperous Victorian coalmine owner, a man with a big, growing family. So in 1860, he built a house of local stone and red brick, big enough for them all and the required army of servants. It was a house with generous proportions, high ceilings and massive fireplaces, a gracious vinery, and a veranda that faced the sculptured gardens and croquet lawn.

The Victorian house had been converted in the late forties, with foresight, into a conference centre. The stables were turned into garages and above them were single rooms. The present management had built on a new dining room, new conference hall and a confusing number of small meeting rooms.

There was also a stone-flagged quadrangle surrounded by bedrooms and two floors of bedrooms above. It was both a suntrap and a snow trap. The family's children had played there in all weathers, their forbidding nanny keeping a stern eye on them. There was even the ghost of a woman in blue who stood at the foot of the main stairs in a cold spot but no one talked about her, not even the domestic staff, many of whom had seen her as they hurried past on some errand.

★ ★ ★

Fancy turned into the tree-lined drive and drove carefully over the speed bumps. Her car was fragile; so was her back. She was exhausted by the long drive. She had turned off the M1 at junction twenty-eight and had then got lost. None of the road signs said what she was looking for. Her brain was not working. She did not know where to go, where she would sleep, where her lectures would be held. And she needed the bathroom.

The drive turned into a circular, tree-fringed area and ahead was a modern glass foyer, built onto the front entrance of the old house. It looked strange, out of keeping with the creeper-covered walls and large bay windows.

A thin woman was hovering in reception, a woman wearing layers of flowing clothes, shades of mauve and pink and primrose, her white hair pinned up with bamboo sticks. She floated rather than walked. But when she heard the car arriving, she turned and her smile of welcome was warm and genuine.

'Hello, Miss Jones? I'm Melody Marchant, your conference hostess.'

Fancy nearly said *Shall I fasten my seat belt?* But she bit her tongue in time. She had a reputation for saying the wrong thing. She put on a sort of returning smile, too tired for anything better.

'Hello,' she said. 'What a pretty name. Middle shelf, lower eye level.'

Melody looked blank, blinking very bright blue eyes. Her lashes were spiked with mascara. She had once been very pretty, but time had added wrinkles and taken away the bloom. But she still had an aura of past beauty.

'Your spot on the bookshelves in Waterstones. When your book is published.'

'Oh, goodness, you mean when I get published. I write children's books, mostly about foxes and hedgehogs. My mother sang in a pop group called Melody once. That's how I got my writing name. They had one hit and then were never heard of again. But I use her name because children can remember it.'

'Lovely story.'

'Did you have a good journey?'

'Reasonable,' said Fancy. 'No accidents. No one threw anything off a bridge at me. No lumps of concrete.'

'I'll show you to your room. Don't worry about getting lost. You'll soon find your way about.'

Melody took some of Fancy's bags and set off at a fast trot, upstairs, along narrow corridors, right turns, left turns, her many chiffon scarves floating behind her. This was obviously part of the original old house. She flung open one of the doors. Light flooded into the corridor, illuminating the walls.

Fancy blinked. The room was vast. It had six single beds in it. A big bay window was draped with brocade curtains and ties. It was a route march to the dressing table on the other side of the room. The huge mahogany wardrobe might be the secret path to Narnia if she could open the heavy doors.

'We thought you might like some space.'

'Am I sharing?'

'Heavens, no. This is all yours. You can sleep in a different bed every night if you like.' Melody laughed.

'Like Goldilocks. Now, if you don't mind, I need the bathroom.'

'Ah,' Melody drew a deep breath. 'Slight problem now. These original bedrooms are not en suite. But there's an excellent bathroom close at hand — bath, shower, very luxurious. You would be sharing that with one other speaker.'

'I don't have a robe,' said Fancy, itemizing her hurried packing. She slept in a teddy bear T-shirt or nightshirt, according to current level of shrinkage. *Sweet Dreams* was printed under the teddy. The other speaker might get the wrong idea. 'Can I have a different room?

This is too big for me. I'd be lost in it.'

And she didn't like it. There was a feeling from the past of agonizing childbirth, pain, death. She was already being difficult. She would get a reputation. They would not invite her back.

'Let me see if there's a vacancy in Lakeside, with a view of the lake. I don't think it's quite full yet. It's very modern. I'll be back in a moment.'

Melody floated off like an errant butterfly, while Fancy took advantage of the close-at-hand, luxurious shared bathroom. It was huge. Another converted bedroom. No towels. She waved her hands in the air. A towel was folded on one of the six beds with token wrapped soap but she dared not use it.

She looked out of the window. The lawn was a hive of bustling people, hugging and kissing each other with shrieks of joy. Old friends meeting from previous years. Others stood about, solitary, newcomers wearing white badges.

Melody hurried back. 'There's a vacant room on the third floor if you don't mind all the stairs. The girls are getting it ready for you. How about a cup of tea first and I can show you around, introduce you to people.'

Tea, flapjacks and ginger sponge cake were being served from trolleys on the glassed-in veranda. Cascades of noise rose from the exuberant crowd. Fancy took a cup of tea and sat with it in the garden. The flower beds were a riot of colour. The gardeners were obviously men who loved their work. It was a joy to look at after the bleak motorway. There was no garden to her church home, only rubble and weeds.

Melody had rushed off to hostess another speaker who had arrived and required her attention. Fancy liked the idea of a room on the third floor. No one could chuck a lump of concrete to that height.

She looked at the printed programme that Melody had given her to study. There were five non-stop specialist courses, lots of two-part courses and even more one-off workshops. Meals, book room, dancing, quizzes and writing time were slotted in with breathtaking persistence. She felt tired just reading the programme.

And every evening there was a guest speaker. Someone famous or who had something to say. She recognized several names, including her own. She wondered now if she had anything new to say in the face of all this talent.

There were five specialist courses. Callum McKay was running the novel course. Fancy had read several of his big Glaswegian sagas.

He wrote under a woman's name for some reason. Brad Hunt was running non-fiction. Maria Lister was talking about children's books and Phoebe Marr was the poetry guru. Fancy knew none of these other names. Her own course, crime, was given equal status.

The chairman of the conference was Fergus Nelson, a semi-retired publisher with a good reputation. Jessie Whytely was the conference secretary and Richard Gerard the treasurer. She knew nothing about either of them or their writing credentials. Then there was a string of committee members.

Fancy gave up. She was never good at remembering names. She had to meet the people first, then she could pin a name to a face.

Suddenly a hand clamped onto her shoulder. The shock tipped her cup and the spilt tea sprayed her knees. The bright sun and sky were blocked out by a tall figure. She shook off the hand, fear clamping her heart, and tried to struggle to her feet.

'Sorry, Miss Jones. It is Miss Jones, isn't it? The crime writer? I didn't mean to surprise you. I thought you saw me coming.'

He was over six feet tall, lean and muscular, dark hair tinged with grey and combed forward like a Roman senator, brown eyes concerned behind gold-rimmed glasses.

He was wearing a crisp navy shirt tucked into jeans. His badge was yellow, which meant he had been to the conference before, but Fancy couldn't read the small print of his name.

'Do I know you?' she asked, dabbing her knees, fruitlessly.

He produced a clean handkerchief and offered it to her. 'Try this.'

'Thanks.'

'I'm Jed. John Edwards. I've been emailing you for several weeks about a cold case I wrote about in your *Macabre Mysteries* magazine. It's a diabolical case and needs solving.'

'Jed? John Edwards?' She sat down, still quivering. It rang a faint bell.

'Schoolboy slang. J Edwards combined and shortened. Complicated email address because of former police connection.' Jed Edwards sat down on the bench beside her and took the cup from her hand. 'I'll get you another cup.'

'Former police connection? You never said that in your emails.'

'Detective chief superintendent, retired. Or rather, semi-retired, not quite on the slag heap yet.' His eyes weren't smiling now.

Fancy looked at Jed Edwards with more interest. 'That's pretty high up,' she said. 'But you look too young to be retired.'

He moved his right hand slowly but it went almost nowhere, flapped around. 'Useless,' he said. 'Can't do anything with it. Can't do the required two-handed gun hold. A couple of bullets shattered the elbow. Permanent damage. And there was bleeding into a muscle, which has led to a stiff arm.'

Fancy was shocked. One never heard of the injuries sustained in the course of duty. Newspapers preferred heroics or grisly deaths.

'I'm sorry, how awful. Can't you move it at all?'

'It has a variable degree of function.'

'Perhaps we could talk about *Macabre Mysteries* some other time.'

'Thanks but I need more than five minutes. The case is a weird one.'

Fancy tried not to look at him. Even for a one-armed, semi-retired police officer, he was very good-looking in an austere way. But she was not interested in men. No way, no more. She would never go through that again.

'How did you know I would be here?'

'It's advertised on the conference website. Not a bad photo of you. I'd know you anywhere.'

Jed Edwards wondered why Fancy Jones suddenly looked scared. It was something to do with mentioning the website and the photo. She didn't like it. He was good at reading people. He had been doing it all his working life.

Fancy shuddered. The website, of course. Anyone could know where she was this week. Whoever threw the concrete, the rucksack, made the thrust in her back. They could find out where she was, follow her. If they were linked. Perhaps she was not even safe here. They might even be here already.

Perhaps if she hid on the high moors of Kinder Scout and Bleaklow, she would be safe. The dry stone walls would protect her from the winds at first, but when she reached the treeless southern slopes, she would be at the mercy of the killing air.

Unless she found a cave. Already her writer's mind was conceiving a plot. She might never use it but she tucked it away in her mental filing cabinet for a rainy day.

# 2

## Saturday Evening

Room 425 Lakeside was ideal. It was high up on the third floor with a view of a wide path below and the single-storey Orchard Room, built on a grassy knoll opposite. Fancy hoped its name didn't imply the destruction of an orchard. Perhaps the ripe apples and plums had rolled down the hill and got trodden on.

The room had a double bed covered in a bluey-green Jacobean patterned quilt that matched the curtains. A polished wood unit along one entire wall acted as a combined desk, dressing table and tea-making area. It had mirrors and lamps above. The wardrobe was an open hanging rail with shelves below. It saved on doors.

Fancy liked the fact that the key tag went into a slot on the wall and the lights wouldn't come on without that activation. It reassured her that she would not leave the room without her key.

The small white bathroom was spotless and compact. The shower had simple controls. She hated showers where she had to read the instructions with her glasses on before switching on the water. Especially if she forgot her glasses.

She began to relax in the safety of the room, hanging up her clothes and putting them in drawers. Everything she'd brought was black or white, or black and white. It was her conference wardrobe. She did not have to think. She took the same clothes everywhere. All her underwear was black or white. The only colour in her packing was the pink teddy bear nightshirt, and a pink leather belt, a blue scarf, a scarlet pashmina and a couple of silk flowers. She had no idea why she had packed the flowers. Mental aberration. She wasn't going Spanish dancing.

At home, when she was working, she put on the first clothes that came to hand. Doorstep salesmen on a cold call often thought she was the cleaner.

She thought about Jed Edwards. She did not trust him, although she wasn't sure why. She did not trust anyone who approached her openly about a cold case story. She did not want to talk about her magazine or cold cases. Yet, he seemed a pleasant man and she was sorry about his arm. He may have been earmarked for promotion, for greater things, before that bullet ploughed into his elbow. Perhaps chief constable next with a salary, smart uniform and pension to match.

Fancy stretched out on the bed and opened the programme again, wondering where she appeared in the complicated grid of events and destinations. She was supposed to be at the chairman's reception now, tutors meeting white-badgers. It would look as if she didn't care or was snooty if she didn't turn up.

She changed quickly into tailored black trousers and a classic black and white silk blouse. She splashed her face and quickly renewed her eye make-up, pulling her hair back into a casual topknot, fingering forward the side wings. A squirt of *Dior Tender Passion* and she was ready. She almost forgot her key and the tutor name badge. The badge hung from a royal blue lanyard and spoilt her colour scheme. She would have to change that. Fast.

There was a lift. A tired, recorded male voice intoned *Doors opening* and then *Doors closing* as if these actions were invisible. Fancy hurried down the path, map-reading at the same time. The reception was being held in another far-flung area. The babble of voices told her she was going in the right direction.

'Miss Jones? Francine Jones? You found us then. Come along in and meet everyone. What would you like to drink? You must be gasping. I'm Jessie, by the way. I know a short cut to the bar.'

Fancy had to squint to read the name badge. It would be rude to peer closely at the woman's bosom. This was Jessie Whytely, the conference secretary. She was a bustling young woman, faintly harassed, badly cut blonde hair in wild disarray, long gold earrings bashing her rouged cheeks. She was wearing purple. Everything was purple. Shirt, trousers, shoes, bangles. Even her nail varnish was purple.

The choice was house red or house white, or should it be called conference red or conference white? The glasses were small, only a few degrees larger than a thimble, she thought. Fancy smiled politely and was introduced to a dozen eager white badgers who flocked around, all wanting to know how to write the next best-selling crime book. Fancy wondered if it was a good idea, telling them how to do it. They might be taking the bread and butter out of her own mouth. And publishing was a cut-throat market. Getting worse by the day.

'There's a big market for crime these days,' she said. 'Readers love it. Yes, do come along to my course. I'll help you all I can. You can ask me anything.'

She trawled in a few more delegates to her

course; she didn't want an empty room. Nothing worse than talking to a spattering of faces, a handful of hopefuls, no vibrant feedback or interaction.

'Let me get you another drink.' It was Jed Edwards. He was wearing the same clothes but had added a blue tie for decorum.

'Thank you,' said Fancy. 'That one went down rather fast.'

'As they do,' he said, weaving his way through the crowd at the drinks table. He returned, managing to hold two drinks in one hand. Fancy took hers before there was another spillage. 'Don't look so worried,' he said. 'I'm not a gatecrasher. I'm doing a two-parter on police procedure. Both talks on the same day. A marathon.'

'I might come to that,' said Fancy, knowing her ignorance about police procedure. She was constantly ringing up the press office at Scotland Yard.

'You'd be welcome. But don't ask me anything too tricky,' he said, echoing her words with a wicked grin. He had good teeth. No nicotine stains. 'You seem a bit uptight about something. Is it this place? Northcote can be overwhelming. All these people, when you are used to being on your own.'

'No, no, Northcote is fine and everyone is being kind and helpful. It's been a strange week in London, that's all.'

He nodded as if he understood when he didn't. 'We all get strange weeks. We'd better circulate among the white-badgers. That's what we are here for. It's why we get a free drink. Or two.'

'How did you get that tie on with your hand . . . ?' There. She'd asked it when she had vowed to herself that she wouldn't. She was too nosey.

'My ties are already tied for me. I loop it over my head and tighten up the knot. Unless, of course, I can find a nice young woman who's good at ties.'

'I'm sure there are plenty around,' she murmured, moving away.

Fancy found she was expected to sit at the committee table for all meals. They had a round table reserved in a far corner of the dining room. Everyone else sat nine-apiece at rectangular tables. It all looked friendly in a big airy room, one side all windows looking out onto the garden. It was divided into areas with arches and low shelves for bags and books. The walls were cream, the tablecloths white, the napkins maroon. The carnation sprigs on the tables were fresh flowers.

'Speakers always sit with the committee,' said Jessie. 'It's a tradition.'

The main course came from the kitchen in

big pie dishes and someone at each table drew the short straw and had to serve out the food. Tonight it was steak pie with peas and parsnips and new potatoes. It was a strange choice of menu for a Saturday night supper but Fancy was hungry and ate the lot. When had she last eaten proper food? But she was not hungry enough for the school-style sherryless trifle with hundreds and thousands on top and opted for a banana from the nearby fruit bowl. The banana was stone cold, like marble, straight from a refrigerator.

There was a thermos of coffee on every table and again it was serve yourself.

'There are packets of tea over by the urn,' said Jessie. 'Lots of herbal teas. Green tea is supposed to be good for you. For the heart.'

'Thank you,' said Fancy faintly. She was already feeling exhausted from the non-stop talking at the table. She had been eating alone for so long. She wasn't used to so much conversation. Words were flung in all directions.

'How did you get your name, Fancy?' asked Richard Gerard. He was an accountant by trade, so perfect for the post of Treasurer. He was trying to write sitcoms for television, so far without global success. But he had sold to regional television. 'It's very unusual.'

'It's another spelling of Frances, though

really my mother named me after Francis of Sales.'

'Who's that?'

'He's the patron saint of writers.' That usually stunned everyone. 'My mother was a novelist. She wrote lots of Mills & Boon romances. It was non-stop hard work, producing at least three novels a year to a deadline. I used to proofread the manuscripts for her. And she paid me. That was my first lesson in writing.'

'And romance.' Everyone laughed.

'And making money.'

'Both useful.'

Fancy nodded. 'I learned a lot from my mother's books. The fiery passion of romance but unfortunately for my personal education, she was a dot-dot-dot writer. The romance always stopped at the bedroom door.'

There was more laughter. Fancy felt she had passed some sort of test. Tonight's guest speaker was timed for 8.30 p.m. but everyone had to be in the conference hall ten minutes early for announcements by the vice chairman. It was all rules and regulations. Fancy felt she was back at school.

The school had had a stream of famous speakers in the past: P D James, Ruth Rendell, Peter Lovesey, Simon Brett, Susan Moody, Gervase Phinn, Leslie Thomas, Gyles

Brandreth. Her turn later this week. Fancy had a lot to live up to.

The conference hall was a cavernous building, with a double-height ceiling like an aircraft hangar with rows of fluorescent lights in the gabled roof. The stage and lectern were along one side in the middle of a wall, so the audience sat in a semi-circle facing the speaker. It was far nicer than everyone sitting in strict rows facing the far end, view restricted and not being able to hear properly at the back.

She was steered to a seat in the left-hand corner. 'committee and guest speakers always sit here,' she was told. Miss Goody-Two-Shoes did as she was told, but she damned well wasn't going to obey the rules tomorrow.

The speaker, no names, even though he was a household name, was full of himself and how famous and clever he was, and quickly became boring. The audience laughed at his jokes and asked lots of questions at the end, but Fancy had heard them all before. She could feel herself nodding off.

Then she found herself daydreaming about her current book, a new scene coming alive into her head, and she desperately wanted to write it down.

Pink pen out and a slim notebook and she was busy writing. The rest of the talk passed happily over her head, and she only came to when the clapping began and the speaker was escorted out to rapturous applause.

'Wasn't he good?' said Jessie. 'Did you enjoy that?'

'Yes. Terrific,' she said, closing her notebook.

It was very dark outside now, with a cool breeze stirring the trees. The paths were lit with knee-high lamps but there were still big patches of dark and shadows. She suddenly felt very isolated. She was with three hundred people and yet she was totally alone. It was time to run for that lift and its reassuring recorded voice and lock herself into room 425. She would be safe there.

'Come and join us in the bar. What would you like to drink? Unless you'd rather go and listen to 'What Are You Doing Now?' It starts in twenty minutes.' It was Fergus, the chairman. He looked like a publisher; bushy eyebrows, bright eyes. He talked like a publisher.

'Thank you,' she said, for the hundredth time that day. 'A red wine, please.'

He brought her a Fairtrade Merlot in a standard bar wine glass. That was a relief — no more thimbles. It was pleasant talking but she was getting a really uneasy feeling for no good reason. The bar area was tucked in behind the glassed-in veranda but she still felt visible and vulnerable. It was a long walk to Lakeside. She wondered how she was going to get there on her own without making a fuss.

The smokers were segregated and had to smoke outside in a gazebo. She caught a whiff of an unusual cigarette, not one she recognized. The faces and bodies in the gazebo were vague and shapeless, coughing and laughing, new cigarettes being lit with sparks of glowing red. They drew on them like tiny red worms.

Fancy leaned back so that she could not be seen clearly. She wanted to be swallowed by the shadows. The wine was shaking in her hand. She needed a good night's sleep before tomorrow's lecture and she had to look over her notes. A group was walking back to the conference hall in the dark. As the hall was halfway to Lakeside, it seemed the right time to move.

'Sorry,' she said, standing up. 'That long drive is catching up on me. So, if you'll excuse me. Goodnight, everyone.'

There was a chorus of goodnights and good wishes.

She caught up with the group walking to the next event, absorbed into their numbers as a protection. She slid into the back of the hall, hoping no one would join her. It was easy to understand the formula. Each person had three minutes to talk about what they were doing now. The organizer had a household pinger to time them.

'Next one, please,' she called out. 'Three minutes only. And I warn you, I shall stop you in mid-sentence.'

It was interesting. It reminded Fancy of her own early days, working far into the night, the constant rejections, the wild ideas she had tried out. She had once been like these young writers. And the elderly writers, still trying, ambition always alive and bright despite the greying hair. For a while, she was lost in their stories, their hopes, their dreams. It was all so familiar.

'Would you like to have a go?' said the organizer, sliding up to Fancy, all smiles. 'Tell us what you're doing now. Everyone would be so interested.'

She could hardly say no. She was an invited speaker.

Fancy found herself being guided to the platform and the lectern. This is where she would be standing later in the week for her main lecture. This was a three-minute practice run. She looked round at the sea of expectant faces, sitting in rows, yet the hall was only a quarter full.

'What am I doing now?' she said, more to herself. 'You are probably expecting me to say that I'm working this novel and planning yet another novel. That I've a serial for a woman's magazine to finish. That my magazine *MM* is blooming and I'm wading through piles of submissions.'

She looked round at the faces and paused. Many looked drawn and white. They were all tired, too, after long journeys by train or car, farewells, responsibilities, desperate for success. Some had even flown in from France and Switzerland.

'But what I am really doing now is running away from someone who is trying to kill me. And I am terrified. He, or she, could be anywhere. They could be here, now in this very hall, or hiding in the shrubbery, or waiting outside my room.'

There was a nervous titter. Fancy had their attention. They didn't know whether to believe her. It could be a trick.

'But I am also terrified of writing my next book. Can I still do it? We never know. It's always a challenge. It still nags me. Have I got that special something inside me or has it gone? We have to prove ourselves over and over again.'

A few heads nodded. They knew the feeling.

'The killer out there could also be true,' she said. 'Or it could simply be the plot of my new novel. Wait and see. I have still got to write it.'

A burst of laughter greeted her closing words. She had not used her three minutes, but she had said enough. Fancy felt a burden roll off her shoulders. She trusted all the writers to help her. They would be there for her because writers were like that. They were there for each other.

The laughter was followed by applause. The event folded and closed. Everyone was drained. Seats shuffled, bags were searched for, programmes consulted. Pens rolled onto the floor.

'I'll walk you to your room,' said Jed. He'd been sitting over the other side and she had not seen him. 'Is that all right? Then you won't be so terrified.'

'I know the way. There are lots of other people.'

'I heard fear in your voice. I've heard fear before. You're frightened.'

'It was acting.'

'No, you weren't. I know real fear when I hear it.' Jed folded his programme with one hand and tucked it into a back pocket. 'But I hope it is just a plot from your thriving imagination. Come on, Fancy Burne-Jones, let me see you to your door.'

Fancy made a quick decision. She had to trust someone and he was over six feet tall. It was a reassuring height, not as tall as the legendary Jack Reacher, but he looked reliable. 'Just to my door.'

He grinned, a twinkle coming into his dark eyes behind the glasses. 'Not a step further.'

★ ★ ★

It was a short walk along the low-lit path but it was a long walk in her life. Fancy had never loved anyone except the heroes in her books. Real men had always fallen by the wayside as they let her down or she failed to be bewitched by their synthetic and predatory charm. She had come to the conclusion that she was too hard to please. A loner. Work took their place. She fell in love with words instead, put them on paper where they completed the landscape of her life.

'Just looking at that trifle made me want to take my own life,' Jed was saying.

'My mother used to make a trifle that dripped with sherry.'

Fancy laughed. She had been letting him talk, listening more to his voice than to what he was saying. She liked his voice, the low timbre, the slight northern accent. It had a musical resonance, yet at the same time, was purely masculine.

'Jelly and custard and hundreds and thousands sprinkled on top,' said Fancy. 'I had a frozen banana.'

'Wait till you see breakfast,' he went on. 'They serve roof tiles.'

'Roof tiles?'

'In normal life, it's called toast. But that isn't fair to them. The rest of breakfast is excellent with a huge choice of cereal and fruit.'

'I rarely eat breakfast.'

'You should. You'll need it here to keep up your stamina. Everyone needs stamina to survive the whole week at Northcote.'

Jed punched in the front door code. Fancy couldn't even remember it though it was something simple. The door swung open to the Lakeside foyer. 'Lift or stairs? I said I'd come right to your door.'

'Stairs,' said Fancy. She didn't want to be in a lift with him. It was far too soon to be so close. 'I need the exercise after all that sitting this evening.'

'What did you think of the speaker?'

'I confess that I was not actually listening all the time. It was pretend listening. I was writing. Something came into my head and

I had to get it down. I knew I would forget it if I didn't.'

'The true professional,' he said, following her up the three flights of turning stairs. 'Even on an evening off. What happens if you are out on a date?'

Fancy couldn't remember when she had last had a date. In the distant past, sometime in The Middle Ages, there had been dates and men.

'Especially when I'm on a date,' she said. 'To relieve the boredom.'

'Ouch,' said Jed, stopping on a landing and looking down at her. 'Did I tread on a sore corn? Sorry.'

Fancy shook her head. 'It was a poor joke. I'm too tired to think up a good one. Tomorrow, perhaps.'

'Nearly there — 425 is at the far end, isn't it?'

'Why is it numbered four, when it's on the third floor?' she wondered out loud.

'It's the way it was designed. Lakeside is built on a slope and the other flank of the building, the wing facing the new lake, has four floors. Your wing is built on the upper slope, so consists of only three floors. Don't ask me what happens in the middle. A sort of empty zone.'

'Or a floor and a half, like the platform in

Harry Potter,' said Fancy.

'You're probably right. Here you are, Fancy. Safe and sound. Sleep well.' Jed turned to leave, almost abruptly. 'Hey, what's this? Someone's left you a present.'

It was a tin of biscuits. The glossy lid depicted assorted tea biscuits, chocolate and plain, made by a well-known manufacturer of biscuits.

'How very kind,' said Fancy. 'From the committee, I expect, in case I'm starving in the middle of the night. But I don't eat many biscuits. You can have them. I've never known a policeman who could resist biscuits.'

'Chocolate digestives. They are my downfall.'

'You have them, then.'

The tin was heavy. For a fraction of a second, Fancy thought: concrete. But the tin was sealed and it hadn't come through a window.

'Thanks,' he said, ripping off the sticky tape. 'I'll leave you with a couple of jammy dodgers in case of unexpected midnight hunger pangs.'

He eased off the lid and removed a couple of layers of grease-proof crinkle paper.

Fancy gasped and staggered against the door, her blood running cold. The thing inside the biscuit tin gleamed an ivory white;

it was a human hand, severed at the wrist, the wrist scorched and burned.

Jed caught her with his good arm, dropping the tin at the same time. The hand spun out of the tin and skidded across the floor. It lay there, obscene and menacing, shreds of tissue scattered.

'Now I know why you're so scared,' he said.

# 3

## Sunday Morning

Fancy had set her digital alarm for 7.30 a.m., ignoring the desperate need for extra sleep. She had slept well, which was surprising after the fright of the night before.

Jed insisted on coming into her room, searching it thoroughly and making sure she was securely locked in for the night.

He dismissed the biscuit tin. 'A very silly joke. It's a plastic model with a daub of red paint. The kind they use for teaching medical students. Forget it.' But he took it away with him, tucked under his good arm.

It surprised her that she slept so well. Sheer exhaustion. The bed was comfortable and she loved the extra space of a double bed, stretching her legs sideways. Perhaps she could move in permanently and go to all the conferences that were held at Northcote. She might learn a lot of new things. Then she thought of all the trifle she would have to consume and filed the idea.

She wanted to be up early so that she could get the feel of the small conference hall where later, after coffee, she would be giving her first crime talk. She needed to absorb the atmosphere of the room, note where the lights were, the windows, screens or walls where she could put her lecture aids.

Her talk was written as a PowerPoint presentation and she needed to check the electrical sockets, microphone, everything, in fact. She did not want to make a fool of herself in front of a crowd of writers with equipment that didn't work. They would be after her blood immediately.

At first, she disliked the room; the windows were too high up. She thought writers should be able to look out of windows, write what they saw outside. They'd need a trapeze to reach these windows. Not a good start. And it was too gloomy until she found the switch for full-on lighting.

Nor did she want the chairs in rows. She wanted a semi-circle. She was so pernickety. The committee had yet to learn what an awkward cuss she was.

She was in her lecturer-ship black, trousers, silk print shirt, funky Portobello Road waistcoat. Her hair was pulled back into her usual high casual knot, pinned with gold combs. The loose wings curved round her cheeks. Simple but classy.

She couldn't eat despite the big choice of

fruit and cereals, even porridge. Writers were tucking into bacon, sausages, scrambled egg and baked beans. She ate half a grapefruit, trying not to squirt her neighbours with juice.

'Sorry,' she murmured, dabbing her chin with a paper napkin.

Jed gave her a nod and a half-wave from across the crowded dining room but that was all. He was sitting at one of the general tables. Fancy knew she was going to move in among the delegates at the first chance. The committee table was pleasant enough but she felt cut off from it, as if there were invisible barbed wire erected round the corner. Some might like the distinction but Fancy did not care for it.

It was an isolated feeling, despite the helpfulness of everyone. The technical expert on the committee came with her to the hall to check that she had everything and it all worked. They tested the microphone.

'Testing, testing,' she said, trying out various distances and heights. She moved the lectern to the back wall. No one would be able to see her standing behind it. She preferred to be with her audience, walking among them.

The technician gave her a hand moving the chairs into a semicircle. 'Anything else while I'm here?' he grinned. 'Like the walls painted a different colour? A quick roller job? How about strobe lighting? I could manage that.'

'What a star,' said Fancy, the adrenaline still pumping. 'Could you manage some arrival music? *Luck Be a Lady Tonight* would be perfect.'

'How about a pipe band?'

'Really?'

'I've brought my kilt and my pipes.'

Fancy laughed. 'I think your kilt might ruin our concentration.'

The gardeners were busy watering and weeding the riot of flower beds. Lawns stretched down to the tranquil lakes. A sleek tabby was sprawled out in the sunshine, waiting to be stroked and admired — his daily routine. Northcote was like Brigadoon, cocooned, a million miles away from the real world.

She took a cup of black coffee into the hall with her, a quarter of an hour before the start of her lecture. She half expected to see another biscuit tin but it all looked normal. Delegates were already arriving, wanting a good front seat.

She made a point of welcoming each group as they arrived, walking among them easily, chatting and putting them at their ease. She didn't have a pipe band or a Sinatra song, but within moments her crime lecture was in full swing.

Fancy knew what she was talking about and she knew how to communicate her enthusiasm. It was not long before ideas were coming fast from the delegates, inspired by her words and guidance, remembering to use her pink pen. She was surprised how quickly the hour went and it was time to troop out, to the chapel on the hill, if so inclined, to pray for success.

She gathered up her notes and switched off the equipment. She had not said half of what she had prepared. Still, it was better to have too much rather than too little. The rest of the day was hers. She could relax. She would go to some of the other talks. It was never too late to learn something new.

'Hear it went well,' said Jed, leaning against the doorway. His back hunched in a way that seemed familiar. It broke her dream. She had dreamed of him last night. How strange when she had only just met him.

'You didn't come.'

It was a statement not a rebuke.

'I might have asked awkward questions or damned your police procedure,' he grinned. 'Come and have a drink. You deserve it. But be prepared. There will be a dozen hopefuls in the bar waiting to ambush you for some private advice. Don't agree to read anything they have brought with them.'

'Thanks for the warning. I might read short stuff. No novels.'

'They'll devour you if you give them half a chance. You're on the menu at Northcote; they'll all want a bite.'

Jed seated her in a far corner and went to queue up at the bar. There was already a stampede from the other course lectures. She wondered about numbers. She reckoned there had been about seventy at her lecture. There were over three hundred delegates and five courses, but the maths was beyond her. The novel and short stories would take the biggest audiences. Non-fiction and poetry were the smallest. She would be somewhere in the middle, even if some delegates went to nothing.

The feeling came to her without warning. One moment she had been happy and relaxed, waiting for her drink, and the next she was washed over in fear. It was like an electric shock, only it was a cold shock.

She shivered violently, almost dropping her notes.

'I'll shut that window,' someone said. But it wasn't just the window. It was more than that. She knew she was being watched. Watched by someone with evil intent. It was

12.39 p.m. Not a time that meant anything.

Jed came back to their table, doing his two drinks in one hand trick. He put them down, only spilling a little. He looked at her quickly.

'What's the matter, Fancy? Seen the ghost?'

She shook her head, trying to shake off the feeling. 'Is there a ghost? No, I haven't seen it. But is there one here?'

He pushed the glass of red wine towards her. 'There are two ghosts, so they say. A lady in blue who stands at the bottom of the main stairs in the old house, next to where the grand piano used to be.'

'How should I know where the grand piano used to be?' she said.

'And the other is a German prisoner of war who escaped from what was the Garden House before they pulled it down.'

'Now that really does make a lot of sense,' said Fancy, sipping the wine. It trickled down her throat and began to warm her. 'A piano that isn't there any more and a Garden House that has been pulled down.'

'All true. I'll tell you all about them one day. It's quite a story.'

'We only have six days,' said Fancy. 'And yesterday has gone already.'

'Why were you shaking when I came back from the bar? Was it a biscuit tin moment?'

'You could call it that.'

He was observant. But then he was a policeman. He hadn't got to detective chief superintendent simply pushing paper on a desk. If she got a chance to get into the computer room, she'd see if he was on Google.

'You won't find me there,' he said, reading her mind. 'Because I'm on cold cases. That's why I emailed you on *MM*. I thought we could be mutually helpful. I could write another case for you, and you might solve the odd case for me.'

'Are you serious about this? I do need help and I do need quality material. I only publish the best.'

'I know. I read it. It's a fascinating magazine. And I've read some of your books. Not all of them because I don't have time, but I like a good crime novel to help me get to sleep. Some of your police procedure is a bit wobbly.'

'And mine send you to sleep?'

'Isn't that the purpose of a good book?'

A woman was hovering by the table, anxiously looking at Fancy, clutching her big A4 memo pad. 'Terribly sorry and all that, Miss Jones, but do you mind if I ask you something? I was at your talk this morning and it was great, but I wondered if you might help me. You see, I've got stuck.'

Fancy nodded and indicated the spare seat at the table. 'Sit down and please call me Fancy. Tell me all about it.'

★  ★  ★

She escaped from the committee table at lunch time. It had been too easy. The evening's guest speaker had arrived plus unexpected wife, so there was no place for her. Fancy slid away quickly and joined one of the rectangular tables.

As she was late, she found she had the last place, at the top and so had to serve everyone. She served the chicken fillets with style, making sure everyone got some of the sauce. The apple pie was also easy to serve, each portion being already cut. A portly gentleman got two portions as a pastry-conscious girl, thin as a stick, opted for some grapes. Frozen grapes.

'I feel sure I was a serving wench in a previous life,' Fancy said, dishing out the food. 'In a tavern, in a low-necked blouse. This comes quite naturally to me.'

The custard was a lurid orange. She had never seen such strange custard. Her criminal mind immediately wondered if it was

53

poisoned with some exotic Peruvian concoction. But everyone had the same. No one fell about, clutching their stomachs, at least, no one in the dining room.

'It's industrial custard,' said the portly gentleman, shirt buttons bursting. Fancy discovered later that he wrote poetry and got it published. 'Everything has a purpose, you know. One of us will write an Ode to Orange Custard and it will be quoted a hundred years hence.'

'Not much rhymes with custard.'

'Mustard.'

'Bustard.'

The table rapidly dissolved into giggles and absurd rhymes. All thoughts of biscuit tins vanished. Fancy enjoyed herself. It wasn't going to be so bad after all.

She spent the afternoon going to other people's workshops and talks. Some knew what they were talking about and others quite obviously hadn't a clue. She wondered why they had been asked to speak. Perhaps they volunteered. There was not much the committee could do to discourage a willing volunteer. And they had a timetable to fill.

She began making notes with her pink pen. She put down all the times of the incidents: the Underground, the rucksack, the lump of concrete, the biscuit tin and two chilling moments. Maybe she was wrong to attach too much to the timings.

Two notes had been put under the door of room 425. They were cheerful pictorial invitations to parties, Monday and Tuesday, both at 6 p.m. One was also in Lakeside but the other was in ABC, and she had no idea where that was. RSVP had been crossed out. 'Just turn up,' they added.

Fancy sat on her bed. She hadn't been to a party for ages, nor did she have any party clothes. What she had with her would have to do. She'd take a bottle, bought from the bar. That would make up for the lack of sequins.

She had a whole hour before supper. A whole hour to stretch out on her bed and relax, think through the day. She made a cup of coffee but didn't drink it all. She set her alarm in case she fell asleep and missed everything.

Something was wrong somewhere — she knew it. Her sixth or seventh sense told her so. Someone wanted to kill her or warn her off. Warn her off what? Her next crime novel? That was a laugh. She never knew what she was going to write till she wrote it. Nor did she ever have more than the vaguest idea how it would end.

She closed her eyes, glad to have a moment to relax.

★  ★  ★

She awoke to a banging on her door. It sounded as if an elephant was trying to barge in. Several elephants.

'Fancy! Fancy! Are you in there? Answer me immediately or I shall get the house-keeper. They have spare keys.'

It was a man's voice but she didn't recognize it. The room was dark, which was strange. She couldn't see anything. She groped about for the switch to the bedside lamp but couldn't find it. She swung her legs over the side of the bed and tried to stand up, but her legs refused to take her weight. They crumbled beneath her.

'Coming,' she mumbled.

'Fancy? Is that you? Open the door at once.'

Some part of her befuddled brain then recognized the voice. It was Jed Edwards.

'Jed?'

'Open the door.' His voice had quietened and was more persuasive. 'It's only me. I want to make sure you're all right. It's very late.'

Fancy staggered to the door and opened it. The room was wavering. She blinked at Jed. 'Late?'

'It's nearly ten o'clock. You've missed

56

supper and the speaker. I was beginning to get worried. You couldn't be that tired.'

'Come in,' said Fancy. She staggered back to the bed and sat down on a corner. 'I must have fallen . . . asleep.'

'And slept through your alarm.' Jed switched it off. 'You set it in time for supper. It's been bleeping for three hours.'

'Surely not? I don't remember.' Fancy tried to shake off the muzziness. 'I feel very strange.'

Jed sat on the chair opposite the bed. 'Did you have any lunch?'

Fancy nodded. 'Orange custard.'

'Tea at tea time?'

'Cup of tea.'

'Anything else?'

Fancy tried to remember. 'I made a drink here, I think. A coffee or something. Yes, I made a cup of coffee.'

'Where's the cup?'

'Over there. I don't know.'

Jed filled a glass with water from the tap. 'Drink this. Now put on a fleece and we'll go for a walk. Have you got a fleece? It's late and it's turned cold.'

'Have I missed everything?'

'Yes, the speaker was good. He writes for radio. He knew what he was talking about for once. No going to sleep in that one.'

Jed made her walk down the three flights of stairs. It was hairy and scary, the dizziness kept returning in waves. Fancy kept her eyes on the broad back ahead of her. He seemed to change direction as the stairs twisted downwards. They were Hogwart stairs. Her free hand gripped the banisters.

Someone told her at lunch that one of the speakers, many years ago, broke her ankle on the dance floor in the small conference hall. Fancy did not want to add her name to the list of casualties. It was late at night and someone was bound to think she had spent all evening in the bar.

The night air was cool and starlit. Some stalwarts were still on the lawns talking, wrapped in ponchos and cashmere stoles. The smokers' gazebo was full of hazy laughter, smoke eddying on the disturbed air. Jed steered her away.

'We'll walk round the lake,' he said. 'It'll be quieter there. And you can tell me what all this nonsense is about.'

'It's not nonsense,' said Fancy, her voice still slurred.

'I'll decide where I hear your story.'

Jed was in his chief super mode. He must have been fearsome to work for. His eyebrows, which were darker than his silvery streaked hair, had a way of drawing together when he was puzzled or angry. They changed his face.

He was taking her to the lake. Fancy did not want to go to the lake. People drowned in lakes. Her victims often drowned in lakes. Supposing Jed was the person trying to kill her? He could push her in and no one would find her till the morning.

She had quite forgotten that she could swim. She could swim rather well. Holidays in Polzeath, Cornwall, surfing all day, had made her a strong swimmer. Padstow Bay with miles of sand to run along was another fond memory.

'We are going to the old lake,' he went on. 'It's in the original sunken garden. It's very beautiful, with weeping willows and water lilies and swans. There a bench by the lake, dedicated to Jill Dick, the Treasurer of the writers' conference for many years. We'll sit there and perhaps her bright mind will help us sort this out. She always loved a puzzle.'

He didn't sound as if he was planning to push her in the lake.

'Is there a new lake, then?' Her mind was beginning to emerge from the fog.

'Yes, didn't you see it when you drove in? The new lake is square, with a path all round it, a verge and a fence. It also has planted water lilies but as yet, no character. The swans won't go near it. Careful, this bit of lawn is steep.'

The path down to the lake was through trees and shrubbery and clumps of flowers. She could smell the heavy scent of an evening primrose. It was a lover's path, the perfect setting for a romantic scene. But she was not with a lover. She was with an interrogator.

The moon came out from behind clouds, on the shy side, and the lake was lit with a silvery gleam. The trees were whispering secrets. The water lilies were closed but their perfume still lingered. It was magical. Writers could write reams here. Poets would be inspired; non-fiction would be lost, wondering how to use the magic in an article.

'Let's sit here,' said Jed, leading her to a polished wood bench. 'Hi, Jill.'

'Did you know her?'

'Everyone knew her. She was very efficient and she loved cats. If you liked cats, she was your friend for life.'

'What did she write?'

'Non-fiction, like me. She was a newspaper journalist.'

Fancy's mind was clearing. She knew she had been drugged. Not seriously enough to put her out altogether or land her in intensive care, though. Some sleeping pill or tranquillizer. Seroquel XL was an anti-psychotic drug they gave to depressives.

'They probably injected a carton of milk,' said Jed. 'They could hardly add something to coffee granules or a tea bag, but it would be simple enough to inject those little cartons with a syringe. You had better throw them all away. Better still, I'll get them all tested and see if the experts come up with anything.'

'You think I was drugged?'

'Classic symptoms. But not enough to kill you.'

'How reassuring,' she said bluntly. 'Just another warning.'

'Tell me about these warnings,' said Jed. 'Take your time, Fancy. Start at the beginning.'

'I don't know when the beginning was,' said Fancy, trying to think. 'I might not have noticed the first signs. Lots of things happen which mean nothing, till suddenly they start to mean something.'

'A very lucid explanation, especially from a writer.' Fancy ignored the sarcasm. She could remember the time of each happening clearly. But there was no logic to remembering the exact time, to the second, almost. Unless one day some explanation leaped out at her.

'I think the first one I remember happening

was on the London Underground, Circle line, at 17.16 p.m.' She went on to describe what had happened or not quite happened. She told him about the rucksack incident on the bus. And the lump of concrete through her bedroom window the night before she left for Derbyshire.

'They got the saint and the lambs,' she added, though he didn't understand.

'Then last night the biscuit tin and this evening, some sort of sleeping pill or tranquilizer,' said Jed.

'I think they're warnings that someone is going to kill me if I do something or don't do something.' Fancy tried not to sound shaken. 'Why should anyone want to kill me?'

'You tell me. A rival author? Someone who thought you had stolen their plot? Plagiarism? A rejected lover? A revengeful husband?'

'None of those. No husband, no lover, no rivals. A disgruntled ex-agent, worried publishers, but that's nothing new in these cashless days. I can't think of a motive, even with my imagination.'

'I'm glad you've told me. I was beginning to think you were a bit weird, one of those eccentric writers who imagine disasters round every corner. Let's go back now and I'll collect the milk cartons for testing. I've a pal in Derby who owes me a favour. He won't mind.'

Jed helped Fancy to her feet. She was stiff and cold, needed warm arms. If they were lovers, thought Fancy, this could have been such a romantic moment. She had almost forgotten what romantic moments were like. It had been so long ago.

'Your hair's nice like that, all loose, instead of that frigid topknot,' he said, his voice changing. There was an unexpected sweetness.

Her hand flew up. She had been unaware that her hair had come loose and was down to her shoulders, tumbled and untidy. His good hand went to touch a dark strand and she leaped back, pushing him away.

'Don't you dare shove me in the lake,' she cried out. 'I can swim. I won't drown. I can swim very well.'

'For heaven's sake, Fancy, calm down. I wasn't going to push you into the lake. Let's get you back to your room before you wake the entire neighbourhood with your shouting. I don't want to get a reputation.'

'S-sorry.' Fancy was tired now, a genuine tiredness, nothing induced. 'Yes, back to Lakeside.'

Jed took her arm and guided her round the darkened path towards the other side of the lake and the quickest way back to Lakeside. It was tranquil but some of the magic had gone. The swans had retired to rest, probably on the little island in the middle of the lake. They would get peace there. Maybe there was a nest.

Jed stopped suddenly. 'Don't move,' he said. He left Fancy on the path and went carefully down the slope, holding on to an overhanging branch of the weeping willow. The reeds stirred.

Fancy watched his sudden alertness; suddenly she was wide awake. The clouds drifted away from the face of the moon again and the lake took on its magical silver sheen. But it was not so magical now. On the surface of the water was something white, slowly turning as it floated. It was a pale feminine arm and around it swirled yards of sodden chiffon.

The chiffon was like a goodbye. The scarves were waving goodbye.

# 4

## Monday Morning

There was a genuine sense of grief at breakfast. The news had spread fast and the committee were in a deep huddle. Rumours flew about that the conference would be cancelled, everyone sent home, money refunded. Two nervous women had already started packing.

The police had been around since the middle of the night. Scene-of-crime tape was flapping from posts all round the shrubbery and the old lake. The drive was littered with marked and unmarked police cars. The police photographer had been and taken his shots. The medical officer had also viewed the body and given his opinion. White-clad forensic experts were combing the scene.

Several of the smaller conference rooms had been set up as interview rooms. Apparently they wanted to talk to everyone: delegates, committee, conference and catering staff, speakers and visitors. It would take days.

'We might as well carry on with the

conference,' said Fergus Nelson, stroking his severe beard. 'It'll help take people's mind off the tragedy, and make it easier for the police if we are all in one place.'

'It'll be in the papers, on the news. Think of the free publicity,' said the committee member in charge of publicity.

'Not exactly an appropriate remark at the moment, Jo-Jo.' Disapproving expressions all round. But it was, it could not be denied, still free publicity.

There was a moment's hushed silence. The drowned woman had been identified. A friend had reported her missing some time after midnight. Apparently they always had a cup of cocoa together on the stairs before retiring.

'It's Melody.'

'Who?'

'Melody Marchant, the speakers' hostess. Always rushing about. She looked after the speakers. Very good at it, too. White hair, floaty clothes.'

Melody Marchant had been a popular delegate, at everyone's beck and call. It was a sobering thought that she had drowned in such a beautiful lake. It had not yet been established if it was an accident or foul play; Jed was keeping his mouth firmly closed and his thoughts to himself.

Her husband, who was not a writer but a farmer, was driving up to Derbyshire straight away. They lived in Cornwall so it was a long journey and he was not expected to arrive until after lunch.

'Everyone wants to know what's happening,' said Jessie. 'We'll have to tell them something.'

'Let's take a vote,' said Fergus. 'Yes, we carry on, or no, we disband the conference. I'm sure Melody would have wanted us to carry on. She loved the conference.'

The vote was taken. The vice chairman made a short announcement in the dining room at breakfast that there would be a special meeting in the main conference hall at 9.30 a.m. All delegates to attend.

There were no late-comers to this meeting. The hall was humming with subdued conversation long before Fergus strode onto the platform. He looked serious and not quite his usual assured self.

'As you will all know by now, our dear friend, Melody Marchant, met with a fatal accident last night and drowned in the old lake.'

There was a universal gasp even though most people already knew who it was. It was the starkness of his words. No padding, no poetic phrasing, no emotion.

'It is a very sad time for Northcote and for Melody's husband and family, but I am sure she would have wanted the conference to continue as per its tradition of taking all disasters in its stride. If anyone feels that they would rather go home, then of course, they may. But the police may want to interview them before they go. Courses and lectures will resume after the coffee break.'

Fancy was surprised that the police wanted to interview everyone. If Melody had drowned herself or if it had been an unfortunate accident, then that could be established without statements from everyone. She would have to change the tone of her lecture: not so many jokes and nothing about death. It was too close at hand.

But Fancy was second on the list for interviewing. She and Jed had been first on the scene. She was shown into one of the small rooms off the main conference hall. It was been transformed with a desk, two chairs, phone, laptop and tape recorder.

'Miss Francine Burne-Jones? Please sit down. I'm Detective Inspector Morris Bradley. I'm very sorry about the circumstances. It must be distressing for you. Was Melody a personal friend of yours?'

He switched on the tape and recited the usual time, date and personnel.

'No, she was not a personal friend. I met her on Saturday afternoon for the first time. She was the hostess to speakers. She met me when I arrived and helped me find my way around.'

'So you are not a regular delegate to the writers' conference?'

He said 'writers' conference' as though it was somewhere custodial for difficult delinquents, a detention centre for rejected writers.

'No, I'm a guest speaker and course lecturer. I write crime novels.'

'Really? So you know all about crime, do you? So we have another Agatha Christie on hand. Maybe we shall call upon you if we need assistance.'

'I don't commit the crimes,' said Fancy. 'Or solve them. I invent plots and use my imagination to write a story. That's what crime fiction is. A story.'

He nodded, steepling his fingers. Perhaps he thought it looked intelligent.

'And do you have a fictional detective?' DI Bradley was enjoying himself. He was a burly ex-Marine, never read a book unless it was a police manual. He tapped his pen on a notebook as if beating time to music.

'Yes. She's known as the Pink Pen Detective, because she always uses a pink pen.' Fancy guessed that this conversation was supposed to be putting her at ease, getting her to relax, but he was making fun of her. Crime writing was never taken seriously by non-readers or reviewers. She wished he would get on with it.

'Ah, such as this pink pen we found by the lake? Does this belong to your Pink Pen Detective?' He pushed a plastic specimen bag across the table towards her. Inside was a pink biro.

Fancy recognized it straight away. It was one of hers.

'No, it belongs to me. That's my pen,' she said. 'I must have dropped it. Or it could be one of several that went missing yesterday after my lecture and someone else dropped it. The lake is not out of bounds to the writers.'

'So you are the Pink Pen Detective? Ah, the plot deepens.'

'I am not the Pink Pen Detective. She is my principal character and I write about her. Now, could you please ask me what you want to know? I have a lecture to give in twenty minutes.'

'Perhaps you could tell me exactly what you were doing by the lake so late at night and who you were with,' he asked smoothly.

'You know perfectly well that I was with Jed

Edwards. We were discussing writing problems.' She was reining in her impatience.

'By the lake? At nearly midnight?'

'It was 11.33 exactly.'

'How do you know the time exactly?'

'I looked at my watch. It's a habit.'

'And why were you by the lake? Had you arranged to meet Melody? Was she upset about anything?'

Fancy groaned inwardly. She was not going to mention being drugged. 'Jed took me to the lake because he thought it was a quiet place to be after a hectic day. No, I had not arranged to meet Melody. I have no idea if she was upset about anything. I hardly knew her.'

'Yet you both found her.'

'Because we were both there, Inspector. If anyone else had been there, they would have found her. I can't see what this line of questioning is supposed to mean.'

'I think it's very strange that you should both choose to go to a remote lake in the middle of a garden so late at night. Unless, of course, you both had a reason.'

'Our reason for going there had nothing to do with Melody.'

'A romantic liaison, perhaps?'

'One-track mind,' Fancy muttered below her breath. 'Hardly, Detective Inspector

Bradley. I'm far too busy to have romantic liaisons, especially here at Northcote. My timetable barely gives me time to breathe.'

'Yet you had time to go down to the lake at . . . ' he consulted his notes, '11.33 exactly. Very strange.'

DI Bradley switched off the tape recorder and stood up. 'Thank you, Miss Burne-Jones. That's all for the moment. I shall probably want to speak to you again, so I would be grateful if you did not leave Northcote.'

Fancy took a deep breath.

'It's plain Miss Jones, please. I have three more course lectures to give, a panel to sit on and my evening talk to deliver. It doesn't look as if I shall be going anywhere, except rushing about Northcote, wondering where I am supposed to be next, losing my way and asking directions.'

But DI Bradley wasn't listening. Fancy could put him in a book. It was always gratifying to put a rude, unpleasant person in a book and make awful things happen to them. She might think up something really nasty for him.

Fancy was glad that her second lecture and workshop went well despite the subdued atmosphere. The group were keen to become crime writers and every word from Fancy

Jones was gold dust. Her books were popular and well read. The delegates were also going to write best-sellers, as soon as they got home, as soon as they found the time, as soon as they got a good idea. They borrowed her pink pens, hoping they contained some magic elixir.

She was amazed at the number of writers who came to lectures and workshops with neither pen nor paper. No writer worth their pepper or salt ever set foot outside their front door without something to write on and something to write with. Even if it was a slab of slate and a piece of chalk.

'Are you avoiding me?' said Fancy as she joined the queue at the bar for a pre-lunch drink. She felt she deserved a drink. It was a long, impatient queue with a cheeky few jumping in by talking to someone well ahead of them.

'No, not avoiding you,' said Jed, looking grave. 'But it might be diplomatic not to be seen together too much.'

'Has the diplomatic Detective Inspector Bradley been hinting at a romantic liaison down by the lake?'

'He asked me if you ever let your hair down.'

'Is that what it's called these days? And what did you say?'

'I told him to mind his own bloody business.'

Jed gave his order for a beer to the bar staff, including a Campari and ice for Fancy. She took the tall pink drink and thanked him.

'I thought you might need something stronger after your grilling,' he said.

'Are we allowed to sit at the same table in a crowded bar or is that too intimate? As you say, we need to be particularly careful. What else did you tell the nosy detective?'

'I had to tell him about an argument I overheard yesterday afternoon. I didn't mean to listen but it was a bit heated. It was Melody and our treasurer, whatever his name is. I can't remember exactly. Richard Gerard? I sent him my cheque in February and that's about all I know of him.'

They found a corner seat in the vinery. The big leaves of the vine were abundant and hung like curtains. It had spread everywhere in the glass extension and they were shielded from calculating eyes. Here the chairs were cane-backed with orange padded seats and the tables topped with round glass.

'What sort of argument?'

'Nothing too spectacular. It was about expenses. She was reimbursed for her petrol costs and they were arguing over one of the receipts. Wrong date or wrong amount, something like that. Perhaps she drove here via Rannoch Moor, researching the Ice Age. I moved on. It was none of my business.'

'Ice Age?'

'Rannoch Moor was once a reservoir of ice, fed by glaciers from the ice cap.'

'How do you know that?'

'I know lots of useless things. I read books.'

'So maybe Melody was depressed. Perhaps she had been fiddling her expenses and was upset about being found out.' The drink was bitter and strong and soothing. 'Or maybe she retaliated and accused this Richard of helping himself to the school's funds. Perhaps she had taken a closer look at last year's accounts and spotted anomalies that didn't add up. Could be.'

'Motives for both suicide and murder.'

'There you go.'

'We are speculating, Fancy, using our writer's imagination,' said Jed. 'We must wait and see what the pathologist says.' He was looking at her over the froth of his beer. 'Is your name really Burne-Jones?'

'I only use the Jones half. I know what you're going to ask. Edward Burne-Jones, the Victorian painter. I am descended from him, but I'm not sure how or from whom. And I do live in Fulham, which is another coincidence, though not at the Grange, which was where he lived and painted his wonderful paintings.'

'You look a bit like his Greek model, Madame Maria Zambaco. She was very beautiful, striking in fact, exotic. Masses of dark hair.'

Fancy was stunned, forgetting her dark hair. 'How do you know this?'

Jed shrugged. 'I like his paintings. I have a few prints. For my eyes only, you understand. I would not have such romantic and passionate paintings on public display. Bad for my image.'

'You never cease to surprise me,' said Fancy. 'An ex-copper who likes romantic Victorian paintings. And knows about the Ice Age.'

'Surprises are what keep a relationship alive,' he said.

Fancy reminded herself to jot down that phrase in her notebook. She would use it somewhere. She did not question whether their brief acquaintance could be regarded as a relationship, though; they were hardly at first-name stage.

'Did you tell DI Bradley why we were at the lake?'

'No, did you?'

'No, I thought it would complicate matters if your strange happenings were linked to poor Melody when they are nothing to do with her. Someone else is out to scare you rigid, for some unexplained reason. I doubt if DI Bradley could cope with any complications. He likes everything to be straightforward.'

'How will we know if it was an accident or suicide?' Fancy drained the last of her Campari. The thirty-seven per cent alcohol was addictive.

'I have a pal — another pal — who might be persuaded to tell me. Ah, the lunch queue is moving. We should sit at different tables.'

'I'll sit at the committee table. I might learn something.'

★　★　★

But she didn't. The committee were keeping their mouths closed. They were not into gossiping today. But Fancy did detect a slight hostility between the treasurer and the conference secretary, even though they were supposed to be long-time conference friends. It may have been her fertile imagination. They were all under a degree of stress. Everyone was guarded.

Lunch was chilli con carne with either noodles, garlic bread or a jacket potato. Fancy went for the jacket potato. She was not really hungry. She slipped away when

77

the dessert arrived, a big, oval plum pie with the statutory orange custard. She could not face more orange.

After lunch she was besieged by writers wanting to talk about what they were working on and hoping that she could magically put them on the right track. She tried, sorted out a few problems. Some even gave her manuscripts to read.

'I can't read anything long,' she protested. 'Only short stories. No novels, please. Don't expect me to read all night.'

'Please, Fancy, just read a few pages, that's all.' The woman had a thick manuscript in a folder. 'If you'd take a look at the first chapter. Tell me if I'm on the right track.'

'A few pages, then,' she relented. 'Put your room number on the top of the manuscript in case I can't find you, Peggy Carter, okay?'

She saw herself slipping work back under doors in the middle of the night. Very cowardly. But she could hardly slip this one back. It looked like three hundred pages at least. And she would be expected to write a few lines of encouraging comment. More work.

Fancy slept for an hour of the afternoon. The night had been disturbed and a nap on her bed seemed ideal. It was bliss. But she set the alarm to wake her for the 3.30 p.m. tea break. She wanted to go to a talk titled 'The Inner Child'. It sounded fascinating. She was prepared to be disappointed, though; she was learning that some speakers had nothing to give beyond a catchy title.

The Orchard Room was packed. Everyone wanted to learn about their inner child or perhaps the IT or politics talks — scheduled for the same time — did not appeal. There were not enough chairs so Fancy volunteered to sit on the floor. She could still get down and get up whereas many of the less mobile could not.

They moved on to meditation. Fancy was not into meditation, even though she lived in part of a church. Still, she closed her eyes and did what she was told.

'Imagine yourself in a nice place, some-where that you really like. Imagine that it is sunny and warm and that you are walking, very happily, and then someone joins you.' The voice was soft and hypnotic. The leader of the group was a sweet and tranquil woman, hair like spun silk.

Fancy had been imagining a beach in the Seychelles. That holiday was a long time ago, when she was young and carefree. An empty beach with no footprints except her own and those of an island dog who had decided to join her for the day. She had swum in the azure blue water and it had been miraculous. A memory to last forever. Her best memory. Yes, it was her best memory.

But her mind drifted away and she found herself walking along this riverside, a kingfisher singing on a branch, the water lapping by. A girl came. She was wearing a blue-check cotton dress with short sleeves and a white collar and her frizzy hair sprang out in all directions.

Fancy lay down in the grass with the girl and they picked flowers and made daisy chains. It was all so peaceful.

'Now I want you to draw this new companion,' the group were told. 'But draw with your left hand if you are right-handed, and with your right hand if you are left-handed. Then write some questions to your companion. Wrong-handed.'

Fancy understood. She drew the girl easily in a blue-check dress and asked the girl questions with her left hand. Who are you?

The girl said that she was me. The girl said she would help me with writing. She said my writing would get better.

Fancy relaxed on the floor. It had all been too easy. The inner child was herself. She had told herself what she wanted to hear. No great hassle there.

'Now I want you to go on a journey with

your inner child. Close your eyes and let her take you where she will,' said the leader.

Fancy closed her eyes obediently. So what. Where would her inner child take her? New York? Paris? Bermuda?

They were on a double bicycle, a bit like the film *ET*. They flew through the clouds and then suddenly took a dive down through the clouds and landed on a barren island. It was dotted about with huge, grotesque statues, sunken into the earth. It was Easter Island. She recognized the statues.

Fancy opened her eyes, shaken. She had never been to Easter Island or shown any interest in it, so why should her inner child take her there?

Why have you brought me here? she asked, using her left hand. Fancy emptied her mind of any thoughts. She did not want to dictate the answer. She wanted her inner child to tell her.

Because they are calling you, came the left-handed answer, the writing disjointed and wild.

The rest of the session was a cacophony of people talking and exchanging experiences. Fancy did not want to join in. She was too shattered. Yet common sense told her this was nothing to do with her recent experiences.

They are calling you. What on earth did that mean?

She opened a new page in her notebook and wrote down all the happenings and their exact times. They were all one minute past the quadrant: one minute past half past, one minute past a quarter to, one minute past the o'clock. It must mean something. There was a pattern, if she could only work out what it was.

They drifted out of the Orchard Room. Fancy thanked the leader, a slim, willowy woman called Tina who lived in some faraway place. Time to shower and change. Fancy was half-sure she had a party to go to if she could find out where it was being held. A numbered room in ABC, the invitation said, and she had no idea where that was.

ABC? Strange name for a building. Were the builders going through the alphabet?

A few of the orchard trees had been left standing and they cast long shadows in the afternoon breeze. Something swayed damply across her face. Fancy brushed it aside without thinking.

Then she looked up, wondering what could be wet on a sunny afternoon. It had been tied to a low branch of an apple tree. Fancy stopped, horrified. It was one of Melody's floating chiffon scarves, slowly dripping water.

The water dripped onto her face.

It was 5.01 p.m.

# 5

## Monday Evening

Fancy hurried to her room in Lakeside, almost running up the stairs, hand shaking as she tried to turn the key in the lock. She was trying it the wrong way in her haste. She slammed the door shut and leaned against it, getting her breath back.

The scarf didn't mean anything to anyone else at the workshop. It was there as a message to Fancy. It was saying: Look what happened to Melody. But she was sure it had not been there when she climbed the steep path to the Orchard Room. Someone was watching her every move.

She had told no one that she planned to go to this talk. It had been a spur of the moment thing. A way of clearing her mind of the day's happenings. And she was always interested in learning something new.

If she didn't go to this evening's party, would they think she was snooty or too successful to mix with ordinary people? Neither of which was true. She liked parties. She liked meeting people. Everything and everybody gave her ideas, sharpened her brain, refreshed her writing. The Pink Pen Detective liked parties too.

She stood under the shower and let the warm water soothe her shattered nerves. Rubbing herself dry helped to jump-start her circulation. She dressed with special care, slim black velvet skirt and white, crinkled, silk shirt, finishing the look with a wide pink belt, some dangling earrings. She wasn't going to be scared off by a bit of flapping wet cloth.

ABC was apparently the large residential building she had walked past several times already, not giving it a second glance. The front entrance door was open. Long corridors stretched ahead either side. She could hear music and headed towards it.

The bedroom was full of people, most of them holding glasses of wine. It was a big room with a double and a single bed. Fancy spotted a bathroom with a bath and shower. Luxury indeed. Music was pounding from a personal transistor radio. It was a bright, cheerful party and the host soon spotted her. In seconds she had a glass of red in her hand and was being introduced to so many people. Some faces she recognized. No committee members present as yet, all delegates, all ages, white badges and regulars, other speakers and course lecturers.

It was a great party. Fancy felt rejuvenated and it wasn't only because of the wine. It was the company. It was talking to normal people about normal things, not always about writing. Callum McKay was a great raconteur with lots of stories. She met Pheobe Marr, the poet, and enjoyed talking to her. Sometimes she wanted to forget that she made her living putting words down in a certain order.

And it was cosy, sitting on beds, leaning against the window, having her glass refilled. Too soon it was supper time and everyone helped clear up the debris before departing to the dining room. They seemed to stay in the same groups at the tables and the good conversation continued. No one mentioned Melody. Her husband had arrived, someone said, but his first stop was obviously Derby Hospital.

'Have you ever wanted to do anything different to writing?' asked Phoebe.

'No, never.'

'I wanted to be a ballet dancer but I grew too tall,' Phoebe said.

Fancy thought about all her dreams and frustrations. She'd never win the Booker or the Orange Prize — not literary enough. She'd never get a film option and walk the red carpet with Johnny Depp, though she often wrote in a part for him. She would be delirious if the Pink Pen Detective got a television series.

'So really you are the Pink Pen Detective,' said her host at the party.

'No, I only invented her. I'm not a detective.'

'I like the way they slash the cover with a pink pen.'

'So do I,' said Fancy. 'The Pink Pen covers are well designed.'

She scanned the heads in the dining room, looking for streaked dark hair and glinting glasses, but he wasn't there. Perhaps Jed had gone home. Perhaps he was dining a young and delightful blonde at a nearby hotel. Fancy gathered that sometimes delegates ate out, tired of stodgy pastry and orange custard.

Tonight's supper was fillet of fish in a white sauce followed by, joy oh joy, a strawberry concoction with a weird name, fresh fruit mixed with crushed meringue and cream. It was unbelievably delicious. Everyone wanted seconds, except the young woman who was on a gluten and sugar-free diet. The kitchen produced something different for her at every meal.

She cut her banana into small pieces to make it last. 'I'd love some of that,' she said enviously.

'You could have had just the strawberries.'

'You tell me now!'

The guest speaker that evening was suitably famous. His books were going to be televised and he was something important in the Crime Writers' Association. He travelled all over the world to conferences and had just flown back from Washington. Northcote must have seemed like the backwoods after the dazzle of a cosmopolitan capital.

Fancy knew him but not well. He bumped into her in the corridor on the way to the main conference hall. 'Hello,' he said. 'I know you, don't I?' He peered at her name badge but couldn't read it properly. 'Lovely to see you again.'

'Glad you found your way here.'

'It looks fun. We'll have a drink in the bar afterwards. It'll have to be a quick one, though, as I've got to rush back to London this evening.'

Fancy decided not to sit in the safety of the elite corner with the committee and other guest speakers. She wanted her independence. She walked over to the other side of the hall, to the 'shelf'. Someone had told her it was called the shelf. It was also called the rebels corner, because once, in ages past, there had been a gang of rebels at Northcote who wanted to change the old stuffy image, and they always sat on the shelf. A kind of clan thing.

The shelf was only wide enough for two rows of chairs but it meant you could look over everyone and get a clear view of the speaker. Fancy had not enjoyed her view being blocked by backs of heads, especially if the heads did not keep still and kept bobbing about.

'Coming to join us on the shelf?'

'May I, please? Do you mind? Is there room?'

'Not at all. As long as you behave yourself. No rowdy behaviour. No wolf whistles or rude noises. Strict rules on the shelf.'

'Promise. I can't whistle.'

'We are a very refined lot up here.'

'I can see that. But you also look as if you enjoy yourselves.'

'We have independent minds. If we think a speaker is rubbish then we clap in an appropriately low-key manner. No overblown hysterics or unnecessary cheering.'

Fancy liked the sound of restrained clapping. For a moment she forgot that they would be judging her tomorrow. They made room for her now, shuffling chairs along so she could sit in the front row. She knew she was going to feel at home on the shelf. She would join them with her dreams and her frustrations.

She had never been top of any best-seller list even with dozens of complimentary reviews. Her website was informative and visited daily by fans. Yet her books stayed stuck in the middle somewhere. W H Smith never put her titles in the number one display spot. She'd never had an advert on the Underground.

But she sold well. And her peers read her writing.

Fancy knew she wrote well. Sometimes she surprised herself with a good phrase or an unexpected turn of words. Her Pink Pen Detective was fun and clever, a woman that readers could identify with. The plots were ingenious and injected with the right amount of warmth and emotion. The weird plots came into her head without any bidding. She had a strange mind.

She made a good living from her writing, which was a lot more than some writers did. Her church lodge was warm and comfortable although she did not really like the location. She supported some starving children in Somalia, but not all of them.

'May I join you?' It was Jed, black shirt, black trousers, jacket slung over his shoulder. Jazzy look.

'Jed. I thought you'd gone home.'

'Not a chance.' Jed never mentioned his home life. She didn't know if he was married, divorced or had a partner. Fancy realized that she knew very little about him. He did not look the kind of person she could ask.

'I've been to Derby,' he said, squeezing in another chair beside her, ignoring a few black looks. 'My friend in the path lab. I did him a good turn once.'

Fancy dared not ask him what he had learned. He would only tell her if he wanted to. 'You missed supper. We had strawberries and cream.'

He groaned. 'Just my luck. My favourite.'

'I've done some homework on my happenings,' she said, opening her notebook and flicking through pages.

'Your happenings. Very Stephen King.'

She showed him the list of incidents and her timing record. 'Do you see anything odd here? A pattern emerging?' He shook his head. 'The times are all one minute past the quadrant.'

'That's a big word for a little girl,' he murmured.

'Don't be patronizing. What does it tell you?'

Jed pretended to think, chin in fist. 'He's a creature of habit. He has to take medication on the hour or the half hour or both. He's set his mobile to go off every quarter of an hour because he's always late for appointments. I don't know why. Perhaps there's a message there. Is he telling you obliquely who he is and you've got to work it out?'

Jed's chief super mode began flicking through possibilities. It was odd. It was as if he was back at his desk, which had been more like home than home. He missed the frantic bustle, being overworked, the hair-raising moments, the rivalry and friendships. Cold cases were the only replacement he could find for a man with one useless arm. Quadrants? It must mean something.

The evening's guest speaker was being escorted into the conference hall by the chairman. He looked at home on the platform; big, muscular, standing firm, no notes. No lectern. He was going to speak straight from the heart.

That'll be me up there tomorrow, thought Fancy, the old nerves rising up into her throat. I shall dry up. I won't remember a word of what I'm going to say.

It was an excellent talk, amusing and informative. It fired Fancy's enthusiasm for her genre. She wanted to get to a computer and start writing a new book straight away. She admired the way he researched police procedure in a practical way, spending days with the force, going out at night with them. She wondered if she should do something like that.

The question time was lively. It would have gone on all night but the chairman drew a halt. 'I must get our speaker to the bar before it closes,' he said. 'And before he goes back to London.'

'He was good, wasn't he?' said Fancy, clapping as the speaker left the hall to applause.

'Very good. But I don't know how he got away with that police work. I wouldn't have let a member of the public come with us on call, even one wearing a flak jacket. You never know when something is going to turn dangerous. We're not insured for the public, not even writers.'

'True,' said Fancy. 'Perhaps he signs some let-out clause before they go out. His books are full of the correct police procedure. Lots of detail about the workings of police stations.'

'Is that what your Pink Pen Detective does? She always seems to be in some sort of danger and requires rescuing.'

They were drifting out of the hall, among the last to leave. Stewards were going round, straightening chairs, collecting lost property, switching off lights, turning off power.

'You'll get locked in,' they warned. 'Only water to drink.'

'And nothing to read,' Fancy added.

'Would you like a nightcap?' Jed asked. 'There's just time before the bar closes. The queue has gone.'

'I don't think so. I need a good night's sleep before tomorrow. It's going to be a heavy day. Two panels in the morning, one-to-ones, and then my talk in the evening. And I need to look at my notes.'

'I shall clap heartily at every word.'

'I'd rather you didn't come.'

'Wouldn't miss it for the world.'

He was walking her to Lakeside, quite slowly, making it spin out. It was another clear night, stars like diamond dust, the trees still and ghostly. Laughter carried from the bar into the still air. Music came from the disco-gyrating in the small conference hall.

'We must go dancing one evening,' said Jed. 'Perhaps tomorrow, after your talk. You'll be feeling relaxed and want to let your hair down.'

'But . . . ?'

'I do a sort of one-armed dancing, holding the lady the other way round. Nothing wrong with my legs. They can still move.'

'Oh,' said Fancy, lost for words, still wondering what he meant.

Jed keyed in the code for the Lakeside entrance door. It was so easy, anyone could have got in. They walked up the stairs, not wanting to use the lift, still stringing out time, stopping on each landing.

They didn't know who saw it first. It was hanging from the door handle of room 425; another chiffon scarf, still wet, dripping a puddle on the carpet. It was the kind of scarf that Melody always wore.

Fancy clutched Jed's arm, the useless one, not knowing what she was doing. But at least his other arm went round her, holding her close. There was some kind of monster out there, walking the grounds.

'Don't look,' he said. 'I'll get rid of it and I'll check your room for you. Then I'll have a look round outside. Whoever put the scarf there can't be far away.'

'One minute past eleven.' Fancy was shaking. 'What does it mean? You haven't told me what your friend said. His report. The pathologist in Derby.'

'There was hardly any water in her lungs. Melody was unconscious when she went into the water. Drugged. Barely breathing. She wouldn't have known anything.'

'Sometimes I think I don't know anything.'

'There's one thing you do know. I'm here. And I won't let anything happen to you.'

# 6

## Monday Night

Jed searched her room. It was getting to be a habit. No wet intruder hiding in the bathroom. Then he disappeared fast, making sure she was locked in. As he said, the intruder could not have gone far. There were damp marks in the lift, as if the scarf had been carried in a leaking bag.

So it must be someone here at the conference. Someone who had followed her to Derbyshire. Fancy had thought that by enduring the tedious drive up the M1, she had shaken off whoever it was that had chucked a lump of concrete through her bedroom window. She was wrong.

It did not make sense. What had she done to evoke such animosity? Written a lot of crime books? All fiction. Edited a magazine called *Macabre Mysteries*?

Cold cases. It must be something to do with cold crimes. Crimes that had gone cold, that had never been solved. Perhaps one of the issues had come too near to the truth. Perhaps someone was scared. They were nervous, worried, running shitless, scared that the case might be re-opened.

Jed had been going to talk about some cold crime in *MM*. She had never listened. She tried to remember what cold cases she had featured in the past but was too tied down with lectures and workshops to concentrate. She must listen now.

Fancy made some weak tea, changed into her pink nightshirt, waited in case Jed returned. He might never return. She was dangerous company. All her life, she had been too bright, too dangerous. Men had left her. Men with no courage, no guts, too self-obsessed with their own looks, their ambition, their place in society.

It was nearly one o'clock before Jed returned. Fancy was in bed, reading notes for her talk the following day. At least her legs were getting a rest.

He knocked on the door of room 425.

'Password,' said Fancy, slipping out of bed.

'Dammit,' said Jed. 'It's Jed. Do I need a password?'

'Yes.'

'Did we arrange a password?'

'Of course, we did.'

'Liar. Campari and ice. Will that do?'

'Come in.'

Jed looked exhausted. He had combed the

grounds, the gardens, all the halls. Nothing. Even the smoker's gazebo had given up coughing and gone to bed. His Roman fringe was standing on end as if his hand had gone through it a dozen times.

'We need to talk,' he said, sitting down on the end of her bed. 'I'm not staying, don't worry, but a cup of tea would be great.'

Fancy filled the kettle with fresh water and switched it on. Jed had taken off his vulnerable glasses and was rubbing his eyes. He looked ready for sleep. He'd already driven into Derby and back that afternoon, missed any supper. She supposed his car was fitted with special controls. Another thing to ask him, one day.

'So what shall we talk about, before you fall asleep?' asked Fancy, making tea. 'I've a stolen banana. Now defrosted.'

'Pass over stolen goods. I need the energy. Whoever it is that's tormenting you with happenings or non-happenings is determined and nasty. He needs to be caught and frightened off, stopped, before someone gets hurt.'

'Before I get hurt.'

'Melody got hurt. Badly hurt. So hurt that she is now in a refrigerated box in Derby.'

'Is there a connection? Is anyone else being sent severed hands in a biscuit tin?'

'I haven't heard any other screams of terror.'

'I didn't scream.'

'Only a tiny squeak,' Jed agreed. 'Amazing self-control.'

Fancy sat on the bed beside him, wrapped in her pashmina. It was like a replay of the pre-supper party that evening, but without the fun and laughter and wine. She made sure there was space between them as Jed negotiated the hot tea with his one good hand. He noticed her precaution.

'You should have seen my handwriting when I had to start learning to write with my left hand. It was like a child's.'

'Like Nelson's.'

He was surprised. 'Have you seen that letter? The first he wrote with his left hand after he lost his right hand?'

'Yes, the one dated 27 July 1797. *I am become a burden to my friends and useless to my country*,' she quoted. 'I went to an exhibition of Nelson's relics and memorabilia at Greenwich.'

Jed looked astonished. 'So did I. Yes, I went to that exhibition. We might have passed each other in the crowd. Brushed shoulders, even.'

'I think you trod on my toe. Someone big trod on my toe.'

'It was probably me. I apologize.'

'I accept your apology.'

'If only I had said hello.'

Jed put the tea down on the floor, being careful not to tip it over. He looked at Fancy with caution, trying to gauge her reaction. She looked calm enough but she was an old hand at disguising her feelings. He never knew exactly what she was thinking. He could gauge the emotion but not the thoughts.

'Would you like me to stay the night? You've a double bed. We could put a pillow down the centre for propriety's sake.'

Fancy imaged that pillow, white and pristine. Jed would be only inches away, that silver-streaked hair on another pillow, breathing his own sleep. She had only her pink teddy bear nightshirt. Not long enough to be entirely modest. She thought of the bleak loneliness of other nights, hundreds of nights, when she had longed for a companion. Anyone, just someone there, being on the other side of a pillow.

'A pillow?'

'No room for a barbed wire fence,' he said, keeping a straight face. 'If that's what you'd prefer.'

'Is this to protect me?'

'I want you to have a good night's sleep, for tomorrow. It's your big day. No more surprises. No nasty surprises. I don't want to find you floating in the other lake. Or floating anywhere.'

Fancy shivered at the thought. She was really frightened. Dew broke out on her skin, not only from a night-chill. Whoever was pursuing her was here at the conference. He was here, at this minute and not far away, watching her every move. It was a relentless onslaught on her nerves. She was supposed to write crime, not be a victim of crime.

'I can swim,' she said again.

'After a blow on the head? Or being drugged?'

'I don't know what to do.'

'If it's a pillow problem, I could go downstairs and get a pillow and duvet from my own room. I would then sleep on the floor, not exactly against the door as there isn't room for my legs, but alongside the bed or below the window. Any space that's six feet long.'

'What do you think is going to happen?'

'I don't know, Fancy. I hope I'm wrong, but something is clearly going on here and you are at the centre of it. What have you done to upset someone so much? Is it revenge? Is it something or someone in your personal life that you haven't told me about?'

'I can't think of anything or anyone. No reason at all. Someone might dislike my books but surely not to that extent. It must be something to do with those cold cases, maybe a case that I have already published. Perhaps I have unearthed a kettle of worms.'

Jed flinched. 'A can,' he said.

'I can't think at this time of night. I'm not one of those small-hours writers. Office hours for me, nine to five, or nine to near midnight. I often just keep on writing, only stopping for tea or a sandwich.'

'I usually write at night. Research and routine work during the day. Work-out at the gym, walk a lot. I have to keep fit. It's only too easy to give up if you have an injury.'

'Will you tell me about it one day?' Fancy asked, blinking. 'You know, what actually happened. Would you mind?'

She might be able to understand him if she knew what had happened. He was an enigma. One moment joking, the next totally distant. Frosted.

'I might. I might not. It was a bit gory. You should get some sleep. There's this pillow question to resolve. Your decision, lady. Make up your mind, before we both fall asleep, where we are.'

Fancy wanted him there but she did not want the reputation. Jed could hardly sneak away at dawn to his own room. It would soon be all over Northcote, a juicy item of gossip for breakfast and lunch. Though it might be forgotten by supper time.

'I shall be all right now,' she said, dredging up the last of her courage. 'This room is safe enough. I'm not afraid of a couple of wet scarves. We both need our sleep. But thank you for the offer. The pillow was very reassuring.'

Jed got up, stretched, obviously relieved. He touched her shoulder briefly. 'I like my own bed, too. But I might change my mind one day and to hell with the pillow.'

★ ★ ★

It was the smell that awoke her. A faint whiff of smoke that eddied round her nostrils and made Fancy cough. The window was half-open and she had not drawn the curtains. She always liked to see the night, the stars, the dark drift of clouds over the moon. Sometimes she got her best ideas in the middle of the night.

She would lay, only half-awake or half-asleep, and a story would drift around in her mind and she would see scenes as if she was watching late night television. She always kept a notebook by her bed. Sometimes she could not read what she had written in the night, lines like wriggly worms. Only this was not late night television, this was not dreaming.

Fancy sat up, coughing. Smoke was curling up under the door, in tendrils of vapour, almost white against the wood panelling of the door. Now her ears caught a faint sound, a crackling of splinters bursting.

Something was on fire outside her bedroom.

She knew that the first rule in any fire is: do not open any doors. It was called backdraught, or something. It only made a fire worse. She had seen a film. But Fancy was on the third floor. It was a pretty long drop from her window even if she knotted sheets together. She only had two sheets and she was hopeless at knots.

She was gambling on it not being a very big fire. It didn't sound like a roaring furnace. She switched on the bathroom light and propped open the door, running the cold tap. She put a wet flannel over her mouth and nose and cautiously opened the bedroom door.

A gust of smoke blew into her face. She coughed and coughed, doubling over, clutching the doorpost, waving the smoke out of her sight.

The fire was burning inside a large bag. On the top of the bag was printed *A BAG FOR*

LIFE, one of those sturdy, save-the-environment projects. The burning bag was settling down inside a bucket from the garden. There was still earth clinging to the sides of the bucket. Flames were beginning to lick upwards and over towards the door of the bedroom.

Fancy ran back into the bathroom, picked up a big towel, plunged it under the running water, came back and threw it over the bucket and the bag. Then she grasped the handle of the bucket and carried the whole thing into the bathroom.

The handle was heavy and hot. She stood the bucket in the shower cubicle and turned on the cold water. A cascade of water hit the fire in seconds.

Fancy jumped back. It hissed and spluttered and the plastic shower curtain melted into shreds like molten sugar.

She leaned back against the tiled wall, gasping and catching her breath. She leaned over the basin and, cupping her hands, drank huge gulps of water from the tap. It was then that she saw that she had red burns on the palms of both hands. Her nightshirt was wet through, clinging to her curves. The shower had sprayed her too.

The fire was almost out. It was drawing its last spluttering gasps, the flames dying, the red ash speckling through the towel as it, too, ate the cotton.

She was shaking now as shock set in. She sat on the side of the bed, making the sheets damp, and unsteadily dialled the number for the night manager. The number was printed on the front of the phone.

'There's been a fire outside my bedroom,' she said. 'Lakeside 425. No panic. I've put it out.'

★   ★   ★

There was such a fuss and commotion in the corridor that it was a wonder anyone got any sleep. Half the inhabitants were up, clad in a variety of nighties and pyjamas, bathrobes and satin gowns, hair in curlers, faces shiny with night cream.

'You were wonderful, Fancy. We could all have been burnt to death.'

'You're a heroine.'

'Back off, everyone. Shock, she's in shock.'

'Everyone make tea! We all need tea.'

Fancy was wrapped in a big dry towel and plied with hot sweet tea. She kept her hands hidden, letting someone else hold the cup to her lips. She was still too shocked to wonder who had started a fire outside her bedroom. It could have been Jed. He knew she was alone and locked in . . .

The night manager was on his mobile phone, waking up the housekeeper and a couple of gardeners. 'Get here, fast. Lakeside 425. I need help.'

He needed witnesses, not help.

'The whole corridor could have caught fire. You saved us all,' said Fancy's neighbour in 423. She was an elderly woman, hardly able to climb out of a window at her age. She wrote very long, involved sagas about country life.

Fancy's heart fluttered down to a steadier beat. She didn't want to be a heroine. She didn't want high blood pressure.

'Don't worry,' said Fancy, reassuring her. 'It was probably a prank. A very silly and stupid prank.'

'Too many parties?'

Fancy tried to raise a smile. 'You've got it. Now you go back to bed.'

'The housekeeper is on her way,' said the night manager. 'She'll get you another room.' He was very young, spiky blond hair, shirt tucked hastily into jeans. He'd never had anything like this to deal with before.

'The bed is all right. I can sleep here.' If she could get to sleep, thought Fancy.

'I think we ought to have to look at the damage or something,' he said. He had no idea, really. This was beyond his normal experience. 'You know, clues.'

Fancy nodded. She was too tired to argue. Perhaps the arsonist had left his room number on a calling card.

# 7

## Tuesday Morning

The night duty manager, hot on the heels of the marathon tea-making industry, was still sweating. When he realized that Fancy had put out the fire and there was no need to evacuate the whole of Lakeside and summon the fire brigade, he relaxed and, to a degree, he began to participate in the event.

He removed the 'evidence'. He said the fire inspector would want to look at it. Another writer with some knowledge of first aid put something soothing on Fancy's burns and bound them up with lint and bandage. She felt like a boxer with two white gloves.

'To keep the air out,' said the first aider. 'Cling film tomorrow.'

The night manager shooed everyone back to their rooms. He was now in his element. It made a change from lost room keys and people locking themselves out. He inspected room 425. There was minimal damage. It needed a new shower curtain and a good scrub, that was all.

'You were very brave, Miss Jones. Thank

you, thank you so much. You didn't panic and that's the main thing in all emergencies. I'm just so sorry that you got hurt. Would you like me to call an ambulance? Maybe you need hospital treatment,' he suggested.

'No, thank you. It's only a little burn. I've done it many times at home, taking something out of the microwave without a cloth.'

'The housekeeper says you can have the room opposite for the rest of the night. The lady who was occupying it has had to go home. Some family problem.'

'How sad. What a pity,' said Fancy, clutching the towel round her. Her damp nightshirt was feeling clammy. And the sheets were damp where she had sat down.

'Can I get you anything?'

Fancy wanted to say a large brandy but that would cement her reputation as an old soak. 'Nothing, thank you,' she murmured, moving across the corridor like a sleepwalker.

She also wanted music. Chris Rhea singing *Josephine* would do nicely. Four minutes of cheer and a pulsing beat.

The room opposite was identical to hers in every way; same furniture, same colour quilt and curtains, except that its view was the car park and the new lake. But it seemed alien. It was not home. It was bare and cold, had none of her things. Fancy wrapped herself in the duvet and tried to sleep. Fire or no fire, there was still tomorrow to get through. But it was already today, she thought sleepily, as she drifted through cotton wool into some haven.

She had the keys to both rooms so she was able to find clothes the following morning and ferry them back to the new room. It was the Question and Answer Panel first so she had to look reasonably intelligent and informed, but relaxed and friendly. A tall order. Black jeans were the answer, with a fitted, black suede jacket. Her shirt was vintage black-and-white striped silk to mini-mize the severity of the outfit. She added a tasselled scarf for jollity.

A fire incident officer came out from Derby and Fancy spent breakfast time answering his questions. The day manager took him to inspect the damage in room 425. Fancy managed to grab some orange juice and a croissant. That was all. She would make up for it at morning break time, indulge in a biscuit.

She thought she might see Jed but he was nowhere around. Surely he had heard about the fire? The grapevine at Northcote was faster than Twitter or Facebook. Again, the awful thought. Perhaps he had put the fire outside her room. He had left her locked in.

He'd had time to set it up. He would know how to do it.

She saw him striding across the lawn, munching on an apple. No time for breakfast either. He waved, then stopped when he saw her hands.

'You're hurt,' he said. He seemed concerned. 'What happened?'

'Nothing much,' she said. 'This is a big fuss. A bit of cling film would have worked just as well.'

'Keep the bandages on,' he advised. 'Milk the sympathy vote. Always useful. Tell me what happened.'

Fancy gave him a rundown of the incident from her viewpoint. He nodded, listening intently.

'You did exactly the right thing in the circumstances, but not if it had been a big fire. Never open a door. Hang out the window and yell for a hunky fireman to carry you down the extending ladder.'

'It was instinct.'

'This time instinct was right but it's not always. I'll examine the fire remains,' he went on. Then seeing her face, he added. 'The fire officer is an old mate of mine. He may ask for my opinion as I'm here. I'll do it immediately.'

'You do have a strange circle of friends,' she

murmured as he walked away.

But he was back before she had stopped talking to some of the writers at her lecture. They drifted away when they saw his serious face.

'Classic incendiary,' Jed said. 'A wigwam built of books of matches, opened up and stood on their end. Torn up paper all around and the whole put in the middle of a big clump of paper. It looks like a typed manuscript. There are page numbers still visible in the corners going up to three hundred.'

'Oh, I hope not. Some poor soul who wanted me to read her novel,' said Fancy. 'Perhaps she left it outside my door. I hope it wasn't her only copy.'

'There are charred bits and pieces left. The fire officer has taken the evidence. Was it a sequel to *Gone With The Wind?*'

'So they just put a match to it?' They were walking slowly towards the main conference hall. Delegates were merging in the same direction. There would be a bottleneck at the door.

'No, a match would just go out without any air. Whoever it was put a burning cigarette down among the books of matches and they went off, one by one, like miniature fireworks. Guaranteed to keep burning.'

'How come you know all about it?'

'Am I a suspect, Fancy? Surely not? True, I was downstairs. I know how to start fires. I've dealt with enough arsonists in my time.'

'I'm sorry,' said Fancy, confidence in tatters. 'I'm a bag of nerves.'

'How are your hands?'

'Feeling better,' she said. 'I might have difficulty in holding a glass.'

'I'll get you a straw.'

When Fancy walked into the main conference hall with the other panellists, it was full to capacity. Questions and Answers were always popular. The chairman, Fergus Nelson, chaired the panel, trying to make sure that each panellist had their fair chance of answering. There was usually one member of a panel who wanted to hog the whole event, thought their words were the only ones that counted, who had too much to say and needed shutting up.

'Good morning, everyone,' said Fergus. 'Settle down. We've a lot to get through.'

Fancy was not one to push herself forward but the chairman made sure she had a fair chance with replies, though she always kept her answers short and sweet. No publicity eulogy about herself and her current work.

When she left the hall for the first break, Jed was waiting outside with a black coffee for her and a couple of biscuits. He looked as if he hadn't slept or eaten for hours. He was drawn and lined, the sparkle gone.

'I skipped the last question,' he said. 'We all know about double spacing.'

'Don't forget some of the delegates are white-badgers. New writers. Never been to anything like this before. It's a revelation.'

'Point taken. Can you manage? I need to get some more coffee. I want an adrenaline fix. I shall go straight to the head of the queue, ignore the looks.'

'We're a bit short of hands, between us,' said Fancy, managing a joke. 'We should invent some no-hands gadget for *Dragons' Den.*'

'And make a million.'

They did not have a minute together. People were crowding round Fancy either to comment on the fire, commiserate about her hands or ask ancillary questions to ones already asked at the panel. Fancy could hold a cup. Her fingers were working outside the clumsy bandage. At least she got a seat on one of the garden benches.

Fergus came up later. 'Can you manage the second session, Fancy?' he asked. 'We shall quite understand if you want a rest. You didn't get much sleep last night.'

'I'm fine,' said Fancy. 'I can carry on.'

She was actually on better form for the second panel session. Her wits seemed to have recovered and her remarks, off the cuff, were hilarious. She even managed to shut up the current trendy know-all, Ms I'm So Famous, with a remark that had everyone laughing.

She couldn't see a silver-streaked head among the audience. Perhaps Jed had gone for some much needed sleep. It didn't matter. She had survived this morning, with him or without him.

It was early lunch today because half of the delegates were off on an excursion to Chatsworth House, the nearby stately home. The other excursion offered was to a factory outlet, buying reject china in bulk, and touring the pottery.

Fancy only wanted to fall into bed and sleep.

Lunch was a rushed affair. Salad and ham, and either grated or cottage cheese was on offer with grated carrot or coleslaw. She couldn't follow what choice she was being given. It was sit and be grateful time.

Delegates rushed out to their coaches. Fancy was left with a whole table to clear. Nobody had touched the dessert — Bakewell tart and orange custard. She went to the frozen fruit table and selected the softest pear.

She had a whole flask of coffee in front of her. And a whole afternoon ahead. She wondered if room 425 had been scrubbed and refurbished. She wanted to be back in her own room.

Jed came and sat down at her table. He looked a few degrees better, less burdened. The landscape of his face had softened. He had had a sleep, even if only for an hour. He could revive on a nap. All policemen could. He poured himself a coffee from her flask.

'No Chatsworth House?'

'I know the history. I've read the Georgiana book. Horace Walpole thought it had an air of gloomy grandeur.'

'Surely it's research, somewhere full of ideas for future books?'

'I don't need any more ideas. My head is spinning with them.'

'So what are your plans for this afternoon? There's some sort of private rehearsal going on in the hall. A writing read-through in the Orchard Room and a last talk on non-fiction at 5 p.m.'

'I've no plans.'

Jed finished his coffee. 'My car's outside. Would you like a drive to Newstead Abbey? It's not far, some part-ruins, some falling down. The poet, Lord Byron, once lived there, though he didn't drown there, he drowned in Italy. Just a walk around, Fancy. Fresh air and nice grounds, somewhere different. A breath of the outside world. No strings.'

Fancy nodded her thanks. It sounded perfect. Especially the no strings.

★  ★  ★

Jed drove well in his adapted car. It was a small, low-slung two-seater with a soft top, dark blue, hardly the right car for a retired detective chief inspector. Extra levers on the steering wheel. Fancy did not recognize the make of car. She was not good on cars. Maybe a Vauxhall Sports? In minutes she had forgotten that he did not have two hands on the wheel.

The afternoon began to warm up. She threw off her jacket and tossed it into the tiny space at the back of the car that might take a child or someone slim sitting sideways. She began to relax, fall into some kind of emotional slump.

The conversation was light, ridiculous, funny.

'I went out for lunch. I remembered Tuesday's lunch is a rushed job. Fish and chips down at the local pub. But no marrowfat peas. They're revolting,' said Jed, taking a right turn.

'You'll never make old age,' she said. 'Fish and chips. All that cholesterol.'

'Don't worry, I will. I'm writing a book of true life cold crime stories. I've emailed *MM* half a dozen times but you never answer. That's why I'm hoping to get some time to talk to you this week. This book is important to me. All those unsolved crimes that deserve to be solved; the villain still out there, walking the streets.'

'I always answer my emails,' said Fancy, indignantly. 'Perhaps I wasn't getting them. Perhaps there's a hacker.'

'But why?'

'Because these cold cases are too near the truth? Because they could be solved if you publish what you know about them? It's a thought.'

'One of my stories featured in your *MM*. It really interested me. *The Missing Cover Girl*. Do you remember that issue? It was one of my first cold cases and one that we have never solved.'

'Yes, I remember. It was alleged that he killed his wife because she caught him having an affair with her twin sister. But it was never proved and her body was never found. So he got away with it.'

'We never cracked it either. Yet there were

traces of blood spatters in the house. The wife was never seen again from that day forward. It was as if she disappeared from the face of the earth.'

'Was it the wife's blood?'

'We could never prove it. Long before the days of DNA. Both sisters had the same blood group.'

'Who reported the wife missing?'

'Her mother. The husband said she had a history of running away and she would probably come back. But her passport and bank account were never touched. And it didn't look as if she had taken anything with her. Even her handbag was still in the house.'

'Did he marry the other twin?'

'Yes, I believe he did eventually.'

'After seven years. When his wife was officially declared dead?'

'I guess so. I was busy on other cases by then, getting slowly promoted. Here we are. This is Newstead Abbey, somewhere behind all those trees.'

He turned into the entrance drive, nodded to the gatekeeper on duty, who waved them through. It was a narrow drive, heavily canopied with trees and shrubs. Many of the shrubs were in flower and Fancy could feel herself relaxing as they left the busy roads and noise of traffic behind.

The house came into view as the drive turned into undulating parkland, dominating a big clearing of grass and paved walk-ways. She could see deer grazing in the distance. Several coaches were already parked near the house, visitors climbing out and stretching. Jed parked the car in a shady spot away from the crowds.

Newstead House was both house and ruin. The ruined abbey walls leaned heavily on one side of the house. The tall stone arches looked precarious, as if they were about to fall at any moment. It was cordoned off with warning notices, keeping the curious at a distance.

'That looks pretty old,' said Fancy, gazing up. So much of the intricate stonework was still intact, a monument to stonemasons of old, carving their gargoyles and angels. The angels were ready to fly. Instinctively she ducked her head.

'Twelfth century, I think. Would you like to see round the house, go on a tour? There's a grand galleried hall where Byron used to do his shooting practice.'

'I think I'd just like to walk round these lovely gardens,' said Fancy. 'My head's too full to take in loads of information and history. I'd rather walk and relax.'

'Good idea. Let's walk, then. I'll keep an eye on the time. You'll want to be back at

121

Northcote before supper. It's your big evening.'

'Don't remind me. Perhaps you could have a puncture or two on the way back. Somebody would fill in for me. The panellist this morning who wouldn't stop talking. She'd do it like a shot.'

'Nonsense. You'll be fine. You know your subject and what's more you're enthusiastic about writing. Everyone loves your course.'

'A course is different to a talk. In a course you're interacting with people, encouraging feedback and batting ideas around. A talk means I have to stand on that dratted platform with three hundred and fifty pairs of eyes glued on me. All my enthusiasm will drain out of me.'

She didn't add: and one pair of eyes who hates me enough to start a fire outside my bedroom. Jed could read her thoughts.

'We might have scared him off,' he said. 'The fire was too public. A lot of people were involved. Everything else has been for you alone.'

They were taking a path towards a pond, lake, river, whatever it was. It was shimmering water. Fancy shivered. Water made her think about Melody. The police were still interviewing everyone but no one was being told anything. The place was alive with rumours.

Some over-imaginative idiot even had the nerve to say it was all a hoax, that the police were out-of-work actors, and Melody would reappear at Thursday night's concert to sing *Auld Lang Syne* and present prizes.

Fancy found the joke distasteful. She could still see the pale arm and the swirling chiffon material floating on the water. That hadn't been a hoax. Someone had stolen Melody's life. She had still a life ahead, children's stories to write.

But the walk through the gardens and the flowers was beautiful. Lots of new saplings were being planted. They dutifully looked at the oldest tree, which had its own plaque. It looked old and misshapen, wizened branches spread, touching the ground, almost too tired to stand up straight. Even the lake was tranquil and wafted cooling breezes across the water.

It was turning into a scorching afternoon, the sun melting down through a cloudless sky. Fancy rolled up her sleeves and Jed loosened his collar. He did not touch her or take her hand. They'd only known each other a few days and had not reached the hand-holding stage though Fancy felt it would have been quite natural if he had reached out to her.

She began to like him, to be less suspicious.

He knew about suffering, his arm and that. He made fun of her but only in the kindest way.

At a steep downward step she went to take his arm but it was the arm that couldn't move and she almost fell. It was Jed who caught her with his good hand and steadied her.

'If you want assistance at any time, you have to walk the other side of me,' he said. 'I'm a one-armed warrior.'

'Sorry. I keep forgetting. I'll remember that.'

'Fancy an ice cream?'

They stopped abruptly and laughed. A meandering middle-aged group on the path looked at them. They were from the coach party. They couldn't see anything funny.

'I've never been called an ice cream before,' said Fancy.

★  ★  ★

They were back at Northcote in good time for Fancy to shower and change for supper. She did not feel at all hungry but thought she should sit at the committee table that evening as she was the invited after-dinner speaker.

She prayed that the menu would be light and tasty. She was getting the collywobbles and feeling sick with nerves. As it was a special occasion, she wore a long, straight, velvet skirt and a ruched-lace printed tunic top with adjustable side ties. It was very elegant. She tied her hair back and clipped on gold dangling earrings.

The dining room was already full and tomato soup was being ladled out at the table into big bowls.

'No, thank you,' said Fancy, seeing herself dripping soup down her front and having to go on the platform wearing red splodges. Nor could she face the steak and kidney pie, so made do with a few fresh vegetables. It was tinned fruit salad and ice cream afterwards, which was not hard to eat. She swirled the lot around her dish into a creamy pink mud. Cold mud. It reminded her of the ice cream they had eaten at Newstead Abbey, the ice cream melting faster than they could eat it.

'Would you like some more, Fancy?' asked Jessie, who was serving that evening. 'You've hardly eaten anything.'

'Sorry, I'm too nervous,' she said.

'You're nervous?' exclaimed Fergus. 'Yet you must have done dozens of these talks.'

'I have, but it never gets any easier. Believe me, nerves never go away. I'll skip coffee too,' she added. 'Don't want to get caught short in the middle of my talk.'

Fancy rose from the table amid a chorus of good luck wishes.

'Bonne chance!' said Jessie.

They knew how she felt, and sympathized. But it was something she had to face alone. She walked outside along the garden path in the gathering gloom. Fergus would join her later and escort her into the conference hall once it was full. The walk to the scaffold.

Jessie came running after her. 'Fancy. You left your belt behind at the table. It must have dropped off. I found it on the floor.'

She had Fancy's pink leather belt in her hand. Fancy took it. She hadn't been wearing the belt. She was wearing a loose tunic top that didn't need one.

'Thanks.'

Fancy took the belt and held it limply. She dare not look at it. She knew instinctively by the feel of it that something was wrong. Someone had been into her Lakeside bedroom and taken it. She did not know what to do. There was a hard lump in her throat and it wasn't a piece of chopped fruit salad.

Jed came up beside her. He was wearing his Mafia outfit, all black, very sexy. 'Break a leg,' he said with a grin.

She held out the belt. It hung loosely in her

126

hand. It had been slashed in several places, slashed with a sharp knife.

'Look at this,' she said. 'My belt. Slashed all along. That knife was meant for me.'

# 8

## Tuesday Evening

Jed whipped a clean plastic food bag from the kitchen and put the belt in it. He had a pal in Derby, another mate apparently, tops for fingerprints. Then he turned his attention to Fancy. She was paralyzed with fright. She stood on the path, in the growing dark, halfway to the conference hall, barely hearing what Fergus was saying to her.

'It's time to go in,' Fergus urged. 'Fancy? Come along, lass. They're all waiting.'

Fancy was not listening to him. That knife would be slashing her next. She could feel its cold blade against her skin.

Jed was beside her again. He looked tall, dark and forbidding. Something different about him. He had put the evidence in a safe place and out of sight. He touched her arm. 'Fancy? Speak to me. Say something.'

'I can't do it,' she whispered.

'Yes, you can,' he said firmly. 'You're not going to let some stupid prankster get the better of you. You know what you're going to say. You're going to give these budding writers hope. You're going to tell them that failure is only an illusion.'

Her heart missed a beat. She was a failure. 'I can't,' she said.

Jed turned to the chairman. 'I'm going on with Fancy. Is that all right? It's going to be a twosome. A kind of conversation. Ant and Dec-style, vaguely. I ask a few questions and Fancy will answer them. We've changed the format. A chat show, an interview-type talk.'

Fancy did not know what he was talking about.

'Anything,' said Fergus, desperate now. 'As long as Fancy goes on that platform. She can't cancel at the very last moment. It would be a disaster.'

Jed took Fancy's arm with his good hand. 'Come along, famous lady crime writer. Show them what you're made of. Let's go blow them off this planet. Put on that gorgeous smile, baby.'

'I'm not — '

'Yes, you are.'

'Failure.'

'I can't even spell it.'

Fancy found herself being propelled into the main conference hall. It was full. A sea of expectant faces turned towards her, many of whom she knew. The shelf was full. They were

129

all her friends. She wished she was sitting up there with them.

A second chair was hastily put on the platform and the lectern removed. Jed and Fancy were both going to sit for this talk. The technical man adjusted the height of the mikes in front of them.

'It's going to be a different kind of lecture this evening,' said Fergus. 'As you all know, Fancy has a couple of bad burns from last night's incident and it is unfair to ask her to stand. And John Edwards, who has some professional experience of crime, has agreed to fire the questions at her. So a big hand, ladies and gentleman, for tonight's speaker, the well-known crime writer, Miss Fancy Burne-Jones.'

Fancy had to admire the way the chairman had made it sound as if it was all his idea. Though 'fire the questions' was a tactless phrase. Her first half-smile of the evening appeared. Jed took it as a good sign and sent her a silent signal of approval. They were ready to start.

'We all want to know the difference between crime writing and thrillers,' said Jed. He looked so good, sitting there, in charge, air of natural authority. 'Is there a difference, Fancy?'

Fancy shifted in her seat, found a more

comfortable position. She could not think of any words. 'The simple answer is . . . that crime writing includes an element of police procedure, whereas a thriller is all action. But the *Die Hard* films explode that theory, sorry Bruce Willis. They are all action yet Bruce is cast as a policeman.'

Fancy was off. There was no stopping her.

Jed had only to steer her towards new aspects. He had an idea what everyone wanted to know. But he did not mention cold cases or her magazine. There was no need to include something which might shatter her present fragile confidence.

'You write every day, don't you?'

'A day without writing is a day wasted,' said Fancy. She paused. She hadn't written a word today yet she could not consider it wasted. She had spent a magical afternoon with Jed, among flowers and a sense of history, words spiralling into her head to use later. Perhaps there would be time tonight.

'My own ninety-day novel course proves that you can write the first draft of a novel in ninety days. And I've done it myself several times. Seven hundred words a day and in ninety days you have a novel ready to work on.'

'Ready to work on? What do you mean?'

'The first draft is the skeleton of your story.

Revising is putting the flesh on the bones. The next revision is honing and whittling and polishing. It's the part I like best. Cut, cut . . . cut.' Fancy's voice was unsteady for a moment. The audience thought it was emotion. Jed knew she was thinking of her pink belt.

'Is that it, then? Two revisions?'

'No, I do a third and final revision so that each page looks right. A reasonable amount of white. And a shining word. Long exchanges of dialogue are broken up. Heavy paragraphs split. Although the typed page is shorter than the printed page of your book, if you get it right initially, it will look right on the page.'

'What do you mean by white?'

Fancy laughed, looking around. 'White paper, white space, a line with nothing much on it. When people go to borrow or buy a book, they flick through the pages. If there is too much black, that is, too much print, it looks heavy going and they may put it back, unless they are an academic. But if there is plenty of white, they know they are going to be able to read it quickly and enjoy it. That's the way to sell books. Unless you rent a stall on Portobello Road and spend your Sundays flogging titles at a discount.'

'You said something about a shining word.'

'I always make sure that every page has a bright word, a beautiful word, an unusual word, something special that shines out like a beacon.'

'Not all of us can write like a beacon.'

'Every one of us has special words hidden away inside or favourite words. Mine are meticulous and serendipity.'

By a quarter past nine, Fancy was flagging. She had talked solidly for three-quarters of an hour, without a single note. Jed passed her a half-full tumbler of water and she took a grateful drink, almost choking on the first mouthful. The taste was sharp: a double gin and tonic.

She flashed him a brilliant smile of thanks. It was just what she needed. A sip of gin now and then kept the energy flowing. She got funnier and funnier. The audience were laughing, enjoying her dry wit and merciless opinion of the book trade She also made fun of herself.

'Burne-Jones is a good writing name. I'm on the top shelf but a bit out of reach for shorter readers. I have a friend whose name begins with W. She goes into W H Smith every morning and moves her books from the floor to eye-level. The staff are getting to know her. Her books are moved back every evening.'

'Writers are very generous people,' said Jed. 'Always willing to share their knowledge. Don't you agree?'

'Of course. In the end it's down to individual talent. Always write from the heart. Writing brings happiness, to you as the writer and then to your readers. Make a contract with your reader. This is the contract: I will give you a book worth reading. All you have to give me is your time.'

The audience broke out into spontaneous applause. Jed thought Fancy had brought it neatly to an end without sounding pompous or patronizing. He leaned across towards her chair. 'Well done,' he said, gravely. Fancy finished her drink.

'Is there any more of that water?' she asked.

'In the bar.'

She pretended a big sigh. 'I'll have to wait.'

A forest of hands went up, each with a burning question. Some questions were almost a major speech but Jed managed to whittle them down into something that required an answer. Everyone wanted to ask Fancy a question. They got some odd-ball replies. She was relaxed now that it was all over and could afford to be a bit flippant. No one minded.

More applause and it was time to leave the hall, escorted by the chairman. People scraped their chairs back. They were going to give her a standing ovation.

Jed put his head down close to the microphone. 'No standing, please. Fancy is a working author, not Nelson Mandela or Terry Waite.'

This brought another wave of applause. Jed had known instinctively that Fancy would hate disproportionate admiration. He was right. She was nodding and smiling in his direction. Their smiles caught like shafts of sunshine, bouncing back to each other.

'The water was wonderful,' she said as she brushed past him. 'From an ancient Scottish spring, running over burns, no doubt.'

'You were wonderful,' he replied.

Fergus took her straight to the bar where there was a bottle of champagne on ice. 'And you deserve every drop,' he said, pouring the glistening foam into a cluster of flutes. The committee gathered round, eager for their share of the unexpected champagne. They didn't get champagne after every speaker. Jed accepted a beer. He preferred it anyway.

'That worked very well,' said Fergus. 'The twosome conversation was very relaxed and enjoyable. Sometimes speakers get carried away by their early struggles and we have to hear about every harrowing rejection.'

'Or they insist on telling us the entire plot

of their latest and then read bits of it out aloud to us. I hate that,' said Jessie. 'And of course, we had two classy people to look at. All the men were looking at Fancy and all the women were gazing at Jed. Like a scene from *Gone With The Wind*.'

Jed did not know where to look. He cleared his throat and sipped his beer.

Fancy unpinned her topknot and let it fall round her shoulders. She felt carefree for once. No more worries about talking.

She had to laugh again as the champagne tickled her nose. Jed looked so put out. 'All the women gazing at such a handsome policeman?' she whispered towards him. 'And I hadn't even noticed.'

Someone topped up her glass. She was well on the way to becoming rather merry. Lots of champagne and a double gin on top of a few carrots and a dish of muddy ice cream. What could she expect? She had freed her fingers from the bandage and could hold a glass very well now. It had taken practice.

There were only two more working days of Northcote: Wednesday and Thursday. She had two more course lectures to do and then she could go home first thing on Friday morning, having fulfilled her contract.

But she did not want to go home. There would be no Jed to support her. What if this belt-slashing maniac followed her back to her church lodge and set fire to it?

'Fancy, you're supposed to be signing books in the book room,' said the book room lady. 'There's a queue forming. I hope you can still sign your name.'

'I'll put a cross,' said Fancy, taking her champagne with her. 'Or a double cross, meaning with love.'

'Tut, tut,' said the book room lady, grinning. 'What we have to put up with, getting authors to sign their books. Next year I'll bring a rubber stamp.'

Fancy spent half an hour signing books. Fergus came through with a refill of champagne. She could hardly remember her name in the feeding frenzy. She had to look at each book cover to remind herself who she was before she signed. But her smiles became lovelier and wider. And she had some words of encouragement to say to each writer. She sold a lot of books.

Jed came to the door of the book room. He had loosened the top button of his shirt, but he looked cold, forlorn somehow. 'Writer's cramp yet?'

She could see that he needed her. He didn't have to say anything.

'Nearly finished,' she said, wanting to wrap her arms round him but remembering in time that she was in company.

The queue tailed away, joining a different queue at the bar. Others drifted off to the late night talks, quizzes and readings. The energetic went to the disco; others stayed in the bar to drink and talk. It was warm enough to go outside and the lawn was dotted with groups talking and laughing. The gazebo was full, as usual, its occupants puffing away.

Jed found the same two seats in the vinery, hidden behind the big leaves. It was perfect for a quiet moment. Fancy needed to wind down. She was still on a high after her talk and too much to drink.

She tried to pin her hair back but her fingers had lost the knack. The bandages were coming undone and she fumbled, unable to retie them. They were looking dingy. Tomorrow she would beg a roll of cling film from the kitchen.

'Thank goodness,' she said, sitting back in a cane chair, ducking behind a leaf. 'At last, a moment alone.'

'You're not alone. I'm here.'

'A moment alone with you, I mean. I've had enough of the maddening crowds. Sit down, Jed. You look worn out.'

'I've been on the phone a lot, finding out things. Do you want to hear about it?'

'Yes, sure. But if you want another beer, the

bar is about to close.'

'Back in a moment. Keep my seat.'

Jed had to wait in the queue but when he returned, he was carrying a beer, a Campari and ice and a packet of crisps. They had lent him a tray. He manoeuvred the tray onto the table top. 'Guessed you didn't eat much at supper.'

'Crisps! Salt and vinegar. Great, this must be Christmas.'

They let the wave of noise wash over them, almost too tired to open the crisps. It was quite dark outside, shadows creeping up over the lawn, great trees looming. Pale faces, a cigarette being lit, flash of a torch. People were dispersing.

Fancy felt the euphoria soaking away, down her legs and into the tiled floor. It was getting cold but it was too late and too far to go to fetch a jersey. Besides, she was afraid of room 425. Afraid of what she might find there.

'Are you warm enough?'

'I'm fine,' she lied.

'Do you remember *The Missing Cover Girl* case?'

'Vaguely.' Fancy was only being polite. She didn't want to talk about a cold case. She was far too tired.

'They were twin girls called Thelma and Grace, born in late July 1950. They were both dark and beautiful, stunners, in fact, but so different in character. Thelma was flighty and flirtatious, got a job as a model, her face on the covers of glossy magazines everywhere. Grace was quiet and studious, went on to Durham University, graduated and became a press officer for one of the political parties.'

'She did well.'

'The husband in the case was Rupert Harlow, a prospective candidate for some seat in the south and they all met at a constituency party. Grace was there as a press officer and Thelma went along to be photographed. A sort of gatecrasher, but Grace let her in. She could hardly turn her own sister away.'

'I can see it all,' said Fancy. 'Rupert fell in love with the glamorous twin and she was dazzled by his political ambition, seeing herself standing on the doorstep of No. 10 in ten years' time.'

Fancy let the words fall around her. She was too tired to take the story in. She was listening out of politeness.

'Exactly. Rupert and Thelma became an item, although I'm not sure who pursued who. Thelma certainly had her eye on being the wife of a Member of Parliament, lunch on the Terrace, dinner in the Members' Dining Room.'

'Did Rupert Harlow ever become an MP?'

'No, he lost at the next election and became a solicitor instead. Thelma and Rupert were married by then, living in Surbiton. It seemed a happy marriage; a smart young couple, dinner parties and trips abroad. Then Thelma disappeared. Rupert didn't report her missing. He said later that she had flounced out in a huff, had gone to visit her sister.'

'And had she?'

'Grace wasn't even in the country. She was attending some conference in Brussels. It was their mother who reported Thelma as missing. When the police went round to the house in Surbiton, they found spatters of blood in the bedroom and on the stairs, which Rupert Harlow could not explain. Thelma's belongings were still in the house, her handbag, car keys, passport, bank book, money. She had taken nothing with her.'

'How strange. It's coming back to me now.'

Fancy remembered the story. The newspapers had called it the case of *The Missing Cover Girl* with lots of glamorous photos of Thelma. Thelma posing at parties, nightclubs, the races, always looking beautifully dressed and radiant.

'Then it came out that Rupert had been

having an affair with Grace for months, cheating on Thelma. He'd got tired of the flighty one and had fallen for the serious one. Thelma had caught them in bed together. There had been an almighty row. It was here that the stories began to differ. Rupert said that Thelma had walked out on him. Grace said that the sisters had forgiven each other and Rupert and Thelma were planning a second honeymoon. Their mother did not believe it.'

'And he was charged with Thelma's murder, despite no body being found?'

Fancy's fingers were itching to make notes. But she had no pen and no paper. Not like her at all. She would have to remember everything.

'The prosecution claimed that the blood spatters were Thelma's blood, but Grace had the same blood group. Grace said she had cut herself on a broken glass. Defence claimed the evidence was flimsy and the case was thrown out,' said Jed.

'Were you on the case?'

'Before my time, Fancy. I know I have grey hair. It was all the talk at the station. They were certain Thelma had been beaten up and buried under the patio.'

'Was there a patio?'

'Police in-joke. Tacky. Poor taste.'

'And why do you think the case might be re-opened?'

'It's the development in DNA testing these days. They can find evidence in the tiniest sample of earth or dust or smear of blood. My digging around to write about the case has stirred things up. And I've a lot more facts about Rupert and Grace that casts a different light on their affair and their subsequent marriage. I want to write about it and put it in my book.'

'*The Missing Cover Girl: Where is she now?* sort of thing?'

Jed nodded.

'If Thelma walked out on Rupert, then she is still around, isn't she? Thirty years older, but still good-looking, I bet. Have you the keys to both rooms?' Jed asked, changing the subject and finishing his beer. Fancy yawned.

'Yes. No one has asked for them back.'

Jed stood up and stretched. 'Do you fancy a dance?'

*　　★　★　★*

The small conference hall was belting out music. It was not Fancy's kind of music — pulsating rock at mega-decibels. She cringed in the doorway. Her ears were protesting.

'Wait a moment,' said Jed. 'Let me see what I can do.'

He went and spoke to the skinny, short-skirted DJ. She turned down the volume and changed the disc. 'By request, ladies and gentlemen, for one night only,' she said. '*Lady in Red*.'

Jed led Fancy onto the dance floor. 'Other way round,' he said. 'My left hand goes round your waist. My right hand can be held anywhere in space.'

'It seems all right,' said Fancy. 'Even if it is the wrong way round.'

'Who wrote the rules? It wasn't Einstein.'

The music was universal. The floor filled. Everyone loved this song of haunted love. Fancy felt herself being held closer. Jed smelled so fresh and strong, as if he showered every hour. She needed this kind of strong man. She had been alone, fending alone, for so long.

'Don't fight me,' said Jed, his face close to her hair. His breath fanned her cheek. 'This was meant to be.'

But she was not sure what she heard. She was floating on a cloud. Moving in time to the music, letting the words wash over her. It was a song she had loved for years. The singer . . . Chris de Burgh. What a mesmerizing voice. He had suffered. He knew what it was all about.

As the music faded away and the dancers stopped swaying, so the DJ pounded her original choice back onto the airwaves. It was ear-splitting, enough to deafen a thirty-year-old.

Fancy and Jed left the dance floor and went outside onto the lawn. The music was still pounding the air. Even the smokers were irritated.

'Do they think we're all deaf?' they coughed.

'I'll walk you home,' said Jed. He still had his good arm round her waist.

They went up in the lift at Lakeside, soothed by the electronic voice telling them about floors and doors.

'Is it all right if I move into the room opposite tonight?' asked Jed.

'Yes,' said Fancy. 'I should like that. If you don't mind. I'd feel safer.'

'The rooms are all alike. It's no problem.'

Fancy leaned against room 425. 'Were you going to tell me something else about the missing twins?'

'Part of my research. I've discovered that the twins' maiden name was Marchant. So Melody Marchant might have been the missing Thelma Marchant. What do you think, Fancy?'

'Melody was very good-looking, even with white hair. Quite striking. But who would want to kill her? The name might be a coincidence.'

'If Melody was Thelma Marchant, then she has already been declared dead. You can't kill the same person twice. That's the law.'

# 9

## Tuesday Night

'Marchant was their maiden name? Are you sure?'

'Yes, but no one remembers maiden names. It never registers. Who would think it important? Their mother, Mrs Marchant, was open about her name and it was there in the records. It was something that went completely unnoticed. Till now.'

'Thelma Harlow disappeared thirty years ago.'

'A long time ago.'

'Melody Marchant could have been from some other branch of the family.'

'Yes, she could. But we don't know yet. They're running more sophisticated DNA tests now. It only takes a few days. It used to take weeks.'

'Are you trying to link this unsolved murder with me, the fire, the lump of concrete and all the other things?'

'I can't see how or why yet, but it is possible. You are here. Melody was here. I'm reopening *The Missing Cover Girl* cold case and you publish a magazine called *Macabre Mysteries*, which ran the story previously.'

Fancy leaned against the wall, her shoulders slumped. It was quite cold now, the plaster chilled and hard against her back. She couldn't remember when she had last slept well. And she needed more sleep.

'I'm too tired to take all this in. Thank you, Jed, for helping me with my talk. I couldn't have done it without you. It went very well, amazingly well, and it was because of your support. It was a great idea and the only way I could have got through the evening.'

'You needed a straight man. I was there and I knew I could shield you from anything unpleasant. I've provided protection in far worse situations.'

'A bodyguard?'

'Did you see that film? Whitney Houston? Great film.'

Fancy didn't want to talk any more. She inserted her key and opened the bedroom door. 'Thank you again, Jed. Goodnight and thank you for a lovely afternoon at Newstead Abbey. It seems a hundred years ago now.'

'It was a hundred years, a completely different world.' Jed saw that Fancy was drooping. 'I'm sleeping in the room across the corridor with the door open, don't forget.'

Fancy absorbed the new arrangement. He

would be near, which was perfect. 'Sleeping across the corridor with the door open seems a good idea. I'll be able to yell for help.'

'I hope you won't have to. I'll check your room first.'

There was no sign of the fire. A new shower curtain had been fitted and every inch of tile scrubbed and cleaned. Even the smell of fire had gone. Her room was back to normal. Someone had put some mauve flowers on the windowsill.

'Are you going to be all right?'

'I could sleep through an earthquake.'

'I don't think your hoaxer could manage an earthquake. Goodnight, Fancy.'

'Goodnight, Jed.'

She could barely drag herself through her normal bedtime routine. She managed to take off her make-up and clean her teeth, but her clothes went into a heap on a chair without being hung up. Bed was a haven and she wrapped herself into the duvet, wallowing in the self-infused warmth. As she slipped into sleep, she started not to care if anything happened to her.

Her best-seller would not get published but that would not matter any more. Authors disappear. They often did. No more working late into the night at a solitary computer. No landfill of tax demands. No more editorial arguments, no more proofreading. Proofreading was her personal nightmare.

But she did not sleep for long. Something woke her in the early hours of the morning. She looked at her luminous bedside clock. It was 2.20 a.m. Not a quadrant. She did not know what had woken her. She dared not move in case it provoked some further unwanted activity.

She moved silently out of bed and stood by the window, keeping well back. A watery moon cast its pale light over the grass verge and path, and the grassy knoll where the Orchard Room stood. Nothing seemed to be happening. No parties. No very late bedfellows. The writers' conference had retired for the night. The manager on the late shift duty could watch television in peace.

Fancy was not sure. Something did not seem right. She needed to find out for herself, to put her mind at rest. She pulled on some black trousers, and a long-sleeved black fleece, black trainers, no socks. She put a couple of pink pens in her pocket; they had sharp nibs. And, as a final thought, she picked up her nail scissors. Not that she would ever use them to defend herself. But they made her feel safer.

Jed's door was open a few inches and she could hear his regular breathing. He was sleeping deeply, worn out by the day's activities. She wished she could stay with him but knew it would be foolish. It would be over by the weekend and everyone would disperse to their homes all over England, many to Scotland. Some would be flying back to Switzerland or France.

She would go home to her church lodge, get the window repaired, get on with her book. So many words a day.

She might never see Jed again. He would go back to his life, maybe to his wife, if he had one. She didn't know. She had never asked. Nor had he ever mentioned a wife, waiting at home, ironing, making jam and chutney.

She crept down the stairs, not using the lift, along the corridor to the front entrance. It was eerily quiet with only a low-wattage light on. It sent no shadows into corners. A few empty bottles and glasses had been abandoned on the central table. Some late-night party that the bar staff did not have the energy to clear up.

The front door opened with the smallest of clicks and Fancy went out onto the path. It was cold and she was glad of the comfort and warmth of the fleece. She had read somewhere that fleece was made from recycled plastic bags. She went down the slope and into the shadow close to the wall of Lakeside. The moon had clouded over and it was dark. She kept close to the wall, hoping she would not wake any light sleepers on the ground floor. She began a circuit of Lakeside, round both sides, through the car park, skirting the older, sturdy ABC building that was clothed in darkness. The main entrance to Lakeside was also closed and dark with only a small bulb glowing over the counter.

Nothing was happening. No one was about. But she sensed something or someone. She heard a noise. Footsteps were crossing the gravel of the main car park, by the entrance hall of the old Victorian mansion. She ducked down behind some bushes and moved between the trees that circled the main driveway to the house.

A man was getting into a car. It was a metallic silver Vauxhall with a roof rack. At two o'clock in the morning? It could hardly be staff and Fancy knew that staff parked way back, out of sight. No one would be working this late.

She tried to fix on some aspect of the man, something to remember, like a detective would. He looked middle-aged. About early fifties, wearing dark clothes, a waterproof parka and a flat cap. She thought she caught the glint of spectacles. He closed the door and switched on the headlights. They beamed away from the school, down the drive. He slid the car into gear and moved away, almost without noise.

The car rolled down the drive, over the speed bumps, towards the entrance gates and the lane that lead up to the main road. In a minute he was out of sight. Fancy breathed deeply. She suddenly felt free. There was something about the man and the car that had spelt trouble, and now he had gone.

Could she put this fear into a book? She had no idea. She needed to get back to her room and rescue what hours were left of the night. She took the shortest way back to Lakeside with complete confidence. She was the only person awake.

Except for the tabby cat who crossed her path. He was also out late, hunting mice from the nearby fields. He twisted himself round her ankles.

Fancy stroked his striped head and back, and he arched, purring. 'I've nothing for you, puss,' she said. 'I'm sorry.'

She took the stairs again. Jed was still asleep, his breathing like an ancient Greek's, strong and regular. If only she could crawl in beside him and curl up against his back. She knew she would sleep as deeply.

But common sense told her not to be so

foolish. She hated common sense. It was so boring. She went back to her room and closed the door, activating the self-lock. But she still put a chair against the door. She made a cup of tea, but later in bed, was asleep before it was half drunk.

★　★　★

Her dreams were weird. A blue thermos flask, a cliff path and the sea lashing against rocks far below. The sea was clear and blue, sparkling. The place meant nothing but gave her a sense of serenity. She did not want to wake up. But she had to.

There was an urgent knocking on her door. And Jed's voice came though her submerged dreams. She floundered in shreds of consciousness.

'Fancy! Fancy, wake up! Are you all right?'

Fancy sat up, blinking. She recognized his voice, the urgency.

She staggered to the door, stubbing her bare toes on a chair, which was extremely painful. She pulled the chair away and opened the door, forgetting the briefness of her teddy bear nightshirt.

'Jed? What is it? I was asleep,' she mumbled.

'I had to make sure you were all right.'

'I'm all right. Why? What is it?'

'Come and see.'

They were standing in the corridor, both less than half dressed. It was idiotic. Fancy hoped no one was watching.

Jed slept in shorts. His chest was brown and bare with a sprinkling of dark hair. He took her arm and pulled her into his bedroom, took her across to the window. 'Look. Down there.'

Below in the car park, a car was ablaze, flames shooting up into the night sky, glowing like a bonfire. It was parked some distance from the other cars, although alarmed owners were running into the car park, anxious to move their vehicles away from the blaze. Sparks could travel.

'Where's your car?' Fancy asked.

'It's safe. Parked on the upper level. Is yours there too?'

'Yes, no point in walking miles with luggage and books.'

'I was worried in case you were in the car,' said Jed, drawing her away from the window. 'So many odd things have happened to you.'

'For heaven's sake,' said Fancy. 'Why would I get into some strange car in the middle of the night? I'm not that stupid.'

'You might have been drugged, taken prisoner, hostage, dragged there. I don't know. I just had to make sure you were okay.'

Fancy calmed down. She could see his point but he had woken her from a lovely dream and that was almost unforgivable. One could never get back to a good dream. It was gone forever.

'Can I go back to bed now?' she asked.

'Yes, sorry to have woken you. I had to check.'

'Was there anyone in the car?'

'No, I don't think so. I couldn't see anyone. Hear that noise? The fire brigade has arrived. Hoses out. Everything's under control now. The night duty manager will be asking for danger money at this rate.'

'Everyone will be glad to go home on Friday morning. All this excitement.'

'Will you be glad to go home?' Jed asked.

How could Fancy answer in all truth? She wanted to go home, longed for her own bed, her computer and books, yet she did not want to leave him. She wanted to stay here with Jed, whatever happened. He had become her rock. Yet she knew nothing about him. He might be a rock of salt.

'I've a window to get repaired,' she said. 'A saint with some lambs. Funny how I don't like my church lodge quite so much any more. No views. Only a few walls and dustbins. And the traffic is diabolical.'

She went back into her bedroom, repeated the locking procedure and drank the cold tea. She had not told Jed that she recognized the car. The blazing car had been a metallic silver Vauxhall with a roof rack.

★ ★ ★

Sleep was more elusive this time. She tossed and stretched, tried going through plot lines, tried to remember her next lecture. She could not remember a word of it. It was going to be a disaster.

'Sorry, folks, I can't remember what we were going to do today. I know I was going to start and then an hour later, I would end.' They might laugh. 'But the in-between bit is a blur. Just talk among yourselves.'

She gave up trying to sleep, switched on the light and found a recent novel. If she couldn't sleep, then she would read. Let some other writer transport her to another world, cast it with dream people, weave some magic.

She must have fallen asleep with the book still open at a page. No reflection on the author or his story; her eyes had given up, refused to stay open. Dawn was filtering through her window, the palest of colours tinting the sky, a brush of light, night bleeding into morning.

'Is this Wednesday?' she asked herself. 'I've lost count of the days.'

Yes, it was Wednesday. Two more days and Northcote would be all over. Life would revert to normal. Everyone would go home to jobs, children, swearing eternal friendship, exchanging email addresses and phone numbers, hugs and kisses. As if life could ever be the same after this time together.

Would Jed kiss her goodbye? Probably not. She would put her cold face on before he could plant a kiss on her cheek.

She showered and put on an easy, crinkled white shirt with her black jeans, with a butterfly cover-up. The weather had changed abruptly; it looked bleak, grey and cold outside. She needed the comfort of warmer clothes. For once she was in time for half a breakfast. Grapefruit, hash browns and baked beans, coffee. No bacon, no sausage. She could not face the cold brown roof tiles, even with butter and marmalade. Everyone was talking about the burnt-out car.

The fire incident officer was around again, prodding the remains of the vehicle, now a pile of soot and twisted metal. 'Looks like you've got an arsonist,' he said. 'There are signs of some sort of fire source. It was thrown over the car. Thank goodness no one was inside. They would have been incinerated.'

'Is it getting worse?' Jed asked. 'Fire in a bucket, now a car on fire?'

'There may not be any connection. Perhaps the car is copycat.'

'Will it be the old house next or the conference hall?'

'Don't look on the dark side, sir. I'm sure there's an explanation for all this. After all, they are writers.'

Jed could have sworn at him, silenced him in a completely unprofessional way. His clenched fist hurt, nails digging into flesh. He swallowed his anger. 'Writers are ordinary, normal people with a longing to write, to create stories, to write something that other people will want to read. They don't start fires.'

'If you say so, sir.'

'I do say so. Would you like some coffee?' Jed tried to be civil.

'No, thank you. I have to arrange for the wreck to be removed for forensic examination. It's still a criminal offence.'

Fancy skipped the first workshop of the day, walked round the garden, talked to a few people, apologized to the writer whose manuscript had been burnt to cinders in a bucket.

'You must let me pay for a fresh photocopy,' said Fancy. The writer wore a white badge, was anxious, wide-eyed, starting out. You never knew, she might be the next J K Rowling or Ruth Rendell. Fancy fished for a card in her bag. 'Send it to me at home and I promise to read it. Every word. And I'll send a critique.'

'That would be wonderful, Fancy. Thank you so much. I do hope you were not hurt in any way.'

'Only my hands,' said Fancy. She had thrown away the corrupt bandages and wrapped her hands in cling film. They were healing and looked pink and healthy. She had good, healthy genes.

The police were still interviewing and were going through the catering and management staff now. No one knew anything. How could they? They were busy cooking and caring for three hundred people. They didn't have time to walk round the old lake in the dark.

Fancy's third lecture flowed. She was not sure why. It might be because she had done her homework and the structure was firmly formed in her head. It might be because she knew her subject. It might be because she liked her group and wanted them to enjoy writing fiction, as she did.

'So today, my friends, we are going to

work. No more jokes. Down to serious work. Pen to paper. Mind in gear. Ideas at the ready. We are going to look for clues and invent red herrings. Has everyone got a pen?'

There was the usual clamour for one of her pink pens.

The hour fled by with hoots of laughter and more good ideas. Fancy thought, fleetingly, that she might pinch some of them. She could use them, slightly amended. She could see short stories, novels, non-fiction, her invisible world. But she sat flat on her greedy appetite and discussed with the delegates how to best use their ideas in their work. How could she have thought, even for a moment, of using their ideas?

Break time on the lawn was welcome. She drank two black coffees. The week was nearly over. She wanted to get back to her current writing; it was too long to be away from her book. It hadn't gone cold on her but she felt a chilly distance. Whereas normally the story lived with her, every moment of the day, now there were whole hours when she did not give it a thought.

'Guess who the car belonged to,' Jed said, trying to balance a coffee and a biscuit in one hand. She did not offer to help. She knew that much now.

'Tonight's speaker?'

'No, Melody's husband. He's the farmer who'd driven up from Cornwall. Not exactly a good week for him. First Melody and now his car.'

'Was he staying here?' Fancy wondered why she had seen the silver car drive away from Northcote at two in the morning, before the fire. It didn't make sense.

'Yes, they'd given him a room in the main house. No one knew he was here. He wanted his presence to be kept quiet, so that the programme was not upset. It was what Melody would have wanted, he said.'

Fancy thought about her arrival and Melody's warm greeting.

'She was a lovely lady. She'd once been very beautiful — it's easy to see that. I only met her on Saturday when I arrived, but she was very kind and helpful. I feel so sorry for her husband.'

'Partner. A bit younger than Melody, I should think. Big strapping chap, typical farmer.'

'A farmer is the perfect partner for a writer. He's out all day, from the crack of dawn, doing farming type things. Hopefully the farm provides lots of good food so she need never go to Waitrose again. Oh dear, Melody need never go shopping again, of course. I'd forgotten.'

'Are you looking for a farmer?' Jed asked. He was disguising a twinkle in his eyes. Did he really want to know? 'Would a farmer suit you?'

Fancy had to pause, think hard. 'I'm not looking for anyone, not even a hard-working farmer,' she said. 'But if one came along, I would kiss the ground, like the Pope.'

'That was the previous Pope who kissed the ground.'

'I don't count popes.'

'I go to a lot of pub quizzes.'

'Does any of this make sense to you?' Fancy wanted to get off the subject. It made her feel vulnerable, a target. 'Melody is drowned and then her husband's car is set on fire in the middle of the night.'

'Nothing about it makes any sense to me, Fancy. And you are a complete mystery.' He sounded annoyed. 'What are you scheduled to do now?'

'Nothing. I've done my lecture. It went well. I think I'm free.'

'Then we can walk around the new lake. Take in some fresh air. The old lake is still cordoned off, scene-of-crime.'

A uniformed member of the domestic staff was running across the lawn towards Fancy. She looked flushed and anxious. 'Miss Jones,' she said, breathing heavily. 'Can I speak to you? Can I ask you something?'

Fancy paused, hoping it wouldn't take long. She rather fancied a walk with Jed when she had nothing to do. And it was a long time since she had fancied anything with a man.

'Yes, of course,' she said. 'What's the matter?'

'One of our maids has collapsed. She's been taken to hospital. Something respiratory. She was doing your room, room 425, and said something about sniffing your flowers and being bitten before she passed out.'

'My flowers? What flowers?'

'Yes, the bunch of flowers on the sill in your room. Do you know who gave them to you?'

Fancy had no idea. The flowers had just appeared from nowhere. A gift from someone. 'No, I don't know. I didn't put them there.'

'She was giving them some fresh water, rearranging them, when something bit her hand. She's quite poorly.'

Jed took Fancy's arm to steady her. Flowers in her room that could bite? She had heard of leaves that were toxic and *digitalis*, or foxgloves, were poisonous.

'You have seriously upset someone,' he said. 'Now they're trying to asphyxiate you.'

'Surely flowers can't kill you,' said Fancy hopefully.

'They can if a lethal spider is hiding among the leaves.'

'That's nonsense. I didn't see any spider.'

He turned back to her. 'Listen, Fancy. None of this is rubbish. Someone has issues with you and it's not funny,' he said. 'You are in serious danger.'

'I'll be going home soon.'

'Want to bet on it? They haven't finished what they came to do.'

# 10

## Wednesday

Fancy didn't want to know anything about lethal spiders. She hated spiders, of any kind. She had trained herself to remove spiders from the bath with a tumbler and a sheet of paper but she had to wear sunglasses during the operation. It was not something to be proud of.

'I hate spiders,' she said.

'Especially ones that bite,' said Jed.

'Is the girl going to be all right?'

'They've taken her to hospital because she's pregnant and they want to make sure.'

'I'd like to send her some flowers,' said Fancy without thinking.

'Surely not flowers,' said Jed quickly.

Fancy felt the colour warm in her face. Sometimes she was so stupid, so unthinking. It was a country from which she found it difficult to return. The words were not there. Maybe they were on paper, but not in her mind.

'No, of course not flowers. A basket of fruit, perhaps? Good for a growing baby. I'll order it online. Can you give me an address?'

'She'd like that, especially you thinking of her. She reads your books, Miss Jones. Loves the Pink Pen Detective.'

'Heavens,' said Fancy, surprised. 'I've never met anyone who's read them.'

Jed guided her down the lawn towards the new lake. It looked raw and unnatural, set in smooth grass with a bank and fence round it. So unlike the old lake with its sweeping weeping willows and plants. No swans.

'It takes time for a lake to merge with the countryside,' said Jed.

'It's man-made, a false lake and looks so artificial.'

'Someone has planted water lilies in it. They are trying. Give it a few years and it'll look different. Let's walk round. The fresh air will do us good.'

The path was new too, of even width and straight. The grass stretched in all directions, verdant green. It was the rich, damp earth of Derbyshire, a dry stone wall in the distance. It had its own untouched beauty. No one had died there. Yet.

'I'd like to give them a tree, a willow, for the new lake. Do you think they'd let me?' said Fancy, seeing a tree growing here, big and sweeping, long after she had withered and gone.

'I'm sure they would like that,' said Jed. He didn't take her hand but he wanted to. Fancy always kept that distance. 'They'd invite you to plant it. Put up an inscribed plaque.'

'Not a plaque, please. Too much like a tombstone. Why did you say all that about the flowers in my room? I've never heard of flowers that can asphyxiate.'

'Neither have I. It was a wild guess.'

'Then why say it?'

They were going to have a row. Fancy could feel it gathering like storm clouds. She caught a quick glimpse of Jed's mouth tightening. His step quickened. He was already a foot ahead of her, not looking back. Fancy clasped her hands behind her, straightening her back. Good for her posture.

'Are you keeping something from me?' she went on. 'I've a feeling you're not being straight with me. What are you not telling me?'

'I've been straight with you all the time. You're the one who is keeping things from me. What else haven't you told me?'

There was a stinging silence. It hurt.

'I don't know what you mean,' Fancy stormed. 'Of course, I've told you everything about the incidents. What else do you want to know? All about my private life? Want to

168

know the details? Time and place? Score rates?'

'Don't you trust me, Fancy?' Jed avoided her questions with his own question. 'Aren't we a team? Haven't I been helping you?'

'Yes, of course, you have, Jed. You've been great and I've appreciated your support but I get this feeling that there's something you haven't told me. It all seems weird. All these things are happening to me and you're always around when they do. It can't be just a coincidence.'

Jed swung back, facing her. 'Are you trying to say that I'm connected to all these unpleasant events? Do you think I'm behind them? Was I on the Underground station, on the bus, throwing concrete through your saints window? So I've had the opportunity, have I? Perhaps it is me, perhaps I'm some weirdo getting revenge because you plagiarized my novel, stole my plot.'

'That's not what I mean,' said Fancy, not knowing what she meant. She was confused, alarmed. She had become used to leaning on Jed. He had been there for her. But how had it happened? He had appeared, come to her of his own accord. He could have arranged it all. He'd had the time, the opportunity.

'Is it about money? Money seems to be at the root of all evil.'

Jed didn't answer.

They were completely alone, by the new lake. Sunlight winked on the water like diamonds, streaks of light reflecting back. There was no one in sight. Fancy was frightened. Jed was tall, strong, muscled, even with only one arm. He could easily put his good arm hard round her throat and drag her back into the hedge. He would know some deadly lock. She wouldn't stand a chance, however hard she fought.

Fancy turned and ran. She kicked off her shoes, felt the grit from the path under her feet. She ran towards the house and the conference hall, towards the lawn outside the vinery to where there would be people. Lots of people. She was out of breath. She didn't often run, not even for a train.

A few people looked at her, thought she was late for a talk.

And she found she was crying. She had trusted Jed. Now all her warm feelings for him had gone. She was alone again. A solitary writer churning out thousands of words to pay the bills. She would stop publication of her magazine. She never wanted to see it again. It would not be missed. Save a few trees.

She could go home. She would pack her things, order a taxi, take any train from Derby

170

back to London, back to her church lodge, get the window fixed. She had forgotten she had a vintage car parked on the higher level car park.

'We're so looking forward to your last lecture tomorrow,' said a group of keen young writers, gathering round her like bees round a flower. 'You've been such an inspiration. You are so enthusiastic about writing.'

Fancy didn't feel enthusiastic or inspired. She felt enthusiastic about going home. She felt swallowed by their obvious admiration, sorry that she was going to let them down. She had to find Jessie or Fergus and tell them that she was leaving. The skin on her hands felt tight and burning. She could blame it on her hands. Delayed shock, sudden urgent phone call from her publishers, anything.

'All it needs is your own enthusiasm,' she said. 'Each of you has got it in you to do it. Make it work for you.'

Fancy didn't really know what she was saying. She was shattered by Jed's sudden change, felt as if she was bleeding into the day. She couldn't remember the time. Was it lunch time? She didn't want any food. Breakfast seemed a hundred hours away. If only she could wake up and find the last minutes had been a horrid dream. Dream was the wrong word. She should have said nightmare.

'I loved your last book,' a fresh-faced young woman was saying. 'It was such a clever ending. How do you think up such endings?'

Heavens, someone else who had read her book. 'I don't really know,' said Fancy. 'It just happens. Sometimes I don't even know how it's going to end. The books take over. They kind of write themselves.'

Everyone laughed, regrouped and let Fancy escape. Richard, the Treasurer stopped her as she headed towards the bar. He was always carrying a file of papers or a clipboard. No change today.

'Hey, Fancy, you've forgotten the pre-lunch drinks party,' Richard said. 'It's the committee's thank-you to everyone who has helped in some way. You are supposed to be there. I'm late too. We can just make it.'

Fancy had no idea what he was talking about but followed him meekly to the reception entrance of Lakeside. It was crowded with people getting their free drink and handful of crisps or nuts. A glass of white wine was put in her hand, carefully.

'Still hurting?'

Fancy nodded, remembering the going-home role she was about to play. 'Still hurting. More than I expected. Thank you.'

Fergus was going to make a speech. She slid sideways to lean against a wall, apart from people. Her strength was draining away. She might faint. The wine tasted of nothing. It could be mineral water. Perhaps it was mineral water.

'Thank you all for coming,' Fergus began, clearing his throat. He was getting conference-throat. 'The committee and I want to thank you all for your support this year in making the conference the great success that it is. So many of you cheerfully help out in different ways and we want to thank you. The book room helpers, the stewards, the DJs, the raffle ticket sellers, the microphone experts, the first aiders . . . ' He went on, listing everyone who helped in some way. It was an endless list.

★   ★   ★

Jed paused in the doorway with a face carved into stone. Fancy folded herself back against the curtain drapes, hoping he could not see her. She didn't want to see him either. What was he doing here, anyway, at the thank-you party? Fergus went over to him with a glass of red wine so she supposed they counted frequent trips to Derby on committee business as worth a free glass of wine.

173

'Don't you like your wine?' asked Jessie. 'Is it too dry for you?'

'A bit dry,' said Fancy, hardly thinking.

'I'll get you something you will like. Come and meet tonight's speaker. I expect you already know him.'

It was Simon Brett, who Fancy knew from the Crime Writers' Association. He was a prolific writer and great entertainer. A sideline was writing parodies of famous books and then acting all the parts himself. She had never seen a performance but the grapevine said they were hilarious.

She wished she could stay to hear it. She would have enjoyed being on the shelf with her friends, cheering and clapping. It was rumoured to be Agatha Christie's turn tonight. One of her famous mysteries.

But she was going home. She would be trying to warm up her kitchen and filling the washing machine. Supper would be baked beans on toast. Lunch would be baked beans on toast.

She found herself being drawn into a chattering group round Simon. He was an amiable man, easy-going, with an infectious laugh. She had second thoughts about going home, and then third thoughts. She could not face another baked bean. Not for a long time, however nutritious.

'I think you'll like this,' said Jessie, returning with a brimming glass of red. 'It's a special bottle we keep under the table for special people.'

'Is that allowed?' whispered Fancy.

'It's a well-kept secret.'

Fancy was laughing at something, half turning, when she found Jed confronting her. He seemed to tower over her, taller than ever. He had drunk most of his wine, which might account for his face being a degree less stony.

'You left your shoes behind,' he said. They were tucked under his good arm.

'Oh yes, thank you,' she said.

'You'd better put them on.'

It was an awkward movement trying to put on her shoes without spilling her wine. He didn't offer to help her.

'I suppose you thought I was going to harm you in some way.'

'Yes,' said Fancy firmly. She took a sip of wine. It was a good one, deliciously grapey. 'And I wasn't going to wait to find out.'

'That's not flattering.'

'It's not supposed to be. Flight or fight reflexes and I've only got a pale pink belt in karate.'

There was a strained silence between them, yet the room was full of noise. Laughter, chatting, clinking of glasses. Even wallpaper pop music belting out from a personal stereo.

Fancy felt that the world could swallow her and she would disappear. She wanted to disappear. The moment was too tense, too unsettling.

'There really is a flower that can kill you,' said Jed. 'It's called monkshood. Sort of mauve or purple. Sickness, nausea, passing out, coma, all sorts of horrid symptoms. It's in books.'

He was trying not to look at her. Looking anywhere, over talking heads.

'But don't you have to eat it, not just sniff it?' said Fancy, her natural interest wiping out the last wall of defence. 'I'll have to look it up on Google.'

'Why were we fighting and arguing?' Jed finished his wine in a gulp. 'You and me? We're not like that, Fancy. It wasn't normal.'

'I've no idea. It was as if some kind of demon took over. The demon of the new lake. We won't walk round it again. It needs an exorcism.'

*Demon of the Lake.* Was that a title?

'Maybe the workmen digging out the new lake disturbed a plague pit. There were plague villages up here. Whole villages were wiped out in the seventeenth century. Eyam, for example, in 1665 and 1666, hardly anyone survived. People were buried in piles.'

Fancy sighed. 'Poor souls. It gives me the shivers.'

Jed put down his glass on the nearest surface and curled his good arm round Fancy's waist. She felt her breasts tighten as he pulled her close. The granite face had gone. He was looking at her with warmth and longing.

'Would it be all right if I kissed you right now?' he asked, his voice low and intense. 'In front of everyone?'

'No, thank you,' she said hurriedly. 'Kissing in public is not permitted.'

'Is that a dare?'

'There's nothing romantic about a noisy room full of writers drinking free wine.'

'It's perfect, Fancy, because no one would notice. Everyone's far too busy queuing up for refills.'

His lips were on hers before she could protest. They were warm and moist. The noise faded into a distant blanket. Fancy leaned against him, feeling the hardness of his chest, the firmness of his good arm, the smell of his aftershave. She clutched the arm that had no feeling, loving it as much as the one that worked. His mouth took hold of hers, drawing her closer. She could taste his wine. He'd been given the special bottle, too. He was special. She was not sure why, but he was.

'Do you think anyone noticed?' he whispered against her ear.

'Well, we haven't been thrown out for lewd behaviour at lunch-time.'

'We must never, never quarrel again. I thought I would die when you ran away from me. I thought you were leaving me forever. And I need you, Fancy. God knows why, but I do.'

Fancy and Jed faced each other, their bodies touching, not caring who saw them. There were a few amused faces, raised eyebrows. Jessie pretended not to notice, but waved the special bottle of red as if it held a magic elixir.

'We know that someone is trying to scare you. You're in danger.'

'*The Missing Cover Girl*?'

'Was Melody one of the Marchant twins? The disappearing Thelma? For some reason you are the target. It could be a sort of revenge for something that happened in the past.'

'But what could it be? I don't know what I could have done.'

Despite Jed's closeness and the good wine, Fancy was shivering again.

'Think back. There must be something. Did you write about the case when you were a reporter or in one of your novels?'

'All my books are fiction. Entirely from my imagination, not even based on real cases. And I was a cub reporter, getting all the menial jobs — obits, weddings, jumble sales. If a good story came along, then my chief reporter collared it. Lineage from the nationals. Anyway, *The Missing Cover Girl* was way before my time.'

'Did your chief reporter cover the story? Think back. Think carefully.'

'I have no idea. It's a million years ago. I can't remember that long ago. Why are we talking about this now?'

'Because you are connected in some way. And whoever has it in for you knew you were coming to the conference, knew they could target you here. There would be more opportunities. You would be vulnerable, away from your normal routine, an easy target.'

'An easy target,' Fancy agreed. She thought of all the things that had happened since she arrived. Not a pleasant memory, yet the bad had been tempered with good. Kind people, sympathy, Jed's protection. And now a wonderful kiss. It was a long time since a man had kissed her with such feeling.

'Is it about money?'

'It's always about money. Money never sleeps.'

'Last drinks before lunch, folks,' Jessie called out from the bar. There was a general movement without looking as if anyone was rushing. Jessie poured out the last of the special wine into their glasses.

'I didn't know you two knew each other,' she said.

'Passing acquaintances,' said Fancy.

'Jed can pass my acquaintance anytime,' said Jessie.

'But you're married, aren't you?'

Jessie looked surprised, then quickly regained her composure.

'I know. But my husband wouldn't understand. We had a big row last week, about money of all things. It's water under the bridge.'

'Have you sorted it out?'

'In a way, but don't hold your breath.'

Fancy understood. Even happily married couples could be on their own sometimes. Couples drifted along their own paths, taking different routes through the woods. It didn't mean that they had stopped loving one another. It meant that they had individual lives, not joined at the hip, not always breathing the same parcel of air.

Jed steered her over the lawn towards the dining room, then let her go. 'You had better go and fraternize with the top table, while I get my nosh with the plebs.'

'Don't leave me,' said Fancy, panicking.

'I can't hold your hand all the time,' he said, inferring that he wouldn't be able to eat if his good hand was otherwise occupied. 'I have to eat.'

'Sorry.'

'What's happening this afternoon?'

'I'm doing an extra workshop. Some of the white-badgers got together and asked if I would do something really basic. You know, double spacing, page numbering, markets, agents.'

'You never stop,' said Jed over his shoulder as he walked away to the far end of the dining room, looking for a spare seat. 'I knew they would devour you.'

Fancy couldn't remember what she ate. It was something cold. Different kinds of salad, sliced cold meats, quiche, cheese — again. The last hour had been a roller coaster and her stomach was in no fit state to accept food. She wondered if she could make a sandwich and slip it upstairs. Room 425 still felt the safest place despite the fire and the flowers.

Perhaps if she was alone, the mist would clear and she might remember some stray bit of information that could be the reason for all these unpleasant happenings. She thought of Melody, floating in the old lake like Ophelia, her face down in the cold water. The police presence was still evident, combing the grounds, but the detective had not spoken to her again.

Except Jed and he was police, wasn't he? He said he was semi-retired. Supposing he wasn't? Supposing he had only said that to reassure her. He certainly asked a lot of questions. Questions that she couldn't answer.

'Stop it,' she said loudly to herself.

'*Comment?*' said Jessie, fork in mid-air.

'Sorry, talking to myself as usual. Bad habit.'

'Don't worry. I do it all the time. Reminding myself of what I've got to do.'

'And I've got to prepare my extra workshop for this afternoon,' said Fancy, rising. 'So if you don't mind, I'll leave you to all this delicious food and grab an apple on my way out.'

Fancy hurried out of the dining room with a chunk of cheese surreptitiously wrapped in a paper napkin, an ice-cold apple and a frozen banana. It might have defrosted by tomorrow. She obviously wasn't going home. She need not pack and warm up the car. No excuses to make. She just hoped she wouldn't find a bomb outside her bedroom door.

She paused at the lift. Would the lift man

still be saying *Doors opening* and *Doors closing*? Or had he been programmed to imprison her in the lift till she ran out of oxygen?

# 11

## Wednesday Afternoon

The police were still searching the garden and the lake, an inch at a time, everything bagged and labelled. The crime scene had been sealed off and freeze-frozen. Now and again there was a glimpse of white overalls. They were looking for strands of hair, flakes of skin, fibres. The lake had even been dredged. It gave up a quantity of empty bottles, plastic bags and rotting debris, even a dead bird. It also gave up Melody's handbag. The sodden contents were being examined by forensic.

Fancy nodded to the white spacemen as they combed the gardens. She didn't ask them if they had found anything. They would think she was going to put them in a book. People were always suspicious of writers, their eyes narrowing. They inevitably asked: 'Are you going to put me in a book?'

No, thank you, she wasn't. She had an unruly crowd of characters romping about in her head, waiting to be given life, stampeding for attention every time she started on a new book. 'Me next!' they shouted, pushing each other out of the way.

She let herself into her room, checking for intruders and anything weird. The flowers had gone. She examined the coffee sachets and milk cartons for pin-pricked holes and decided that the Nescafé was uncontaminated. She refused to make a nest of her own fears. Both fruits got a hot water wash before she ate them. She munched the chunk of cheese with relish.

As she sat at the desk, eating and drinking, she drew a sheet of A4 paper forward and started to write down all the possible connections with the Marchant twins. As she worked out the dates, she realized that it was almost impossible to find a connection. It happened before she was even born. The trial, the disappearance, the subsequent investigations. The case had rarely been written about in the last twenty years. Only her magazine had dredged up the mystery.

She opened the lid of her laptop and went onto Google. *The Missing Cover Girl* case was on Wikipedia and had several other empty sites. One site covered the trial of Rupert Harlow. She made a note of all the names mentioned in court, the judge, the barristers. The dry mechanical details. None of them rang a bell, not even the merest tinkle.

Then something caught her eye. The Marchant money was mentioned. 'Money never sleeps,' Jed had said. Wasn't there a film, with that title? She hadn't been to see it. *Wall Street* was of no interest to her. She clicked on the link.

The twins' father, Eddie Marchant, had owned a family brewery in the Midlands, which he sold to a big northern conglomerate for a tidy fortune. The money was left equally to both girls in Eddie's will, on condition that when one daughter died, her share of the brewery money should go, without question or qualification, even if she had married, to the remaining daughter.

This clause caused a great deal of trouble. Thelma could not be declared dead for seven years because her body was never found. Grace, therefore, had to wait for Thelma's share of the inheritance. Lawyers made a lot of money out of the proceedings. But again, there was no link to Fancy.

She put the banana skin and apple core in the bin. Now she had a basics workshop to do, showing budding writers how to take the bread out of her mouth. She would be surviving on the Public Lending Rights in her sixties. No mileage left in you, her publisher would tell her, by email, his eye on her diminishing royalty returns.

This thought of the future shocked her. She did not want to grow old, wrinkled and die, even if it was some way off. She did not want Jed to reach seventy, his hair turning white, crippled with arthritis. He might die before her. That would be devastating. The taste of grief enveloped her, even though she might never know what happened to him. They might not be together. She might read his obit in the *Police Review*. That seemed even worse.

Her only link with the Marchant twins was that it was a cold case and her *Macabre Mysteries* magazine had featured it some months earlier. Perhaps someone thought she was getting warm. She had a quick wash and changed into a plain white T-shirt to show that this workshop was in casual mode.

On her way to the Orchard Room, she passed Jed walking the other way. He was talking earnestly to an elderly, white-haired gentleman with a stick. Her heart lurched at the sight of him. This was getting ridiculous.

'Is it the Marchant money?' she asked as they passed.

'I think you're getting warm,' he nodded.

She focused on climbing the steep path to the Orchard Room. 'You knew all the time,' she threw back over her shoulder.

'I'm a detective, remember?' he reminded her with a wink.

Fancy wondered if Jed was really retired. They could still employ a one-armed detective, couldn't they? It made no difference to his ability to detect, only for the required two-hand hold on a gun.

'You are not really retired, are you?' she continued, catching her breath.

'Whoever said I was?'

'You did.'

By now he had moved on, still talking to the elderly gentleman. She'd heard that the old gent was famous, had written a war-time thriller, which had been made into a film called *633 Squadron*. It was still re-shown every Christmas on television with big stars, David Niven or Dirk Bogarde. She wasn't sure which actors.

'She sounds nice,' she heard the old man saying. 'Can't see too good these days. Eyes going. Go by the voice. She's always pleasant.'

'She is nice,' said Jed.

Fancy bounced into the Orchard Room. It was full. They were all waiting; big white A4 ruled notebooks from pound shops at the ready. Eager to fill them with her words of wisdom. They were determined to be on the next best-sellers list. They saw themselves mounting the steps to collect the Booker Prize.

'Settle down now, chairs in a semi-circle, please. This is not a lecture. Shoot questions at me, not all at once, and I'll answer them. Only don't ask me how much I get paid. Never enough for the amount of time and midnight candles burned.'

They laughed. Chairs scraped on the floor. It was a non-stop hour of giving information, words flying through the air. They asked questions they'd been too embarrassed to ask earlier with everyone listening. A lot of them were wearing white badges. They were also using her pink pens. Fancy wondered if she would get them back.

Fancy covered a dozen issues: presentation, titles, character names, covering letter, synopsis, agents, PLR, conferences, postal courses. She was truthful and concise. No point in making it sound easy. Should it be 1.5 spacing now, in order to save trees?

'But what does double double-spacing mean?' she asked the delegates.

'A passage of time,' they chanted back.

'So many beginners make that mistake. Putting an entire line of extra space between paragraphs. This shrieks that the writer is an amateur. Not necessary unless it's a passage of time.'

Fancy looked at her watch. 'I can hear the rattle of the tea trolleys. Buns and cake time. I hope this has been useful.'

'Wonderful. Thank you.'

'Great. I can't wait to get home and get started.'

'Just what I wanted to know.' The words flew, fragmented through the air.

They followed her out onto the lawn, still finding more questions to ask. Some of them didn't listen. She moved with people, hustling towards the forming queue. She was dry-mouthed, dehydrated, longing for a cuppa.

'You know you said you'd look at my manuscript when you got home, Fancy? Well, you didn't give me an address.' It was the woman whose manuscript had been burnt in a bucket. Today her tow-coloured hair was in plaits and she had entwined flowers in the braiding. She wore big sunglasses with pink rims and a yellow flowered caftan.

'Ah, flower power,' said Fancy, digging in her bag for a card. 'Glastonbury. All that mud. Singing and dancing.'

'Before my time,' the woman said, cutting short the pleasantries.

'I'm sorry,' said Fancy. 'I've forgotten your name. Is it Maggie or Meggie?' The woman had been to all her lectures, sitting at the back, taking notes earnestly, not saying much.

190

Her name on the white badge was too small and cramped to read.

The woman shook her head. She was annoyed. 'Peggy. Peggy Carter.'

'Nearly got it right. I've met so many people, you'll understand.'

Peggy Carter took the card and shrugged. Fancy sighed. No top marks on the feedback form from this delegate. Fancy had met over a hundred people in the last few days. It was a wonder she could remember her own name.

Only one more full day to go and then she really could go home. If her car was still in one piece and not vandalized. She had an awful premonition of another night fire lighting the sky. There were two more nights to get through, though, as everyone left on the Friday morning. The domestic staff had a quick turnover day: sheets out in the corridor promptly, please. Seeing the coach off to Derby station after breakfast on Friday was apparently a tradition, noisy and tearful. Jessie had told her that she should be there, to show an element of bonding.

But she could sneak off home on Thursday evening, after supper, join the M1 when the southbound traffic was minimal. Nothing in her contract said she had to stay for the last night's entertainment, whatever it was that they had been planning. There had been mad and secret rehearsals going on behind closed doors most days. Doors of the hall vibrating with laughter.

She could plead a deadline. The committee would understand that. Work came first.

Peggy Carter was at her side again, holding out a cup of tea. She looked contrite. 'Sorry, I was a bit sharp earlier. Stress, you know. Rushing everywhere. It's starting to get to me. Northcote fatigue, they call it. Here's a cup of tea for you. I didn't know if you took sugar.'

Fancy took the cup. 'How very kind of you, Peggy. It's been a hard week for all of us. People don't realize the stress. Everyone writing up notes, having to concentrate and still do their own writing in any spare time. Not much sleep.'

'If you can find any time to sleep.'

'Exactly. Thank you for the tea.'

Fancy wandered onto the lawn, holding the tea, looking for a seat. They were all occupied. She sat on a bank of grass, hoping it was dry. If it wasn't, she decided, she would just have a damp bottom.

Jed sprawled out beside her, not looking at her, gazing across to the croquet lawn where a game was going on. Not strictly according to the rules, by the sound of laughter.

'Still mad at me?'

'No,' said Fancy. 'Life is far too short to take offence.'

'Did you recognize who I was talking to?'

'Not his name, but I know him by reputation. He wrote the *Squadron* book that was made into a film, didn't he? He's famous, then?'

'That's right. And he was around at the time of Thelma's disappearance and Rupert's trial. I wondered what he could remember.'

Fancy heard the tantalizing promise. 'And could he remember anything?'

'His memory is as sharp as a pin. And he was working for a newspaper in south London at the time, a reporter, writing features in his spare time, as well as his novels.'

'Like most of us, he still needed a day job.'

'But you don't have a day job. So you make enough to live on from your books?' Jed looked at her as if for pound signs on her forehead.

'That may change, any day soon,' said Fancy. She wanted to steer the conversation away from her perilous finances. 'So what did he tell you about the Marchant twins?'

'Lots of interesting stuff. It was not all sweetness and light between the twins. There were stories of quarrels and fights, of the girls being thrown out of nightclubs, parties. They made headlines in all the tabloids. Once, Rupert Harlow was taken to hospital with a broken nose after a fight. He didn't know which twin hit him so didn't press charges. They both looked so alike.'

'So I wonder which was the twin with the aggressive temper? The glamorous Thelma or the clever Grace? Perhaps Rupert was innocent after all and one twin turned on the other twin.'

'It was Thelma who disappeared,' Jed reminded her.

'She could have been murdered by Grace and the body disposed of by Rupert. Don't ask me how. Then Grace and Rupert married, eventually, when the law allowed. To keep each other quiet, sharing the proceeds. All that Marchant money.'

'A bit far-fetched. There must be a simpler explanation. The trouble is that there is no one to talk to, no one to question.' Jed was sipping tea, thoughtfully.

'What about Melody's husband, the farmer from Cornwall? Surely he must know something about his wife's past? Especially if she is related to the Marchant twins. She must be, with the same surname.'

'I can't seem to find him. I want to speak to him.'

'Has he got a name?' Fancy asked.

'Marchant was Melody's writing name.'

'I'll find out.'

'Thelma disappeared sometime around 1975. That's more than thirty years ago. Who told you that Melody's husband had arrived from Cornwall?'

'Someone on the committee, I think. I'll check my notes.'

'It doesn't make sense. So who *was* Melody? Is she related to the twins? We know so little about her. This gets more and more complicated. It's a cold case that can stay frozen, for all I care. Except that someone thinks I am implicated. Shall I make a placard saying *I am Not Involved* and parade about the grounds?'

'If you want to add *Mad Writer*, it might work,' said Jed, pulling Fancy to her feet. 'Shall we meet for a drink before supper?'

'No parties tonight?'

'I've turned them all down. Too much work.'

'I've another bedroom party to go to in the ABC.'

'Tell me the room number and I'll gatecrash.'

Fancy almost lost her footing on the grass slope. Jed caught her, held her steady. A wave of dizziness came over her.

'You should take more water with it,' she

vaguely heard him saying. The joke did not appeal to her. She'd heard it before. Old as the hills. The lawn seemed to rise up in contours; trees swayed, flowers wobbled, above was a thunderous black summer sky. Like an earthquake. Did Derbyshire have quakes?

'Cliché,' she said, blinking. 'Boadicea,' she added, not knowing why she said the woman warrior's name. 'AD Sixty, Queen of Iceni.' Her brain was not working properly. Something had happened to it. It was as if the mass of cells did not belong to her any more. 'Massacre,' she added.

'Fancy?' said someone. She was not sure if it was Jed. She couldn't remember who Jed was. 'You're talking nonsense. I'm taking you back to your room. I think you ought to lie down for a bit.'

'What room?' she asked. 'My room at home? My church bedroom? Please stand still. You are making me . . . dizzy.'

'Fancy, do you remember where you are? This is a writers' conference in Derbyshire. You're a lecturer here. Tell me where your home is.'

'My home? It's . . . it's . . . over the rainbow.'

The man was shaking her now. Fancy did not know who he was. She was so tired, she wanted to sleep forever. She closed her eyes.

'Walk, Fancy. I'm taking you to your room in Lakeside. Do you know what number it is? Tell me the number of your room.'

'I'm not a number. Squadron Number Something.'

'*Doors opening*,' said a male voice. '*Doors closing.*' The lift rose.

She was being propelled along a corridor, one foot in front of another, like a robot. The walls of the corridor were caving in, ceiling receding in waves.

'Stay awake, Fancy. Don't go to sleep on me. Where's your key? Is it in your bag?'

Fancy didn't answer. She was swimming now in deep, deep water, her nostrils filling. She was drowning, like Melody, in the lake. She had forgotten how to swim. But she knew she could still swim.

Jed opened the door and pushed her inside. She fell onto the bed. He filled a glass with water from the bathroom and tried to make her drink from it.

'Open your mouth, Fancy, and drink this. Drink some water, damn it.'

The water trickled down her chin and soaked into her T-shirt.

'What's happened? What's the matter with Fancy?' It was Jessie at the door, looking in anxiously.

'I think someone has slipped her the date-rape drug, Rohypnol. She can't remember anything. Rambling. She'll be asleep in a few moments.'

'How dreadful,' said Jessie. 'Thank goodness she's already done her evening talk.' That was her first thought. Always the conference. 'I'll stay with her. We'll organize a rota. Will she sleep it off? Does she need a doctor? We've got a doctor among our first-aiders.'

'Yes, get the doctor.'

'This is awful. Poor Fancy. Another accident.'

'Not funny, Jessie. Not an accident.' Jed's voice was firm.

# 12

## Late Afternoon

The doctor, Dr Arthur, wrote obscure poetry in his spare time. When he had any time, that is, which was hardly ever. The conference was his holiday, his break, his own personal extravagance. But he came immediately and pronounced Fancy to be in no danger. The pupil of her left eye was dilated, the other a tiny speck. He agreed that she had been given a mild form of the date-rape drug, Rohypnol.

'We even give low dosage of Roofies to kids on the wards to quieten them down,' he said. 'She'll be very still, very quiet. The short-term memory goes. Won't remember much when she comes round. Pity, she'll miss supper. Celebration supper tonight. I think we get a complimentary glass of wine.'

'I think we'll both pass on the celebration supper.'

'So how was the drug administered?'

'I don't know. It could have been slipped into her cup of tea,' said Jed. 'Or in the bottled water on the speaker's table in the Orchard Room. Fancy had a workshop there earlier. I guess the kitchen will have put everything through the dishwashers by now, but I could check the water bottles.'

'Her hands are healing nicely,' said the doctor, looking at the pink skin under the cling film. 'Good sign.'

'She's pretty fit.'

'For a writer,' the doctor added. 'It's a mystery. Why slip her the drug? And in full view of everyone. Not exactly a date scenario. Unless you are dating her. Though I doubt if you would need a drug to get a date with this young lady. She'll be very obedient now. That's the point of this drug.'

'Obedient? That's not like our Fancy. I doubt if she's ever been obedient.'

'It'll flush out very quickly. Make sure she has plenty of water to drink.'

'It's either another warning or they wanted to stop her going to tonight's party.' Jed looked at the invitations, which Fancy had fixed to the edges of the mirror. Tonight's party was in the ABC building, the posh one. The room number meant nothing to him, nor the host names.

He would be going, he decided. He took the invitation card down and put it in his pocket. No one would check that it was addressed to Fancy. Someone might be there who should be prevented from meeting her.

He wondered who it was. Well, he was going to find out.

Jessie, in her usual efficient way, had put together a rota of carers. No one was asked to do too much because so many other things were going on. Her rota was in twenty-minute shifts which she reckoned meant that no one missed the whole of a party, or the whole of supper, or the whole of that evening's speaker.

'There's such a lot going on this evening,' she said. 'I don't want anyone to miss anything.'

'If the shifts change on time,' Jed said.

'I'm making sure everyone knows that prompt arrival is essential. It would not be fair to be late. Shall I put you down for a shift, Jed?'

'No need. I'll be popping in and out all the time, to see how Fancy is getting on. I shan't leave her for long.'

'Ah,' said Jessie, knowingly, remembering the public kiss. 'Of course.'

'Thanks, Doctor,' said Jed. 'Hope we haven't kept you from anything.'

'Going to a poetry workshop in the lounge. A few of us poets getting together.'

'Enjoy yourself, and thank you again.'

Jed did not expand on the kiss. That kiss had been an impulse, part of an excess of emotion, making up from the new lake quarrel. He did not regret it, not for one moment. But he did wish that it had been less public.

Too late for any regrets.

He went down the stairs to his old room in Lakeside. He needed a shower and a change of clothes. Living in two separate bedrooms did not make life easier. He never knew where anything was, upstairs or downstairs. Not that he had brought much in the way of luggage. A canvas carry-on held all his belongings.

He sat on his bed and switched on his laptop. He had some reports to send. They had not heard from him today. They would be wondering what was happening. He typed in his password. He wished he could tell Fancy. One day she would know and then she might never speak to him again. And that would be devastating.

He never thought that he would meet someone that he liked so much. He had been alone for so long it was a way of life, not needing female companionship. Work was busy enough. Any spare evening was spent writing reports, examining cold cases, listening to jazz. He rarely went out after work. And, like Fancy, he was always tired, short-changed on sleep.

He typed fast. There was a lot to report. Wheels were moving fast. Fancy must not know. She would be too alarmed.

He also sent an email. He needed backup. He couldn't protect Fancy on his own, all the time. The conference was becoming a dangerous place. Too much had already happened to her. He might not be able to save her if they got any nearer.

*   *   *

The bedroom party was in full swing by the time Jed arrived. It was crowded with happy, sparkling people, drinking and laughing. Music was blaring from a portable stereo. It was playing Jeff Hooper, the Matt Monroe of today, who had won *New Faces* when he was seventeen. Jed had brought a bottle of a good red as an offering. The room was already hot with body heat, stuffy with mingled perfumes, hair spray, deodorants. The scent was overpowering, stifling.

'Come in, come in,' welcomed the hosts, two friends who shared a room, offering bottles of red and white wine in each hand. 'Did you bring a glass? Never mind, we can find one for you. We'll wash out the toothpaste first.'

'I might like toothpaste,' said Jed. 'It would

make a change.' Their wine was vintage supermarket. Few writers were flush with money but they had generous hearts. They brought what they could afford.

He cruised the room, bumping knees, treading on toes, raising his glass in greeting. He knew most of the people at the party. There was no one who seemed a particular threat to Fancy, or someone she should not meet. She knew everyone here, had already talked to them frequently during the week.

'Where's Fancy? I thought she was coming. She's such a fun person,' said a white-badge magazine writer, crunching crisps. 'I want to ask her something about *The Lady* magazine. She might know the right person.'

'She'll be along soon,' said Jed. 'Unless she has another party to go to. I think there are several on the go this evening.'

'What it is to be so popular and so successful.'

'It's the price you pay.'

So why the date-rape drug? It would not harm her, only send her to sleep for a few hours. Something must be planned to happen in those hours. He didn't like it at all. So was someone else protecting her? Nothing made any sense. Jed felt out of control, facts and acts swimming in his head in an attenuated way.

It was the heat of the room, as well as the warmth of his dark alpaca jacket. He had to get out. He hurried along the corridor and the sloping path to Lakeside. There was no light on in Fancy's room, which was strange. He went up in the lift to room 425 and flung open the door.

The room was empty. Fancy had gone. Her bed was empty.

Where was the rota of carers? This shift of volunteers giving up twenty minutes of their time in turn to look after Fancy.

Jed ran across to the opposite room, to the one he had been using. No one there either. No sign of occupation.

He ran down the stairs, two at a time, and out onto the lawn. People were drifting around, those not invited to parties, drink in hand to show that they didn't care too much. He knew the feeling.

'Where's Jessie? Have you seen Jessie?' he asked. 'Have you seen Fancy?'

He drew a blank everywhere. No one had seen Jessie, or her rota. No one knew anything about a rota. They thought Fancy was at a party or having a rest.

'There are several parties. You might have gone to the wrong one or maybe she's cruising between two parties. People do that.'

He saw Richard, earnestly talking to Fergus

— some conference business — at the corner table reserved for them near the bar.

Jed gatecrashed without thought. 'Have you seen Jessie? Have you seen Fancy? She's missing. She's not in her room.'

The two men looked at him, blank-faced, surprised, slightly put out at being interrupted. 'Don't know what you're talking about, old boy. Is she supposed to be in her room? Nothing to do with us.'

'Not in trouble again, is she? Not another fire?'

'Jessie set up a rota to sit with Fancy,' said Jed.

'News to us. Don't know anything about a rota. Do you know, Richard?'

'Never know what Jessie's doing,' said Richard. 'She's a mystery to me. She doesn't even answer her emails. No idea at all. Ask someone else.'

Jed backed off. This was a waste of time. He left them to their cold beers. He didn't know where to go, or what to do next. He could hardly phone for backup. Backup for what? A crime writer who had gone walkabout? She might have gone home. Fancy had seemed a bit fed up, homesick, perhaps.

He began combing conference rooms. They were all empty. His imagination was in full flight now. Perhaps she had a new lover, had fallen for someone younger at the conference. Perhaps she had faked the drug and was even now under the duvet in a different Lakeside room. But he knew it wasn't possible. Her collapse had been genuine enough. And so had that kiss.

He checked her vintage car. It was still in the car park. Empty. Locked.

He ducked under the crime-scene tape and hurried through the shrubbery to the old lake. The swans were still circling the water, unperturbed by the day's activities. The willow's leaves glistened in the fading sunlight, a rosy glow in the sky. There was going to be another glorious sunset.

Then he saw movement on the far side. It was only the faintest stirring, a water vole or underwater fish, maybe? He ran round, almost slipping on the damp path.

'Fancy,' he shouted.

She was in the water, trying to swim, feeble paddles of her arms barely keeping her afloat. Her weight was pulling her down and she was gulping water, her head falling under, her feet stuck in sludge. She was still half-drugged and only the coldness of the water was fighting it.

Jed strode straight into the lake, water up to his knees, put his good hand under her armpit and round her back and heaved with all his strength. A one-handed rescue was a struggle. For the first time he cursed his lack of dexterity. He bent down and gripped her sodden T-shirt with his teeth but the cotton ripped.

She was starting to struggle, unaware of what he was trying to do.

He cursed again. Standing on one knee, balancing himself, he brought his other knee up under her body so he could get a better leverage on her. It seemed to work. He staggered back, pulling her along, keeping her head out of the water.

'Wake up, Fancy. Wake up, give us a hand. I can't do this by myself.'

'Can swim,' she muttered, coughing.

'I know you can, girl. Come on, do some swimming. Show us how well you can swim,' he said, gritting his teeth, and heaving her through the weeds towards the further side of the lake.

She did nothing. She was a dead weight, still drugged, her own body and her own shoes dragging her down. But she was breathing, coughing and choking, her dark hair slicked across her face. He tried to bring his useless hand up to clear her mouth, but it was impossible. It wouldn't move beyond a vague wave on the water.

'Blasted arm,' he shouted.

He struggled out of his jacket, one-handed, and somehow got it under Fancy's body, thrashing around in the water to grab a sleeve from the other side. Clutching both sleeves with his good hand, he pulled on his jacket, using it as a sling. The way Iron Age people used to move things before wheels.

She began to move like a sluggish parcel.

It wasn't what he had bought the expensive jacket for, but he reckoned it was worth the sacrifice as Fancy began to move towards the side, inch by inch. He took a deep breath, using every ounce of strength, and was able to lift her over a clump of weed, cutting his wrist on something sharp as he did. She lay face down on the path, water dribbling sideways out of her mouth. She was not a pretty sight. The sleek and elegant novelist was a sodden mess.

She was breathing, gulping great gasps of air. Jed began rubbing her arms and legs to get the circulation going. She seemed to be coming round, the cold water helping, the cold air giving her goose pimples. Jed had nothing warm or dry to put round her. He was soaking, too.

Everyone had gone in to supper. The lights in the dining room were bright and welcoming, but Jed steered Fancy clear of the festivities. No supper tonight. No orange custard. He fancied getting Fancy into a tepid bath before she died of hypothermia. And he might well join her in the bath.

Not how he had envisaged their first bath together, but it would have to do.

# 13

## Same Evening

Jed had done his first-aid training and was up to date in hypothermia treatment. He had twice fished would-be suicides out of the river; once in Liverpool, once in Manchester. Both had jumped off bridges in an alcoholic haze.

No hot baths and no alcohol. Both methods damaged the already cold blood.

First he had to get those wet clothes off Fancy, but not here in the open, somewhere warm and indoors. She might not appreciate a semi-conscious striptease, but she wouldn't know about it.

He carried her back to Lakeside, her own feet doing some of the walking in a semi-drunk fashion. Anyone seeing them would think they had been to a very inebriated party. Keying in the door code was difficult with only one hand.

'Ouch,' said Fancy.

It was a good sign. They stumbled into the lift, dripping water everywhere. *Doors closing*, said the voice. Fancy slumped against

Jed, their wet bodies so chilling. *Doors opening,* the voice said again at the third floor.

The door to room 425 was still open, No anxious volunteer sitting there, white-faced and panic-stricken. Jed kicked it shut. He drew the curtains and put on all the lights. They would generate some warmth — he knew that the radiators were turned off for the summer. He plugged in the hairdryer and propped it up on the desk. The hot air fanned into the room.

Peeling off Fancy's wet clothes was not easy without her cooperation. He left her bra and panties on, taking his eyes off their lacy feminine curves now tinged a murky lake-water shade. He dried her gently, knowing that roughness would damage her skin. Her feet were torn and bloodied but they would have to wait.

Then he wrapped her in both sheets and the duvet, rolled her into the centre of the bed. She didn't have a coat to add on top and the towels were damp.

He left her for a moment and collected the duvet from the opposite bedroom. He laid it over her carefully. He had a feeling that her shivering was already becoming less violent. Her own body heat had to work to warm her up.

He was the one beginning to shiver.

He stripped off his clothes, took a quick warm shower to get rid of the lake water and the musty smell. Then he dried himself and climbed into bed with Fancy. He slid under the second duvet and put his arms round her, holding her gently, in a loving but dispassionate hug. It was not how he had imagined their first night together either. But it was good to hold her, to be able to put his arms round her.

The warmth generated by his body was helping, as he knew it would. The room was warming up, but not excessively.

'Nice,' she murmured.

He wondered if she would remember anything. How she had got to the lake. Who took her, who pushed her in. Would she have any clues locked away in that sleep-drugged brain? Her writer's mind might have latched on to something, noticed something, remembered a voice or a sound.

The shivering was gradually subsiding, and Fancy lay in a restful slumber, occasionally murmuring and licking her lips. Her hair was drying into untidy peaks. She would have a fit when she saw it, Jed thought grimly. He picked off stray mauve petals of loosestrife, the willowherb that grew in the lake.

'Would you like a drink, Fancy?' he whispered.

She nodded, eyes still closed. 'Dr . . . ink.'

He got up carefully and turned off the hairdryer. The room was really warm now. He made two cups of tea, one only warm, his hot. He saw a little pot of honey purloined from the breakfast table and put a spoonful into Fancy's tea. It was going to be awkward giving her the drink.

He tucked a towel round his waist in case she woke up.

He took the warm tea to Fancy and helped her to sit up. She was able to drink some of the sweet liquid and seemed to appreciate it. Then she lay back and dozed off again. He drank his own hot tea, then climbed back into bed with her, folding his body against hers, his warmth bringing her temperature back to normal, slowly and gently. He could almost have fallen asleep in the comfort and the company.

She had stopped shivering now. She was going to recover without hospital treatment, but he would find the good poet doctor as soon as he could. And he needed some dry clothes himself as soon as possible.

Leaving Fancy was a problem. Jed did not trust anyone now. If he locked her into room 425, she might wake up and panic. And there were spare keys floating around if you knew how to get hold of them, and whoever had taken Fancy to the lake might have that knowledge.

There was a long enough lead on the telephone to take the instrument into the bathroom. He did not want to disturb Fancy. He phoned management and got the duty manager, as the day staff had already left. It was not the night manager but some in-between person.

'I wonder if you could find Dr Arthur for me. He's probably just finishing supper in the dining room. It's not an emergency so no announcement, please. Someone will know where he's sitting. Just say that Jed Edwards would like to see him again. He'll know what it's about.'

'But no announcement, sir? It would be quicker to do it over the tannoy.'

'No, thank you. No announcement, no emergency. I don't want anything public. I just need to see him.'

'I'll do my best.'

He did his best very quickly and in less than ten minutes, Dr Arthur was in room 425, holding his supper napkin. Jed opened the door, still with the towel tucked round his waist.

'Good heavens,' said Dr Arthur, eyeing the

bare chest and legs.

'Good heavens, indeed,' said Jed. 'Not what you think. Come in and shut the door. I found Fancy in the lake, the old lake. Someone tried to drown her.'

★ ★ ★

Dr Arthur was satisfied that Fancy was recovering from her immersion in the lake, thanks to Jed. Her pulse was almost normal and her breathing regular.

'We need to get her moving about,' said Dr Arthur. 'Some small activity would help. Nothing strenuous, some walking. The Roofie hasn't helped. Perhaps some more warm sweet tea.'

'Can I leave her with you while I go downstairs and get myself some dry clothes?' Jed didn't like doing this but he had to trust someone. He could hardly suspect every single delegate at the conference.

'Of course, dear boy. Mind who you meet in the corridors. It'll be tomorrow's top gossip. That towel — not exactly Tarzan.'

'Tomorrow's gossip. Delegate caught *in flagrante delicto*. I'll put my wet clothes back on. Nasty but necessary.'

Dr Arthur caught the apprehensive look on Jed's face. 'Don't worry,' he said. 'I'm not your lake murderer. I'll look after the young lady till you get back.'

'Thanks,' Jed said. 'I'm getting paranoid about everyone.'

★   ★   ★

It was the fastest change in the West. Jed had another shower, towelled off and put on jeans and a black polo-necked sweater. He grabbed black socks and trainers and raced back upstairs, half expecting Fancy to have gone again. But she was sitting up in bed, a jersey round her shoulders, drinking more tea, with the doctor holding the cup. There was a rosy hue to her face.

'Would you like to read some of my poems?' he was saying. 'I don't let many people see them. They might think I've gone off my rocker.'

'I would love to see them,' said Fancy, her voice dry and hoarse. 'It would be a privilege. Please let me have some.'

She sounded almost normal. Normal words, even if the voice was rough. She smiled at Jed as he came into the room. 'I've been in the wars, apparently,' she told him. 'And I hear you saved me again.'

He wondered how much the doctor had told her.

'How are you feeling?'

'A bit weird. I don't actually remember much. I remember drinking tea on the lawn and we were talking. I don't remember what we were talking about but I expect it'll come back.'

'I think I can leave you in good hands,' said Dr Arthur. 'I'd rather like to hear tonight's speaker. I understand he's very amusing. A parody of an Agatha Christie play, I hear.'

'Is it evening already?' asked Fancy, a bit puzzled. 'Is supper over?'

Jed nodded. 'You missed it. We both missed it. We might get a meal rebate at this rate.'

Fancy lay back against the pillows. 'I'm so nice and warm, I can't be bothered to get up. What a pity. I would like to have heard this speaker, too. Another time, perhaps. I can't even remember his name.'

Her head was still fuzzy and she could not remember anything beyond being with Jed on the lawn. She was aware that she had very few clothes on and presumed that a nurse had taken them off her, though why she was not sure.

She was in her room, not in hospital, so that was reassuring. She seemed to be wrapped in a sheet like a mummy, a bit odd. And she did not smell the same. She smelt musty, and her hair felt awful. Surely she'd

218

washed it only that morning?

'I'll say goodnight, young lady. No more gallivanting around the grounds unless you are with someone, preferably Jed. It might do you good to get up soon and move about the room or the corridor. You need some gentle exercise to keep your circulation going.'

'What about food and drink?' Jed asked.

'No alcohol but a snack won't hurt her, if Fancy feels like it.'

Dr Arthur hurried out of the room and closed the door. He wanted a seat near the front for a good view of the play. The week was going by too fast.

Jed had brought his laptop. He opened the lid and turned it on. 'Will you mind if I do some work while you sleep?' he said. 'I've got some catching up to do.'

'Are you writing a story?' Fancy asked, sleepily. 'Did you come to my lectures on crime writing?'

'No, I didn't come to any of them. I hear they were very good.'

'I've got one more to do, the last one, and then I can go home. Home, sweet home. To my church lodge. Did I tell you I lived in part of an old church?'

'Yes, you did. Do you want to go home?' He was watching her face. She looked very peaceful, the colour coming back into her cheeks, her lashes sweeping. He hadn't noticed before that she had long dark lashes.

'Oh, yes, I think I want to go home,' she said. 'I'm used to my little place. It's part of an old church, you know, so it's blessed and holy. Very holy.' She giggled, as if it was a joke. 'Full of holes. But I don't like all the traffic.'

She snuggled down, back in the bed, pulling the second duvet round her.

'I need to get back to work,' she went on, drowsily. 'I have a December deadline. My publisher knows I always meet my deadlines. He relies on me. And I've been getting a new idea for a book while I've been here. I need to write the outline down before I forget it. I think I've already forgotten it.'

'You could dictate some notes to me if you like, and I'll print them out for you,' Jed suggested.

'I can't do that,' she said. 'It spoils the magic to talk about a book before it is written. It has to stay here, inside me, till the first draft is down.'

'The magic?'

'Oh, yes, every book has its own magic.'

She was half-asleep again and Jed kept quiet, knowing sleep was the great healer. He made sure she was tucked in and warm. He went back to his laptop and sent in a report of the current events. He repeated his request for backup. 'A WPC is also essential. I can't stay with Miss Jones all night.'

Though he would have liked to stay wrapped round Fancy. He knew that now.

\* \* \*

Fancy woke an hour later, wondering where she was. Daylight had faded and there was only the desk lamp on. Jed was sitting at it, working on his laptop. She could hear the click of keys. It was soothing to have him there, though why he was there, she was not really sure.

It was her bedroom at the conference, she realized now, recognizing the Jacobean print curtains and the duvet. She saw the invitations she had stuck round the mirror and they reminded her that she had a party to go to that evening. Then there was supper and tonight's entertaining speaker.

She lay there, wondering what to wear. She wanted to wear something special, something that Jed would like. Perhaps the black velvet skirt again and a white silk top that was decorated with tiny seed pearls. It was classy and elegant. He might take her dancing. She would like to go dancing again. One-armed dancing was easy to get used to.

'Hello,' she said, her nose peeping over the edge of the duvet.

'Hello, sleeping beauty,' he said.

'Have I been asleep a long time?'

'Quite a long time; several hundred years.'

'Do I get a kiss to wake me up?'

'If you would like one,' he offered.

'Sorry, I need the bathroom.'

She swung her legs over the side of the bed, trying to free them from the sheet.

'I should keep the sheet on,' said Jed. 'You haven't much else on.'

She took a few unsteady steps, Jed holding her arm. He guided her to the bathroom, put on the light. She saw a pile of damp towels on the floor but there were dry towels hanging on the rail.

'I brought some fresh clean towels up from my room,' said Jed. 'I thought you might want a shower once you'd woken up.'

'What do you mean? Have I been asleep? How stupid of me.'

Once she had woken up? She had no idea what he was talking about, but when she saw her face and her hair in the mirror, she decided she certainly did need a shower. Her hair was a horrid mess of tangles and mud. It was a disaster.

'I look dreadful,' she muttered. 'Excuse me,' and she shut the door.

She barely had the strength to turn on the shower but somehow she managed it, lathering herself with jasmine gel and shampooing her hair. She didn't take long over it as she felt too weak. She wrapped a bath towel round her and tottered back into the room, sitting heavily on the bed.

'That was hard work,' she said. 'I'm worn out, exhausted.'

'Are you feeling better?' He noted the soft glow to her skin, the wet hair hanging over her shoulders. 'You're looking a lot better.'

'I'm feeling a bit weak. Perhaps I'm hungry. I don't remember when I last ate. It seems a long time ago.'

'Do you fancy some chips?' he asked with a grin.

'I haven't had chips for years. All that salt and fat. Lethal.'

'Then it's time you did. Get dressed and I'll drive you to the pub down the road and we'll have some chips. I'm ravenous. I missed supper, too.'

'But I've a party to go to, in the ABC.'

'You've missed the party, supper and by the sound of the clapping, we've missed the speaker too.'

Fancy swallowed the information. She began drying her hair. Jed turned back to his laptop while she put on clean underwear, not looking in the mirror, though he knew he could watch her reflection in it. She was pulling on jeans, a white T-shirt, shrugging into a black fleece and slip-on shoes.

'I'm ready,' she said. 'If you don't mind wet hair.'

'I'm getting used to wet hair. It seems to happen a lot.'

★   ★   ★

Jed's car was also parked on the higher level so Fancy did not have far to walk. She turned her face to the fresh night air as they went out of the back entrance of Lakeside. The moon was partially obscured by fingers of cloud.

'That smells good,' she said. 'It's honeysuckle.'

'Enjoy it,' said Jed, pointing the digital door key at his car. They heard the click of the doors unlocking. 'The pub will be stuffy and smelly.'

'But full of real people.'

He held the passenger door open and she climbed into the small two-seater. She was still a bit dizzy but regaining her balance with every step.

'I had a friend who forgot where she had parked her car in a big multi-storey. The only way she could find it was by clicking that remote thing,' said Fancy.

'There's a story there.'

'There's a story everywhere. Are you going to tell me what has been happening?' she went on as he drove carefully over the speed bumps in the road. 'I don't remember anything.'

'All in good time,' he said. 'I need some food first. I can't work on an empty stomach.'

Not exactly true. Many times he had done a twenty-four-hour stretch without a break, surviving on coffee and the odd stale biscuit or Mars Bar.

'So I've missed a party, supper and tonight's speaker,' said Fancy, repeating his words in the hope that it would prompt her into remembering something. 'What was for supper?'

'I have no idea. I missed it, too.'

'Did you miss the ABC party?'

'No, I went to the party. I took your invitation.'

'What a nerve. You mean you gatecrashed with my invitation?'

'No one seemed to mind. They were all very friendly.'

'And what was I doing while you went to the party with my invitation?' There was an edge to Fancy's voice. For some irrational reason, she was annoyed.

'Unfortunately I have no idea. I thought you were asleep but subsequent events indicate that you were not exactly asleep.'

Fancy let out an exasperated gasp. 'I don't want to get angry but somehow I don't think you are telling me the full story. I want to know exactly what has been happening and why I was such a mess and wet and muddy.'

'You're not ready for it,' he said, turning into the car park of the pub. It looked pretty full. The pub was going to be packed. He eased into a tight space between two badly parked cars. He wished that driving instructors would give basic tips on parking. It would make the streets much tidier.

He helped Fancy out of the car and for a moment she stood unsteadily on the tarmac. He caught a whiff of jasmine gel. She regained her balance and nodded. 'I'm okay.'

It was a pleasant old pub, several farm workers' cottages knocked together and opened up. It had low ceilings, smoke-darkened beams and faded hunting prints on the walls. The area was divided into nooks and crannies and Fancy wondered if they were ever going to find two seats together. But they were lucky. A couple on a bench seat near an open hearth got up and Jed was there in a flash.

'What would you like, Fancy?'

'Red wine, please.'

'You're not allowed alcohol.'

'Who said so?'

'Dr Arthur. No alcohol tonight. I don't know about tomorrow.'

'That's nonsense,' said Fancy, unfastening the zip of her fleece. It was warm in the pub even though the fire was imitation flames. 'There's nothing wrong with one glass. I should know. I'm always having one glass.'

Jed shouldered his way to the bar and ordered fish and chips, a side salad, a beer and a Rainbow Punch. He got the name from the drinks list hanging in the bar.

'Exactly what is this Rainbow Punch?' he asked the barmaid as she drew his beer. 'Is it non-alcoholic?'

She nodded. 'Pineapple juice, orange juice, Grenadine, soda water and a slice of lime. I'll bring the food over to you,' she said, ringing up the till. Jed handed over a ten pound note and some coins. 'Table seven by the fire.'

'Yes, thank you.' He walked carefully back with the two glasses on a tray. Fancy took the brightly coloured orange-and-red striped drink in a sling glass. It had a slice of lime balanced on the rim.

'What on earth is this?'

'Taste it and see. Time you tried something new.'

Fancy took a sip through the straw. It was delicious. Lots of fruity tastes and it had quite a kick, though she had no idea what was in it. 'Lovely,' she murmured. 'Is it a sort of gin sling? A Derbyshire gin sling?' It took away the taste of mud and tea that lingered in her mouth. She had no idea what she was supposed to be remembering. It was enough, for the present, that Jed was with her and he was looking after her in this comfortable old pub.

'The red stripe is the De Kuyper Grenadine. It's made of red currants and pomegranate syrup. That's the sharp taste.'

'Mmm,' she agreed. She looked at him over the brimming glass. He looked dishevelled, his Roman cut untidy, the fringe flopping. His glasses needed cleaning. They were smeared with something muddy. Hadn't she suspected him of being involved? Hadn't she stopping trusting him? It was all lost in the mist of her mind. Thoughts swirled round like fragments of sound, disjointed and incoherent. She was almost dizzy with indecision. And this annoyed her too.

'It feels funny to be back in the real world,' she said. 'The conference is so cut off from everything, as if we are living in a fictional world. I'm not surprised that people go out for a meal now and then, to get their feet back on solid ground.'

'You remember that you're at a conference, then?'

'Of course I remember that I'm at a conference. I'm giving talks, aren't I?' She looked at Jed's face, trying to get some clue from his expression. 'I am, aren't I? Or have I imagined it?'

'No, you're at a writers' conference in Derbyshire and you've been giving lectures. You're a crime writer. You have one more lecture to give tomorrow.'

Fancy almost choked on the straw. 'Tomorrow? But I can't. I can't remember anything.' She remembered a nightmare dream when she stood up in front of a room full of people and couldn't remember a word of what she had to say. Perhaps she was still living that nightmare.

The girl was coming over with a big white plate for Jed. On it was a huge, steaming cod fillet covered in golden batter and a mountain of glistening chips. It smelt wonderful. She put down cutlery wrapped in a paper napkin and a small bowl of standard salad. No imagination. Lettuce, tomato, sliced beetroot and a sprinkling of cress and a small ramekin of dressing.

'Enjoy,' she said, without expression, as if she had been taught to say it.

'The salad is for you,' said Jed, pushing the bowl towards her.

'Thanks a million,' said Fancy, helping herself to a glistening chip. It was hot and nearly burnt her fingers and her mouth. But the taste was fantastic. She had been denying herself this taste for years — too much salt and too much fat. But this was a special occasion. She was beginning to realize that she had survived something and hoped that soon Jed would tell her. Meanwhile another little chip wouldn't hurt. Forget cholesterol.

'Don't mind me. Help yourself,' said Jed, adding a dollop of tomato sauce to the plate. They still had bottles in this pub, not plastic sachets, impossible to open.

He took some of her salad, to counteract the fat, he told himself. Fancy ate a few more chips, savouring the forbidden food, wiping the fat off her lips with a paper napkin. She also munched some limp lettuce, to show willing.

'So what's been happening to me?' she asked between sips of her Rainbow Punch. 'You said you would tell me when I felt better. I feel better now.'

Jed forked up a mouthful of succulent fish, wondering if she was strong enough to hear it all. He leaned forward, carefully, as if shielding her from all the people in the pub.

She was looking at him, her dark eyes full of trust.

'You were drugged with a date-rape drug, but it wasn't a big dose. Then someone tried to drown you in the lake. They left you to drown. The old lake. The same lake where we found Melody Marchant.'

# 14

## Wednesday Night

Fancy thought she would faint. It was like a macabre plot from one of her own crime novels. She could have written it. But could the Pink Pen Detective have solved the mystery? Probably not. She wasn't that smart.

'Is this true?' she said in a low voice. 'Is that why I can't remember anything?' She was frightened and bewildered.

'The drug blanks out all your present memory. But not forever; it does come back sometimes. In time for your lecture, we hope. But you will never remember what happened to you while you were under the influence of the drug. You won't remember who dragged you or carried you down to the lake. Or who pushed you into the water.'

'Someone wants to kill me. The lake wasn't a threat like the biscuit tin or the fire in a bucket. This was a definite attempt to kill me. But why? What have I done? What's the motive?'

'If only we knew,' said Jed. 'Then we might

be able to help you.'

'Have you been assigned to me?' she said, sharply.

'Yes.'

'Did you save me, pull me out of the lake?'

'Yes.'

'So you're not here at the conference because you're a writer?'

'Not exactly.' Jed sighed. She would hate him even more now. 'I do write. I like writing. I am writing a book about cold cases in my spare time. But this cold case has been erupting like a long-dead volcano. Your magazine article led us to opening up the case of *The Missing Cover Girl*. We've been investigating the money side. It's a fraud investigation. Where has the money gone? All those brewery millions?'

Fancy shivered, but from fear, not the cold. 'And I am in danger. Perhaps it's revenge for publishing the case and attracting your attention to it.'

'I've arranged for a WPC to come up from Derby, to keep you company, all the time, day and night, twenty-four hours.'

'I don't want a WPC, however nicely mannered and well behaved.'

'You are going to have her around for twenty-four hours. I can't sleep with you, can I? But she can.' Fancy didn't answer at first.

'What's her name?'

'WPC Richmond. Dorothy Richmond. A very pleasant woman. You'll like her. And she's one hundred per cent reliable.'

'There isn't space in my bedroom. You know that.'

'It's only for one night. You can go home on Friday if you're up to driving. I'll be getting in touch with CID near where you live. They'll keep an eye on you.'

'What a busy little bee you are,' said Fancy, sucking up the last of her punch. She laid emphasis on the *bee*. 'Don't you ever go home?'

There was no answer. Jed wasn't going to tell her.

★ ★ ★

WPC Richmond was waiting in reception in the main house. Even though she was in civilian clothes, regular jeans and a grey anorak, there was no disguising that she was a policewoman. She was sturdily built, strong-looking, with minimal make-up, her brown hair pulled back into a short, stubby ponytail. She was carrying a briefcase. No handbag or anything feminine like a scarf. No earrings, no jewellery.

But she had a pleasant smile, good teeth.

'Miss Jones?' she said, coming forward briskly. 'I've been sent here for the next twenty-four hours. I may then be relieved by another WPC.'

'Good heavens,' said Fancy. 'I've never had a bodyguard before.' She was feeling considerably better, though some areas were still completely blank. She couldn't remember how she had got to the lake. 'What fun. I feel like Whitney Houston in that film..'

'Not exactly a bodyguard,' said Jed. 'A companion.'

'I hope you can do karate and all that self-defence stuff,' said Fancy. 'You see, I keep getting attacked in some form or another. It's very disconcerting.'

She knew she was rambling nonsense, but she couldn't seem to stop. She turned to Jed, who was trying to distance himself. He was obviously irritated with her flippancy. She'd annoyed him again.

'I bet the disco has started by now. Shall we all go? A threesome would be awesome. Raise a few eyebrows.'

'I don't think you're in a fit state to go dancing,' said Jed. 'You can barely walk. A good night's sleep and you may become your normal, rational self.'

Fancy opened her mouth to speak, then forgot what she was going to say. Her mind still seemed to be going round in circles and it certainly wasn't the punch, even one laced with redcurrants and pomegranates.

'If you say so, Mr Edwards.'

'Perhaps we should go to your room and make a nice cup of tea,' said Dorothy Richmond, taking charge.

'A nice cup of tea,' said Fancy bitterly. 'That's all I seem to have heard today.'

'It always works.'

'Tell me more. I'm agog.' She was rambling again.

★ ★ ★

Dorothy Richmond took Fancy upstairs in the lift. Jed disappeared, anxious for some time on his own. He had things to do. He'd had little chance to search the ground near where he had found Fancy in the lake. At least the crime tape was still in place and the lake out of bounds to the conference delegates.

There should only be traces of his feet, Fancy's and her assailant's. He was hoping to find other significant traces. How was Fancy taken down there? She was a tall girl. Surely not in a wheelbarrow? The gardeners had several of those around. If it was some kind of vehicle, then there would be signs.

He had a flashlight with a strong beam. He made sure he had enough specimen bags in his pocket and his good hand was gloved. He hoped he wouldn't meet anyone.

He did meet the roaming tabby who had adopted the conference centre as being marginally more interesting than his nearby domestic owners. Nobody talked to him at home, whereas everyone here petted him between lectures. Occasionally he got a morsel of ham or cheese from lunch.

'Hello, Tabs,' said Jed. 'Don't get in my way.'

★ ★ ★

'I don't know what we're going to do about sleeping arrangements,' said Fancy. 'It's a double bed but I'm not used to sharing with a complete stranger.' Nor was she used to sharing it with anyone, she could have added.

'Don't worry, Miss Jones,' said WPC Richmond. 'I'm not going to sleep. My remit is to sit up all night and make sure you're safe. I've brought some paperwork to do.'

'That's all I ever seem to hear these days.'

Fancy tried to tidy the room. It looked as if it had been hit by a cyclone. The bed was heaped with crumpled sheets and duvets. She straightened them out.

'Good heavens,' said Fancy. 'Then we must get you a decent armchair. There's only an upright chair to use at the desk. You can't sit on that all night. I'll phone management and get them to bring up something more comfortable. They'll be glad it's not me reporting another fire.'

The duty manager was glad. He promised a more comfortable chair in ten minutes. It arrived while Dorothy was making the tea. It wasn't ideal, but at least it had arms and was padded. Bright orange. Clashed with the room décor.

He was puffing and blowing. 'Not used to carrying furniture,' he said. 'We have porters for that. But you are special, Miss Jones. Our heroine.'

'Very kind. Much appreciated,' said Fancy, with what she hoped was a winning, heroine smile. 'We won't bother you again.'

She hoped not.

Fancy donated a couple of pillows to the basic armchair and took herself to bed. She had had enough of today and whatever had happened to her. Tomorrow might be better.

'Goodnight, Dorothy,' she said.

'Goodnight, Miss Jones.'

'Call me Fancy.'

★ ★ ★

Jed had no trouble in finding out how Fancy was taken down to the lake. The evidence was there on the ground, the path of crushed grass, the broken stems, the muddied track. She had been dragged down in some sort of sling. Maybe a rug, a blanket or a tablecloth. Something strong and big enough.

An owl hooted in the distance. It had spotted prey.

He couldn't find any other evidence, except for another of Fancy's pink pens. But it could have fallen out of her pocket.

The ground by the edge of the lake was churned up and told him nothing, but might reveal something to the forensics team. They would be down in the morning with their eagle eyes and tweezers and specimen bags. There would be soil particles on the soles of the shoes worn by the killer, but the thought of examining the shoes of all the delegates was daunting. Half of them had walked round the lake at some time. They would all be carrying evidence.

He heard the crunching of footsteps coming towards him. They did not seem to be trying to conceal the sound. It was the heavy tread of a big man.

'Stop,' said Jed. 'Police.'

He flashed his torch in the direction of the intruder.

'Police, eh? Are you going to arrest me for taking a midnight stroll? I'm only walking off an evening's drinking before I take to my bed. Too many parties.'

Jed recognized the burly figure of Callum McKay, the lecturer on the novel. He was wearing the tweed jacket he had worn all week, with a fawn check shirt. Jed wondered if he had brought any other clothes.

'Didn't you see the scene-of-crime tape? You're not supposed to be here.'

'Of course I saw it, old boy. But I'm not going to let a bit of plastic stop me from walking round the lake; it's my favourite place at Northcote. I'm sure your lads have done all the combing for evidence that they need. It's only a small shrubbery and a small lake — hardly Kew Gardens.'

'Did you walk round your favourite place this afternoon?' Jed asked, lowering his flashlamp. 'Sometime before supper?'

It was a shot in the dark. He might have seen something.

'Yes, I did. It's a wonderful place for ideas. I'm really stuck in my new book. It's about a couple who swap houses and then the husband of one finds out he had affair with the wife of the other when they were both students. But I won't bore you with the details. It's very complicated.'

'Did you see anything unusual or anyone else walking round the lake?'

'No,' he shook his head, shaggy hair falling over his brow. 'Nothing.'

Callum McKay was a big man, muscles like an ox. He could easily have dragged Fancy down to the lake. But if he had wanted to drown her, he would have held her head down till she stopped breathing. He wouldn't have left her floundering. And a plausible motive was missing.

'Did you see Fancy Jones at all, alone or with anyone else?'

'Fancy? No, I didn't see her. Lovely woman. Writes terrific books. I've read them all. Can't put them down.'

'Did you see anyone else?'

'Well, I thought I saw someone . . . but then I didn't, if you know what I mean. Queer thing.'

'Are you sure?'

'Are we ever sure of anything?' Callum laughed. 'I have a hell of a time remembering how to spell my own name. I can never remember how many l's it's got in it.'

'Remember hell and spell and then you'll always know,' said Jed.

'Say, that's damned clever, old boy. Thanks. Hell and spell. I'll remember that.' He chuckled. 'Hell and spell. All these years and

I've never thought of that.'

Callum had seen something even if he couldn't remember what it was.

The author lumbered away, muttering to himself. Jed gave up. It was too late, too cold and chilly to do any more. It would have to wait till the morning. He needed sleep. He texted Dorothy Richmond.

'Is Miss Jones okay?'

'Sleeping like a baby,' was the reply. 'No snoring.'

Jed shut off his mobile. He was missing out on life. It was time he pulled himself together. The damage to his arm had had more of an effect than he thought. He had decided to opt out of normality. The gremlins needed to be banished.

★ ★ ★

In a far corner of the grounds, where the drive went over the first speed bump, a figure was bending over a mound of cloth. It was one of the Jacobean patterned curtains that hung in all the Lakeside rooms.

The figure was cursing, striking match after match, but failing to ignite the material. It was wet and muddy, stank of lake water. The figure emptied out a rucksack of papers and books and began tearing pages out of the books, crunching the pages up into balls, piling them into a pyramid. The pages caught fire easily, curling tongues of flames licking the edges and racing along the print. It blazed into a mountain of heat, fuelled by more paper and then the rucksack itself.

The curtain began to steam, held over the fire, shielding the bonfire person from the fire itself. His fingers got cramp and he almost dropped the curtain. Coughing and choking on the smoke and the fumes, there was no respite from the roar of the flames.

Suddenly the curtain caught, flames devouring the dry hem and then the side seams like a wall of fire. It was dropped to the ground, where the material folded into itself, hissing and steaming.

Balls of burning paper skittered about, scorching dry leaves and stretches of grass. Plenty of those after the hot summer.

A sheet of flame shot up as the folded material ignited, sparks flying upward in a fireworks display. They showered the surrounding ground. Little fires broke out, greedily eating anything dry and crackling. A low-lying branch caught fire, the leaves curling in the heat.

The fire was spreading, running along the dry grass, leaving the smouldering curtain and half-burnt rucksack. The figure began to run. Not in the direction of the conference centre but towards the road.

Then it began to rain, quite heavily.

★ ★ ★

Jed stopped walking. He could smell the acrid burning but it was also raining. He'd already been thoroughly soaked once this evening. It wasn't going to happen twice.

He gave up being a detective. Whatever was being burnt could wait till morning.

# 15

## Thursday Morning

Fancy woke early, remembering everything, or almost everything. There was a missing gap after taking the cup of tea from white-badger, Peggy Carter, and then Dr Arthur talking to her about his poetry. Jed seemed to be around a lot, on and off, coming in and out of her room like a weather man.

She remembered the fish and chips, especially the succulent taste of the forbidden chips. And that brightly coloured drink with a kick, but no alcohol.

She turned over and saw a strange woman asleep in an armchair by the radiator, some papers on her lap and more fallen on the floor. The woman looked very uncomfortable. Then Fancy recalled her name, WPC Richmond — also a town on the River Thames — deployed by Jed to guard her through the night.

Some guard, fast asleep.

Thoughts eddied through her mind. Someone had drugged her and then left her to drown in the lake. Was it the same person or different people? Fancy shivered though she was not cold. She was more scared. It was no longer weird happenings and threat. Something had happened which could have killed her. And Jed had rescued her. She did not like the twists and turns that this drama was taking.

Perhaps she could be taken into protective custody. She might be safer in a police cell. She would demand all mod cons: her own shower, television, daily menus, and access to a private gym. Or perhaps inmates got all this already.

Her last lecture was this morning. Her head had cleared and she could remember what she planned to say and the area she would be covering. A quick look at her notes and she would be nearly word perfect.

But did she want to do it? It meant getting up, getting dressed, facing the world. It meant addressing a hall full of delegates, any one of whom might be Melody's killer. She wanted to do a declining lady stunt. Stay in bed for ever.

Or the killer might be one of the other lecturers. Forsaking the committee table at meal times had not been a good move. She knew some of the other lecturers thought she was antisocial and acting above herself. It was not true. She liked to mix with everyone at the conference.

'Good morning, Fancy. Did you sleep well?'

Dorothy Richmond had stirred. She was picking up her fallen papers.

'Oh hello, I thought you were asleep.'

'Just dozing. It's a trick. Not actually asleep. Ears still alert even if eyes closed.'

'You must have been awfully uncomfortable in that chair.'

'Not exactly the Ritz. Do you mind if I have a hot shower? I'm feeling rather stiff and sticky.'

'Of course not. Help yourself to anything. I'll make some tea.'

'The cups need washing.'

Fancy did as she was told. Dorothy Richmond was used to being obeyed. Fancy washed the cups and made tea while Dorothy was in the shower. The shower curtain was opaque so all secrets were kept secret.

Fancy stood at the window, drinking the fresh brew. The jogging brigade were already up and out, keeping fit, running around the misty grounds, wearing regulation jogging gear. Perhaps she should take more exercise. Exercise was supposed to be good for depression. Writing was a solitary occupation; bum on seat for hours, eyes glued to the screen, days and weather passing by in an endless stream of nothing. She only had the clouds for company.

But this lecture was something she had to do. She decided she would say no to all future invitations, however flattering.

Her last lecture. She had survived drugging and near drowning. Her appearance had to be stunning. She was a survivor. She peered among her limited wardrobe, looking for something that she hadn't worn before but everything had had an outing or two.

She went for the slim black jeans and fitted jacket with a plain white shirt. She did look stunning, the sweeping wings of her dark hair hiding the pain in her eyes. A white and silver scarf tied in a Chelsea knot went round her throat. Maybe someone would try to strangle her with it . . . But who? She was suspicious of everyone. Even Jed. He only said he had rescued her. He could have been disturbed by someone and put on the rescue act.

Maybe Dorothy Richmond was not a genuine police officer at all. Fancy could have been suffocated in her sleep. There had been plenty of opportunity, plenty of pillows.

'For goodness' sake,' Fancy told her mirrored self. 'Snap out of it, girl. You're becoming paranoid.'

Dorothy came out of the bathroom. She had dried and dressed again in the same creased clothes. 'Talking to yourself now, are you?' she said. 'That's a bad sign.'

'It's a good sign,' said Fancy, putting on a soft pink lipstick and mascara. 'It shows I'm still sane enough to talk to myself.'

'Let's go and have some breakfast,' said Dorothy.

'Are you going to be my taster?' Fancy asked. 'In case someone injects a dose of arsenic into my grapefruit?'

Fancy knew she was being unnecessarily caustic but she couldn't stop herself. What was the matter with her? She was not usually so rude.

'Not in my job description,' said Dorothy, putting on her serviceable lace-up shoes. Her coral lipstick was a quick swipe in the region of her mouth. It was not a good colour for her skin. She needed a make-up makeover.

The early birds were already queuing outside the dining room, determined to get their favourite table or sit with friends. Fancy never minded where she sat or with whom, usually cruised around to find an empty seat. Now she would have to find two empty seats.

'Let's take a walk,' said Fancy. 'I don't like queues. I'll show you around the grounds.'

'There's no need,' said Dorothy. 'The super showed me around after the woman drowned in the lake at the beginning of the week.'

Fancy stopped, puzzled. 'You mean you've been here before? Detective Chief Superintendent Edwards showed you around? Why didn't you say?'

'You didn't ask me.'

There was no answer to that.

'Looking forward to your last lecture, Fancy,' said a group of young writers, eager-faced. 'Everything you've said has been so helpful. What have you got in store for us this morning?'

'It's a surprise,' said Fancy. 'Wait and see.'

'So you're giving a lecture this morning,' said Dorothy, helping herself to a packet of cornflakes, a packet of muesli and a banana. She piled the lot into one cereal bowl. Fancy, who had pounced on two empty seats like a predator, sat looking at her half-a-grapefruit.

'My last. And my last ever, I hope. You can sit at the back of the conference room and stop anyone rushing in with a grenade or a stink bomb. Also watch out for any irate delegate who thinks I've stolen their priceless plot. They may have brought one of those sharp grapefruit knives in with them. I'm not wearing body armour.'

'How many people do you expect at your lecture?'

'Between seventy and eighty.' This was a slight exaggeration but Fancy was past caring.

The numbers always varied. Some delegates were itinerant. They cruised from lecturer to lecturer. And now she was a sort of novelty factor.

'I'll need six pairs of eyes,' said Dorothy. 'Perhaps I should phone Derby for backup.'

'I thought you were backup.'

'There's a limit to what I can do,' said Dorothy, going back to the fruit bowl for another banana. 'I'm not a miracle woman.'

Dorothy put away a good-sized breakfast, including the bacon, egg and beans fry-up. She passed on the toast. Fancy stuck to half a grapefruit, an apple and black coffee. She had not seen Jed yet this morning. She hoped he had got a good night's sleep. He needed it.

★ ★ ★

The room was crowded for her last lecture. There were some new faces, delegates who had strayed from their original courses, wanting to sample something different.

Fancy spotted Phoebe Marr, the poetry lecturer, sitting at the end of a row. She was a petite woman, fairy-like, with a halo of fine blonde hair. She smiled at Fancy and waved.

'I hope you don't mind,' she said. 'I've

brought all of my lot to your talk. I thought they ought to know more about real life for their poems.'

'They are welcome,' Fancy said. 'But I'm not sure if they will learn anything useful. My motto is: write plain. Cut all unnecessarily flowery words.'

Phoebe laughed. 'We could all learn from that.'

'Perhaps we'll learn something from you. Better words, brighter images.'

Fancy launched into her lecture. There was so much to say and so little time left. She was concentrating this morning on how to weave in clues and red herrings and how to resolve all the loose ends. She wondered if there was such a thing as a criminal poem. Perhaps Phoebe would write one.

'We're now going to do some practical work,' she said. 'You're all going to become detectives. Please go out into the grounds of the conference centre and search for anything you think might be a clue. You can't go into the taped-off area, of course. That is still, sadly, an out-of-bounds crime scene. Remember the clue must not be contaminated. Either bring it back, untouched by hand, or write a description of it.'

'We're going to be real detectives!'

'Wow!'

'Ten minutes. That's all you've got. Poets as well. No slacking. Back in ten minutes, everyone, please.'

There was a scramble to get out. Fancy knew they would be gone fifteen minutes. She sat down, exhausted by the effort. She had not recovered from yesterday's ordeal as much as she thought she had. She stretched out for a drink. She had brought her own bottle of water.

'Do you want me to go out and search for clues?' said Dorothy, amused. 'Uniformed might have missed something.'

'No, you're supposed to stay here with me. I don't think they've tried poisonous gas yet.'

'I'll tell you if I sniff anything obnoxious.'

'I hope I don't smell obnoxious,' said Jed, coming into the hall. 'Some of these new aftershaves are pretty weird.' He walked to the front row and sat down, stretching out his legs. 'So, come on, Miss Burne-Jones, lecture me.'

'Why aren't you at your course?' said Fancy, trying to hide her pleasure at seeing him. He looked fresh and showered, and well groomed, his silver streaks brushed forward tidily. Straight from a senate debate at the forum. No toga; jeans and a sweater.

'My course has run out of steam,' he said. 'I thought I've give you a try.'

'You are not supposed to do that, change courses.'

'Phoebe's here.'

'They're going to write a poem about clues and red herrings,' said Phoebe quickly. 'This is work experience.'

Jed grinned. 'Neat. Mind if I have a word with Dorothy?'

'Go ahead. Ask her what she had for breakfast.'

Jed and Dorothy went into a huddle at the back of the room. They seemed to have a lot to say. Phoebe was scribbling on her notepad, inspired by something. Fancy had bought one of Phoebe's slim volumes of poetry. She could write funny verse as well as the emotional stuff. Almost another Pam Ayres.

The newly appointed detectives began drifting back with their finds wrapped in paper or a clean handkerchief. The noise was horrendous as they swapped stories.

'Settle down, please,' said Fancy, going back onto the platform. 'Now let's hear what you've found. One at a time, please.'

'As I was crawling about in this Peruvian swamp, I found a bent brass hairpin. DNA shows that belonged to the murderer.'

There was a general groan and laughter. It was the class clown. He could be relied upon for a joke in any circumstance.

'And I found this torn up email, stuffed into a crevice in the wall.'

'This is a tiny screw that has been sharpened. Could be a lethal weapon.'

'My clue is a red one. A map showing where the treasure is hidden.'

And so it went on. There was general laughter and amazement at what people had found in the grounds. They had a few minutes to translate their finds into writing and a few more minutes to hear some of them read out. Time was flying.

Fancy then talked about resolving issues, tying up loose ends. One part of her mind was saying: Tie up your own loose ends, idiot, resolve this issue.

No one wanted to leave, even though they could hear coffee being served on the lawn. There was a charming, eloquent vote of thanks from an articulate writer with good manners and loads of clapping.

Fancy was touched by his kind words. 'Thank you, thank you,' she said. 'It's been a pleasure. You are all very talented and I wish you well in your writing careers.'

Phoebe had taken her group to a corner of the lawn, with coffees, to discuss their thoughts and inspiration. They were all talking non-stop. Definitely inspired. It was good that the poets also found her talk enlivening.

Fancy surveyed the conference room, now that it was empty of people. Most of them had left their clues behind. There was always some lost property. Cardigans left on backs of chairs, notebooks, bags. She gathered them up to take to the office.

Jed was rummaging through the clues, not touching, but looking. Someone had found part of a credit card. It had been cut in half. It was the left half with the gold chip that validated the card. The imprint said: Mrs G Harlow. He recognized the bank logo.

Jed picked it up carefully, using a handkerchief. 'Look at this, Fancy. I think this means that Grace is here, too. The card numbers are incomplete but I should be able to identify the card from this amount of information.'

'Grace? Thelma's twin sister?'

Fancy felt all her elation from the talk drain away. Not the other twin sister here, the serious one who had married Rupert Harlow. It was too much to take in.

Jed pulled out his BlackBerry and keyed in some numbers. The amount of databases stored on the device was phenomenal. He also phoned the CID room at Derby and waited for an answer.

'Leave all the clues in there,' he said to Fancy, over the top of his mobile. 'Dorothy will pack them up. The bent hairpin from the Peruvian swamps might be just what we've been looking for.'

She tried to laugh, but it was difficult.

He seemed to be a long time on his phone, listening and talking. She didn't move away. She didn't want to go out on the lawn on her own. She knew she would be besieged by writers and she really was too tired to talk any more.

Jed came back to her, his face grave, and took her aside. 'The pathologist has some interesting revelations. He tells me that the cut marks on the drowned victim's finger tips were made by a serrated edge.'

'A grapefruit knife?'

Jed held out the cut credit card, now in a plastic specimen bag. 'Don't touch, but I can assure you that edge is very sharp. It's an excellent defence weapon if you are ever assaulted.'

'Sure, I always carry a cut-up credit card in my pocket when I'm out.'

'You should.'

'So someone tried to destroy Melody's fingerprints,' said Fancy, noting this small fact for some future plot. 'But why?'

'So we couldn't identify her. The victim's

body had a very faint scar on the lower right abdomen. An appendectomy incision made a long time ago. Probably when she was a teenager. This pathologist is a curious man and he made some enquiries. It took some time to find medical records that went back that far.'

'So Melody had her appendix out.'

'No, Melody didn't. But Grace did.'

Fancy felt the cold returning to her body as she took in Jed's words. 'Are you telling me that it wasn't Melody that we found in the lake? Are you telling me that it was Grace, the other twin sister?'

'Yes. The drowned woman was Grace Marchant, known here as Melody, which was her writing name. So is Thelma still alive, or was Grace killed by someone else?'

'And where do I come into all this?'

'I'm sorry, Fancy. We have no idea. I only wish I knew.'

# 16

Still Thursday

Fancy stood and felt like Alice in a blue gown, looking down a large hole and wondering where it would take her if she fell. It would be cold and dark and hollow, no Red Queen waiting with a chopper.

'Not Thelma?'

'No, she was not Thelma,' said Jed. 'It was Grace, the other twin, the serious one. There's no doubt about it. Even with the damaged fingerprints. The scar is the conclusive identity evidence.'

'Why did Grace call herself Melody?'

'It was her writing name. Melody Marchant, their mother's name when she was a blues singer. Grace wrote children's stories. Lots of writers have different names for writing, don't they, *noms de plumes?*'

'I use my real name.'

'Lucky you. It's a nice one.'

'So where does this leave us now?'

'I honestly don't know. Perhaps Thelma is still alive and out there somewhere, despite the court case and being declared dead. Perhaps it is someone else after the brewery money. The revenge theory is still possible.'

'Do I have to stay here? I've done my last lecture. I could go home now.'

'But the mystery will follow you. It had already begun in London — the Underground, the bus, the slab of concrete — before you came to Derbyshire. You're safer here with me and Officer Richmond.'

Fancy could see integrity in his eyes. And the concern.

'So who is the farmer who came up from Cornwall saying he was Melody's husband?'

'We believe he's Grace's husband, that is, the writer, Melody.'

'But Grace's husband is Rupert Harlow.'

'Yes, so this must be Rupert Harlow and it was his car that was set on fire.'

Fancy collapsed on a nearby seat. 'This is all too complicated. So Rupert Harlow is now a farmer in Cornwall with a wife who writes children's stories? My brain has gone into stress mode.'

'Why not? He was sick of Surbiton and being a solicitor. And when Thelma disappeared, he decided to start a new life, miles away, with Grace. They moved to Cornwall, bought a farm with her half of the inheritance, started rearing sheep.'

'Save me,' said Fancy. 'From mental overload.'

'I need to talk to Rupert Harlow. Let's go out and get some fresh air. Show your face. It might worry a few people.' Jed took her arm and propelled her towards the door. 'Coffee? You need the caffeine.'

'Yes, but I'll get it myself.' She knew he would not like her saying this.

'You don't trust me?' He looked appalled.

'It's not that I don't trust you,' she said carefully. She needed him. 'I think I would feel happier if in future I check everything first myself. It's not that I think someone would tamper with a big flask of coffee and drug a dozen random innocent people. That would be totally at odds with what has happened to me. It's always been directed solely at me. Frankly, after all this, I don't trust anyone.'

Jed nodded. 'Fair enough, Fancy. Richmond and I will do what we can to ensure your safety. We're relieved that everything has failed so far.'

'So far? That's hardly reassuring.'

'What else can I say?'

'But I was in the lake, half-drowned. If you hadn't come along . . . I might have been in the Derby morgue this morning in a box. It's a nightmare.'

'But you're not and that's what's important,' said Jed firmly. 'Be positive.'

'I'll get your coffee. You can trust me,' said WPC Richmond. The sturdy officer had a glimmer of warmth in her eyes. Perhaps she was starting to bond with Fancy. 'Black?'

Fancy nodded. 'All right, thank you.'

'I started reading one of your books last night. It's good. The heroine, the Pink Pen Detective, is a lot like me. Same kind of thinking.'

Fancy and Jed said nothing as WPC Richmond joined the queue at the coffee trolley. They exchanged the shadow of a smile.

'Wow.'

'You've another fan.'

'I'll give her a pink pen.'

'She'll treasure it.'

★ ★ ★

Jed told Fancy nothing about his meeting with Rupert Harlow. The man seemed resigned to the situation, slumped in a chair, his face grey with fatigue, as if he knew Grace would be murdered one day. All traces of the London solicitor, the prospective MP, had long gone. He was all farmer in tweeds and waterproof, without the mud.

At first he was difficult to pin down to a meeting, was uneasy. He gave Jed a dozen reasons why he was too busy.

Jed did not give up. He was relentless. 'We are trying to find out what happened to your wife. It doesn't help if you won't talk to us.'

'I knew this would happen one day,' Rupert said. 'It was a disaster waiting to happen. Thelma hated Grace. Even when they were children, they were always fighting. Thelma was jealous of Grace, of her beauty, of her brains.'

'But Thelma was beautiful too.'

'It was a different sort of beauty. Brassy, more glamour, superficial. Grace was really lovely.'

'I'd like to know everything, right from the beginning,' said Jed. He had his laptop open. 'This is an informal meeting between you and me. No tape recorder, no caution. I am helping DI Bradley who's in charge of the case.'

'Once upon a time I wanted to be a Member of Parliament,' said Rupert Harlow, in a resigned, bedtime story sort of way. 'A foolish dream. I wasn't cut out for politics. But I did meet Grace at constituency meetings and that was the best thing that ever happened to me. She was a press officer and most efficient at her job.'

'And you fell for her?'

'Not exactly. I was always a slow mover in that department. I admired Grace tremendously but she was so busy, she didn't have time for romance. I felt it was important to establish my career first, so that I had something to offer her.'

'Then you met Thelma?'

Rupert's face relaxed momentarily. 'I can't explain what happened. It was at a pre-election party on the Terrace at the House of Commons. A party for new prospective candidates. Thelma blew in like a display of fireworks. She was dazzling, her hair like spun gold. So glamorous with such confidence. I even remember what she was wearing — a sort of white Grecian thing with high-heeled gold sandals. I've no idea what Grace was wearing. Her usual black, I think.'

'And you were bowled over?'

'She bowled me over. She made a beeline for me, stayed with me all evening, on my arm, made it look as if we were an item. It was heady stuff, I can tell you, especially for someone like me who had had little success with women in the past. As I said, I was a slow mover.'

'Go on.'

'In no time, we were engaged. Don't ask me how it happened, but it just did. Looking back, I think she was seeing an illustrious career ahead for me and for herself as my wife. She loved the glamour of politics, being photographed with me everywhere, night-clubs, parties. And she was putting Grace in the shade. That was the real motive. She wanted to snatch me away from Grace. And I let her.'

Jed made his notes discreetly. 'So you got married?'

'Before the election. She wanted to make sure of me. She knew that once I was elected, I might become a very eligible bachelor MP. And Grace would still be working with me. It was a very posh wedding, at St Margaret's, Westminster. Thelma looked like a dream in white satin, flowing veil, tiara. That dress and the honeymoon cost me a fortune.'

'Was Grace a bridesmaid?'

'No, I don't think she was asked. Thelma left her in the shade. Grace would have looked lovely, might have stolen some of the bride's limelight.'

'But you didn't get elected.'

'No,' Rupert let out a long sigh. 'I had neglected my electioneering, too busy going out to nightclubs with Thelma and being photographed for the tabloids. My constituents decided I was a playboy, not serious about their problems and worries. They voted with their feet, in the other direction. I came second in the polls.'

'A disappointment for your new bride?'

'She was furious. I've never seen anyone so angry. She screamed and yelled at me. We'd bought a new house in Surbiton and I thought she would wreck it. But eventually she calmed down when I said I would stand again at the next election, and work a lot harder. Next time I would get in. Meanwhile I had a job with a reputable firm of solicitors, and the money was coming in — for her to spend.'

'You had lots of nice holidays?'

'Lots of nice holidays. Crete, Barbados, the Seychelles.'

'But you were still seeing Grace?'

'Of course I was still seeing Grace. I was working with her. She was helping me with my new campaign, when she had time. She had been promoted to Tory Head Office in Great Smith Street and was making a name for herself there. The girl had brains as well as beauty.'

'Thelma didn't like that.'

'I made sure that Thelma didn't know. She would not have been pleased. She was always very jealous of Grace. It wasn't even about the money; they both had an inheritance, left to them by their father. They were neither of them short of money.'

'Then what happened?'

Rupert looked uncomfortable. He was restless in his chair. 'Do I have to say any more? Why do you have to know?'

'I would remind you that your wife, Grace, has been found drowned. It was not suicide. She had been drugged. And that is murder. If you want us to find out who did it, then you have to cooperate, Mr Harlow.'

'I'm not proud of it but I suppose I had always loved Grace, right from the beginning, and then Thelma came along and bowled me over. And they both looked alike. It was uncanny and so confusing. Sometimes when I was with Thelma, I would half close my eyes and imagine I was with Grace.'

'So you began an affair with Grace,' said Jed, getting Rupert back on track.

'Yes. I couldn't stop myself. Grace was the one I had really wanted. She was bright, intelligent, good company, as well as looking so beautiful. And she seemed to like me. I couldn't believe it. Stupid old me, who married the wrong sister.' Rupert seemed to slump even further into the chair.

'Would you like to stop now?' asked Jed. 'Have a cup of coffee or something? We can take a break.'

'No, thank you. It wouldn't help. Grace has gone now. I don't know how I'll manage without her.'

Jed gave Rupert a few moments to recover himself. 'Then what happened?'

Rupert wiped his face. 'Thelma found us together, Grace and me. She went berserk. I thought she would kill us both. She had a knife in her hand and Grace did get hurt. Those blood marks on the stairs. Grace was running down the stairs, out of the house, her cut hand smearing the wall.'

'So Grace got away?'

'Yes, she had her car. She drove off, leaving me to deal with Thelma. Her presence only made Thelma more furious. I don't remember much more of the evening, except that it was one row after another, shouting, yelling. The next morning she had gone, completely disappeared. The wall was still smeared with blood.'

'She took nothing with her?'

'No. She wanted it to look as if I had killed her. But I knew that I hadn't. The police thought otherwise.'

'Why didn't you report her as missing?'

'I thought she had gone off in a huff. Gone to stay with one of her model friends, or with her mother. I was glad she'd gone. I wasn't going to make any moves to get her back. I didn't want her back. Look, I've had enough of this.'

'So it was her mother who reported her missing?'

'Yes, that was my mistake. I should have done it. I was so glad to get a bit of peace and quiet. I had my job, a busy office, something to get on with, no domestic conflict at home. Peace and quiet.'

'Did you see Grace during that time?'

'Not on a personal basis. But during pre-election work, occasionally. We let it cool down. Can I go now?'

'What happened after that?'

'When I was charged with Thelma's murder, of course I was dropped as a candidate. You could hear the clang all the way to Surbiton.'

'And you went to court?'

'The Old Bailey. It was a scary experience. But there was no evidence. It was all circumstantial. Thelma wanted it to look as if I had murdered her, but I hadn't. Even the blood streaks were not conclusive. No body was ever found. The case was dismissed for lack of evidence.'

'Did you take up with Grace again, after the court case?'

'Not straight away. She was upset about our affair and upset about her sister disappearing. But eventually after the trial, we got together again, though quietly at first. It was inevitable. And that was when we decided to make a new start to our life in Cornwall. It was the best decision we ever made.'

'What about the money?'

'The money?' Rupert looked surprised as if the money had nothing to do with it. A sort of curtain came down over his face.

'Yes, the brewery money. The fortune left to both sisters.'

'Grace had her half and part of it went towards buying our farm in Cornwall. She was tired of politics by then, and only too happy to get away. Thelma's half was untouched until seven years had passed, and she could be legally declared dead. Although the money then passed to Grace, she did not touch it. She felt it was tainted. It's still in an account, earning a bit of interest. Not much these days.'

'But still a lot of money?'

'Yes, I suppose so, a great deal of money.'

'Who gets it now?'

'Me, I suppose. I don't know. I suppose Grace left a will. It's not something we talked about. I never thought it would happen.'

Jed closed his laptop and stood up. 'I should watch your back, Rupert Harlow.

Someone is out there, determined to get to that money. Money is always the root of crime. Money and revenge. Be careful. Have you any children?'

'No. Couldn't have any. Grace only had half an ovary.'

'Thank you. I'll be in touch. I'm really sorry about Grace. Really sorry.'

★   ★   ★

Jed found Fancy on the lawn, talking to a group of writers. She felt safer out in the open air, among colourful flower beds and trees and a quilt of mist. Her coffee had gone cold beside her. Her group surrounded her. She was safe with them.

'Have you got a moment, Fancy?' Jed stood over the group, dark and tall and authoritative. There was no arguing with the man.

'Okay, folks, see you all again later. It's time you went away and did some writing. A day without writing is a day wasted.' Fancy turned to Jed. 'What is it?'

'We need to look at Grace's room. I've got the key.'

'Let's go, then.' She didn't ask why.

She followed him into the main house, the mansion that had brought up the Victorian coal-owner's big family. It all seemed vaguely familiar. Fancy remembered the curving staircase and the wide corridors and then the bedroom with the six beds. But Jed was not taking her there. He was taking her to the room opposite.

The bedroom was on the other side of the shared luxury bathroom Fancy would have been sharing with Grace.

'This was Grace's room, or Melody as we knew her. She had a room in the main house because she was the conference hostess.'

It was a pleasant room with large windows on two walls and facing views of the garden and the fields. It had a double bed, made up with quilt and cushions and modern cedar wood furniture and fitted beige carpet. Grace's personal belongings were strewn around. Lots of make-up, a portable radio, lots of files about the guest speakers who needed to be escorted.

'I was supposed to be in the room opposite,' said Fancy. 'But I refused it. I didn't like it.'

'What a difficult speaker you are.'

'Very awkward. A pain.'

Fancy opened the double wardrobe door. The first few hangers contained long, floating dresses and skirts, pale pastel colours, very Melody. But on the last few hangers were plain skirts, navy and brown, with blouses and a couple of plain jackets. A very different style of dressing.

'And look at these,' said Fancy. There were three wig stands on a shelf with different wigs arranged on them; a golden one, a dark-brown short-cut and a wiry grey.

'Three wigs,' said Jed. 'What does all that mean?'

'I've no idea. But Grace was a complicated person. Two kinds of clothes and three wigs. She was playing a part.'

'Amateur dramatics? Perhaps she was in the end of conference show.'

'Maybe. We need to find out.'

By the side of the bed, on the nightstand, were several manuscripts. Grace had brought some of her children's stories to work on. Fancy was full of admiration for anyone who could get a children's story published. It was well known that it was the hardest of all the writing genres. People thought it was easy because of the shortness of the stories and because they were for children but those were exactly the reasons for the difficulty in getting published.

Fancy scanned a couple of title pages and gasped. 'Good heavens,' she said, echoing Jed's amazement. 'Listen to this. Her heroine is a girl called Pinkie. The blurb is that she is a pen-pushing girl detective. Look. Pinkie, the

Pen-pushing Girl Detective.'

'But you write the Pink Pen Detective books, don't you?'

'And Grace was writing something quite a bit similar. I've had eight Pink Pen crime books published. I don't know if these Pinkie stories have been published or are newly written. Maybe Grace thought I had somehow pinched her idea, but quite honestly it looks as if she had . . . well, adopted a form of my idea, but written it for children.' Fancy tried to word it diplomatically.

Jed thumbed through the manuscripts. 'Why bring them to the conference, though, if they have been published? It looks as if she was hoping to meet a publisher here or find an interested agent.'

Fancy turned the pages, reading the odd paragraph.

'Perhaps she was trying to get rid of me, put an end to my books, so that her stories could have a clear run. It's possible. Writers can be incredibly paranoid about their work.' It was difficult to believe; Melody had been such a pleasant woman.

'Paranoid enough to push you under a train? A sheep farmer from Cornwall?'

'Grace had money. She could have paid someone to do it. Given them some other reason. I don't know. But it is possible. It's the first link we've found. The first possible reason for the attacks on me, however odd it may seem.'

'But the attacks have continued long after Grace was drowned.'

'I don't know. But the police could look into Grace's bank accounts. See if she has recently paid someone a large sum of money to get rid of me in London. Maybe some criminal who owed her a favour. Perhaps the attempts were meant to injure me, not kill me, so that I couldn't write any more. Remember, there were three attempts. It's a possibility.'

'Does this discovery make you feel any better about the recent events?' said Jed, still half-reading another manuscript, flipping over the pages.

'In a way, yes. It's a reason. Some writers go to great lengths to get their work published. Grace may have thought it unfair that I got published and she didn't. I don't know. We can't ask her.'

'Or we could ask her husband, Rupert Harlow.'

'He's not likely to know. Writers keep their feelings closely to themselves.'

Jed closed the pages. 'So I've noticed.'

# 17

## Thursday Afternoon

Lunchtime at the conference that last day was buzzing with excitement. All the main courses had finished, wrapped up. There were no more talks or workshops. It was time for fun and relaxation, cementing friendships. Also time for packing, making arrangements and phoning home.

Officer Richmond and Fancy sat at a corner table where Fancy could have her back against a wall. It seemed the safest place. Dorothy had a good view of the whole room from her seat beside Fancy. They let someone else do the serving for a change. Lunch was lasagne and salad and new potatoes.

The discoveries in Grace's bedroom had shaken Fancy. No one had stolen her ideas before, as far as she knew. Pinkie indeed. It was a blatant lift of her themed crime books. But it was not an offence. She could hardly sue. There was no copyright on ideas or titles.

Before lunch they had made a brief visit to the IT room and looked up Grace's website on the internet. It was pretty bare of details, not even a grainy photograph. Nothing about writing or publishing Pinkie books. She had had two children's books published. One called *Jumping Bean* and the other *Hedgehog with Hiccups*. And both published some years back by a reputable house, about the same time that Fancy's first Pink Pen mystery came out. There was nothing more recent.

Fancy's detective books had generated a lot of publicity, daytime TV sofa shows, reviews in the newspapers. Even a couple of magazine articles with touched-up glossy photos. It had been a heady time. Fancy had thought for a while that she had arrived. She soon discovered that she hadn't. She had merely touched fame with the tip of her pen.

Perhaps Grace had read the books and decided she could 'borrow' the idea for a children's series. Then, if she put an end to Fancy's crime series, her own might stand a better chance of being published.

And putting an end to the crime series meant putting an end to the author. It became a possible motive.

Officer Richmond's appetite had not diminished. She put away seconds of everything. Fancy declined the Bakewell tart and orange custard. She fingered a few black grapes. Drank some black coffee. Her mood was black. She didn't often feel so down.

Depression: the writer's curse after writer's block.

'It's their annual general meeting, right after lunch,' said Fancy with little enthusiasm. 'It's traditional.'

'Do you have to go?'

'Not really. But my friends on the shelf said that support for the AGM by visiting lecturers always goes down well.'

'Goes down well with whom? Then what happens?'

Fancy shrugged shoulders. 'Collecting books from the book room, paying any bills for the phone, packing and then dressing up for the dregs party on the lawn. In the evening there's entertainment, whatever they've been rehearsing all week. No idea what it will be. Probably a revue. I know someone who has brought bagpipes.'

'What's the dregs party?'

'Any drink that's left over from the private parties during the week is put out on the lawn. Or you take along anything that you have in your room and don't want to cart home. A horrible mixture of drinks, I expect. Not good for the stomach. I think that is what they said.'

Fancy had little enthusiasm for this party either. She had been or not been to enough parties this week. It was easy to lose count, especially having lost slices of time. She wanted to go home to her own place, put on some comfortable clothes and lock the door on the world.

She would become a recluse, never go out, order food online, communicate by email. She need never see anyone again. Get a cat. It sounded good.

This would suit her. She would become mysterious and unavailable like Miss Haversham. Except that she would change her clothes, wash and eat healthily. Occasionally dust and vacuum the debris.

The AGM passed in a sort of haze. Fancy sat with her new friends, only half-listening. She was already back in her current book, longing to get her fingers on the keyboard, phrases coming into mind.

Officer Richmond also had a glazed expression. She wasn't listening to what was going on. Why were they were arguing about the voting rights of new delegates, the quality of the soup in the dining room, or the prospect of higher prices in the future as forecast by the treasurer in his report? Maybe she had to write a report.

Fancy didn't vote; she wasn't a member. The procedure was all properly carried out, as far as she could see. No one could complain. But there were murmurs and complaints about whether it should be a cross or a tick. Were all AGMs so tedious? She had attended very few.

'I'm going to pack,' said Fancy, as they spilled out onto the lawn for tea. 'Then change for the party. What are you going to do?'

'I ought to report back. They need to hear from me regularly.'

'I'll be fine. You do what you have to do and I'll see you later. Nothing can happen now. It's time to go home.'

It was easier to pack going home. Once the clothes rail was empty, the drawers empty, bathroom cleared of all but essentials, there was nothing else. She left her travelling clothes out and the minimum of cosmetics for the morning. She was looking forward to going home.

But where was Jed? He had disappeared as usual. She was getting used to his double existence. She knew he wasn't telling her everything. Perhaps he thought she would be frightened or dismayed.

She knew she must get used to not having Jed around. He was not permanent. He was part of the writers' conference and an element of the disturbing events. Once she got back to London, he would be gone from her life.

She did not believe in love at first sight. She believed that love grew, that a long friendship sometimes tipped over into passionate love. And could be perfect.

The dregs party. Not the most inspiring name to give a party. It gave her mouth the taste of stale wine and unwashed glasses. She barely wanted to go but she knew it would be expected of her. To be seen to be mingling with other, less successful writers, still giving them hope and inspiration.

She put on the same black trousers and her favourite seeded white pearl top. Low slip-on shoes, no more heels. Especially on the lawn. A rope of pearls. A white flower pinned in her hair. Was that party-ish enough? She took a bottle of good red bought from the bar, not left over from anything.

The lawn was crowded. Many of the women had dressed up, black, sequins, gaudy tops, see-through chiffon, long dresses, dangling earrings. A couple of men were in dinner jackets, very smart. Others had ignored the dressing up, still wore the day's grimy T-shirts and crushed fleeces, stained trainers.

Officer Richmond was close, faintly flushed from her labours over a laptop. 'Do you want a drink?'

'Try to get me a drink from the bottle of

wine that I brought. Nothing that is already opened and days old. I've a long drive tomorrow. I don't want to be scurrying to the nearest loo every five minutes.'

'Trust me. I'll find you something decent.'

'Thank you.'

Fancy turned to a woman who was talking to her. She had been on Fancy's course, writing historical crime. An interesting idea because historical crime is about dark deeds that have already been committed. No need to invent or plot anything. Fancy was genuinely interested, especially in the research.

'One has to juggle true facts with the fictional writing,' the writer said, twirling a glass of Coke so that it fizzed over her fingers. 'It's horrendously difficult at times. Especially these days when readers can check many facts on the internet.'

'I admire the amount of research that must go into writing historical crime,' said Fancy. 'I don't think I have the stamina.'

Someone gave her a drink. She thought it was Dorothy. It seemed like Dorothy was at her side, but she did not actually look. She was giving her full attention to the historical writer. A nod of thanks. People were talking round her, laughing, drinking, a milling crowd of people having a good time.

One moment she was looking at the sturdy

Victorian mansion, the red brick walls, the sloping gables, tall chimneys and the expanse of manicured lawns with their colourful beds of flowers in careful shapes. She could smell cut grass from the gardeners' labours that afternoon and a hint of rain. She could smell crisps, salt and vinegar, chilli being handed round. In the distance was a haze of Derbyshire fields and woods, dry stone walls meandering like a child's drawing.

She had become separated from the main partying throng. But she did not know how it happened, turning and talking to someone different, changing the grouping.

Then there was a sharp pain. Somewhere on the back of her head. The sky became washed in complete blackness, only lines of dark branches changing the pattern. She could only register the darkness — if she could see anything at all. She did not remember the glass slipping out of her hand. The glass of a good red.

Even the party voices had disappeared. There was a buzzing in her ears as if a wasp was caught in her hair.

'Get her in the car,' someone said.

# 18

Evening

She first became aware of the confined space. Barely room to move, and if she could move, knees bent, she knocked into some hard surface. She discovered that her wrists were bound together with figure-of-eight duct tape, and her ankles. This bent over conformation gave her a slight degree of movement, but was more secure than simple round-and-round binding.

There was a strip of duct tape across her mouth. No point in making a noise. There was nothing across her eyes, thank goodness. She stared into the darkness, trying to control her fear. No one knew where she was. Jed didn't know. Dorothy would think she was cruising the party.

There was a lot of movement and bumping. From the jolting and the smell of fuel and rust, she guessed she was in the boot of a car being driven somewhere. She was doubled up, her head hard against the outside metal.

It was definitely the boot of a car and she

recognized that they were driving over the speed bumps at the entrance to the centre. The friction and hardness of the interior jolted her spine with a series of painful shocks.

It was not Jed's car, for sure. Which was a relief. Jed's two-seater did not have a proper boot, only a space for a briefcase and a raincoat. Maybe room for a couple of bulky files. Strange, how she was always suspecting Jed. It was irrational and unfair.

Fancy kicked hard at the lid of the boot with her heels but the noise just echoed back to her. Hopeless. She was wasting precious energy. She would need every ounce of it if she was to survive this kidnapping. She thought of Jack Reacher. He always conserved his energy, measured his breathing. Not easy to do when you were terrified.

That's what it was. She had been kidnapped. One minute she had been at the dregs party, and the next, she was trussed up like a dummy and folded into the boot of a car.

Her head hurt. It had been a glancing blow, only enough to knock her out for a few moments. A faint glimmer of light lined the edge of the boot lid. It was badly fitting. An old-model car. New cars had power mechanism for closing the lid.

She was being shaken from side to side. She would be black and blue by tomorrow. If there was a tomorrow. This might be the last day of her life.

Fancy felt quite calm about it. The death day came to everyone at some time. Some early, some late. Her life had been productive and happy, apart from an obvious lack of permanent success in the romance department. Something she regretted but it had been out of her control. She had a row of books on library shelves. She would be remembered as long as they stayed there. At some point they would be taken off, pages dog-eared, and sold off at car boot sales for fifty pence each.

Copies would remain in the British Library and at the Bodleian Library in Oxford, underground and gathering dust, unread.

She had lost track of where they were driving after the first few turns. She had never been any good at navigating, even in the passenger seat with a map. They turned onto a smoother surface, a main road, leading somewhere, up and down dales. It would be sensible to try to rest, to restore energy. That's what the Pink Pen Detective would have done.

But first she searched around the interior to see if there was anything that could be of use to her. No knife or handy screwdriver. But she did find some loose screws and a length of wire which she managed to coil and manoeuvre into her trouser pocket. Then she found a crumpled-up plastic supermarket bag, which she pushed around with her nose until it was pressed under her cheek and gave a slight degree of relief from the hardness of the side panel.

She felt a crunching over a driveway, a turn and several parking manoeuvres. Then the engine was switched off and the silence folded down like a blanket. She strained to hear voices but whoever was in the car, one or two people perhaps, neither were speaking.

The boot lid was opened and a rush of air came with the smell of moorland. She was somewhere high, feeling the wind. Hands clamped over her eyes and for a second she thought they were going to blindfold her. But it was something softer. Then she realized that it was her own scarf, twisted and tied. She recognized the *Dior Tender Poison* perfume.

She was dragged out of the car and dumped onto the ground. There were two people. She heard two sets of footsteps, one lighter than the other, with shorter steps. A man and a woman. She decided not to struggle or try to scream. Not much point.

Better to let them think that she was still unconscious. But to stay alert.

The crunched-up plastic bag was in her hand, half-hidden. Might be useful. She might go shopping.

She was being dragged over a rough surface. Her best black jeans would be ruined. Gravel tore at her cheek, rough and smarting. She heard a door being unbolted, heavy rusted bolts drawn back and hinges creaking open. Where were they putting her? In a barn? A shed? Was it some derelict old building, out in the wilds, where she would rot until the foxes found her?

Suddenly the darkness was even darker and an icy blast of cold air hit her skin through her thin clothes. It was like mid-winter. This was some weird barn.

She heard an exchange of low muttering. They were trying to find something on the walls.

'Dammit,' she heard. 'It must be somewhere.'

She did not recognize the voice. There was a slurred edge to the words. As if he did not have much time. He had to be somewhere else quick. Was he doing this as a favour, or being paid?

She heard a switch and saw a cross beam of light against an archway. Her scarf was not that thick. She glimpsed a low, arched roof, glistening stone walls. It was not a barn.

They were dragging her across a floor, then there was a bump, down a hard step. Then another bump, down another step. The steps were different heights, different widths. Fancy tried to relax, to minimize the agonizing pain, the bruising to her body as she fell awkwardly, half-rolling, half-sliding.

It was a flight of steps, with a series of little lights on the walls, like islands. She could see the pinpoints of light through the scarf. But they had blown in several places, leaving ragged areas of gloom. Her captors were holding onto a hand rail, pulling her down after them. Even they were gasping for breath.

Fancy tried counting the steps, but lost count after fifty or sixty. The air was getting colder and colder. She would die of pneumonia. She completely lost count. It might be in the hundreds.

They were way, way below ground level by now. Fancy decided that they were in one of the disused mines that had once thrived in Derbyshire. It had been a great mining industry, especially the Blue John mines, which were a tourist attraction even today, and still mining the precious Blue John mineral to sell, fashioned into jewellery, in their craft shops.

But this was no Blue John mine. This was a derelict lead mine. Probably from the Victorian era. Fancy's heart fell. No hope of rescue. No one would ever find her. It had probably been shut up for years. She may as well think of the women of old who worked down here for a pittance, clearing the rubble, or the children who stood with candles in the alcoves for sixpence a week and worked the bellows.

She was no different to them. Flesh and blood. Slave labour.

There was a series of grunts when she realized that they had reached the end of the long flight of steps. They were out of breath, drawing in deep gulps. She could hear a strange, slapping noise. The air felt fresher. No bad gas.

Fancy then realized that the slapping noise was water. That was how they transported the lead ore in those days. It was heavy stuff. They pulled it along in boats before heaving the ore up those stone steps.

They dumped her onto some sort of wooden platform, towards the edge of which they were pulling a boat. She was bundled into the shallow wooden vessel. They cast off and pushed away from the platform.

It was a kind of bliss. The smooth, painless gliding over the water. It was almost calm, although Fancy was still bound and still blindfolded. She tried to relax into the pain of her aching joints. There were definitely two other people in the boat, guiding it along with their arms and their legs against the mine walls, grunting with the effort, much as it had been guided long ago by the workers.

It was like being in a gondola but without canals and Venetian palaces. No singing, no sunshine, no spaghetti.

They reached some other place and hauled her onto another hard flat expanse. Stone this time. She was left, curled into a foetal position, her head on the stone. She breathed hard air, felt a high roof above, a few vague lights moving. It must be a huge cavern in total blackness.

Then she heard the two people retreat. They were getting back into the boat. Still no talking. They were leaving her. This was her last place of rest. Silence came down into the air. And more blackness. They had taken their torches, turned off any lights.

It was the loneliest moment. She was completely alone, in darkness, hundreds of feet below the surface of the earth. And no one knew she was there. Except those two. She trembled with cold and fear.

Fancy was not one to give up easily. She might be battered and bruised but her brain was still working. Goodness gracious, great balls of fire, the Pink Pen Detective had been in worse situations. And somehow she had got out of them.

She crawled about on the platform on which they had left her. It had edges, which seemingly dropped away to fathomless bottoms. It was important to keep moving. There was some sort of path leading away from the platform along which she crawled on her elbows, hunching up her knees, her feet dragging, sloughing into the floor.

At a curve, she managed to haul herself up, almost sitting upright. Everything hurt. She was leaning against rock. She found a sharp bit that was level with her wrists and began to saw against the duct tape. Up and down, the jagged rock catching her skin. She felt a lessening of the tension and kept sawing. Then the rock finally bit through and her wrists were free. The relief was immense. She rubbed back the circulation.

She tried to renew circulation in her back and legs. She could not find the end of the tape on her ankles, feeling around. She sharpened one of the screws from the car boot on the rock face and then started cutting through the duct tape that bound her feet. It took longer but eventually worked. She was free, took off the scarf over her eyes. But she was still in total darkness, hundreds of feet down a disused lead mine.

Deep breaths. Sit and think. This is not the end, she told herself.

She felt round the walls till she found an alcove. There was an old stump of candle, barely an inch, left by some child. And a vesper. One strike left. She struck it carefully on the rock. It flared in the night, like an angel flame. She moved it carefully towards the candle wick, praying that it would not go out, but it took hold and in a moment, the pathway was lit with holy light.

'Thank goodness,' said Fancy. 'Bless you, some poor, hungry child.'

The meagre light cast strange shadows. She was in a tunnel, low ceiling, hewn walls, rough and hacked at by miners from long ago. She could only move along it, hoping there was some other way out. She found another alcove and another candle stump. She put the stump in her plastic bag and licked at the condensation on the walls. She knew the bag would come in useful.

Or she could retrace her steps. Except that they would have taken the boat back to the steps they'd brought her down and there would be no way out for her, except to swim in the underground canal and climb those hundreds of steps in the dark.

More stumps, which Fancy collected, saved, relit, each time her current candle flickered and threatened to extinguish.

It was a juggling act. Candle and flame. Her bad hands again, nearly burning. She found a loose lump of rock and set the next candle on it, pushing it firmly into the last warm stump. She didn't want another accident.

The path was leading upwards; she could feel the incline. But the archway was getting lower and smaller. Soon she would be back on her knees. No more children in alcoves. It was petering out. The miners had lost the seam, stopped working it.

She was already very weak. The blow on the head had not helped. No Jack Reacher-sized skull to ward off the blow. They had knocked her out. They meant to kill her this time. Eventually. She was struggling. The tunnel was getting smaller.

Soon she would be totally unable to move forward.

She was down on her knees, crawling. Rough-hewn rock scraped against her shoulders, bumped her head. This couldn't be the way out. Exit for a mouse, perhaps. Nor could she feel any fresh air. It was just a tunnel leading deeper and deeper into the rock.

It grew narrower, closing down on her. She could not move an inch further forward. She craned for a glimpse of light ahead but there was nothing. If there was a way out then she couldn't see it, nor could she reach it. There had either been a rock fall or the tunnel simply petered out.

She turned her head and hit her face against a jagged jut in the rock face. She felt a tell-tale wetness dropping from her nose. Now she was bleeding. On her favourite white beaded top.

# 19

## Later on Thursday Evening

The nosebleed continued for several agonizing minutes. She had no tissue to stench the flow. She could only pinch her nostrils and hope that it worked. Blood trickled down her top, inside her bra. No time to grieve about best top, best Wonderbra.

In a vampire novel, she would have cupped her hands and drunk her own blood. No such extreme measure now.

She dared not move until the bleeding had slowed, had started to congeal, to form a scab over the broken membrane. There was no other sound, only the slow drip of her own blood and her breathing. The quietness was eerie. She waited till it had slowed and she felt safe to move.

She began to slowly shuffle backwards along the way she had come. No room to turn round. It was slow and laborious, painful. Her jeans were ripped at the knees by now and her skin scraped.

She had no sense of time, no clock in her head; beyond tears. Surely someone would have missed her at the dregs party by now? Officer Dorothy Richmond, perhaps, with a second glass of good red wine? Or Jed, when he returned from his mysterious errand. He would have appeared by now, to enjoy the last night's festivities — the entertainment, revue, pantomime, or whatever it was they had been rehearsing in secret for days. Surely he would want to take her for a last drink in the bar, if their friendship meant anything to him? Surely he would be looking for her?

Fancy had no idea. He was an enigma. A man she hardly knew.

The brain was getting confused. Had she been conked on the head? Not enough to knock her out for good, but long enough to remove her from the dregs party and bundle her into the boot of a car. Dorothy had brought her the drink. Or had it actually been Dorothy? Fancy couldn't remember now. She had not looked round. Only a voice and a hand offering her a glass. It could have been anyone.

She'd give anything for a glass of rock-bottom, the pits, any leftover, only-good-for-gravy wine, right now. She was so thirsty. Her lips felt cracked. Rainwater vintage would be the tops. A Scottish burn, a tumbling waterfall.

She moulded half-warm stumps of old

candle into usable lumps, with torn threads from her scarf as wicks. Women of old used to make their own candles. Now she had a constant flickering light. It was cheering, less intimidating. She was in a mining tunnel with long dark shadows. She could see axe marks on the walls. Men had worked here, hacking out the mineral. Somehow their spirits were around her, cheering her on.

The tunnel grew larger, wider. Now she could sit thankfully, rest with her back against a rough wall. Now she could stand, walk unsteadily, one hand on the wall to guide her. Walking took the edge off her fear.

She was back on a flat platform of rock. It was a vast cavern, with soaring walls of darkness in all directions, glistening with running water. She dared not look down. There was no need to look down. Again, she licked the walls.

The canal ended here, the murky water blocked by a man-made dam. There was no boat because her captors, whoever they were, had taken the boat back to the entrance. A chill rose from the dark water.

If she called out there might be an echo. But they might hear her and return.

Fancy took the crumpled wire out of her pocket, straightened it out and tied a small rock to the end. She would use it to test the depth of the water. She did not fancy a swim in those cold, dark depths, especially as she would lose the light from her life-saving candle stumps. She needed light.

It was not more than three feet deep. Her wrist went into the water, holding the wire. It did not need to be any deeper to transport the lead back to the exit of the mine in the shallow boat. Three feet was up to her thighs. But what would be on the floor of the canal — centuries of sludge, debris, the bones of long-dead children?

She was only wearing little slip-on, ballet-style shoes. She bound one foot up with the same wire to make sure the shoe stayed on and gave her more grip. She used her stylish scarf to bind the other shoe. It would have to do, though it would soon become soaked and slide off. Goodbye, scarf. She added a Roman-type twist round her ankle in the hope that it would stay on longer.

Then she stepped cautiously into the water, levering herself down over the side, holding the candle stump aloft. She gasped aloud. It was freezing, dark and ominous. She tried not to think about what she was treading on. It was slippery with moving stones. The water almost came up to her waist, shocking her with its intense cold. She kept her free hand on the left-side wall, as the boat people had, when using their arms and feet to propel the boat along.

Fancy tried to remember how long she had been in the boat but her memory was playing tricks. Had it been five minutes? Ten minutes? A real detective should have been keeping track of the journey. Jack Reacher would have instant recall.

She waded carefully along the canal, not hurrying. A fall would be disastrous.

She had to find that entrance, those hundreds of uneven steps leading to the surface and air. The candlelight wavered with every step she took, casting shadows on the wall.

She felt a change of direction, the canal she was in began veering to the left. Ahead in the murky darkness, she glimpsed another canal leading off to the right, to another mine seam. Which one? Which one had they come along? How could she possibly tell which canal led to the steps?

She decided to keep to where she was, feeling the wall along her left side. If she was wrong, she would have to come back. No way could she find her way over towards that right canal without something to hold onto midstream.

It felt right, this direction. Something told her. There were more of the alcoves in the rock face where children stood with candles for sixpence a week. The canal washed against her body, centuries-old water, surges of wet and cold. It had never been renewed. Perhaps some rain had washed down, but essentially it was the same water that had been transporting lead since the Victorian times.

Fancy kept going. Her spirit was determined to keep alive. She was not going to die yet. She had books to write, characters to bring alive, plots to evolve and solve. Maybe even a brood of children to conceive. It was not impossible. There was still time. She never knew who she might meet one day around a corner, across a crowded room. If only she could see someone, waiting for her.

She could hardly believe it when she bumped into the end of a moored boat. It looked like the same one she'd travelled in. She had reached the end of the canal. She had made it. She had walked the water. She hung onto the end of the boat, gasping for breath, letting out a long sob of relief, releasing the emotion.

Her candle was flickering in its last moments of life. She crushed the hot wax into her hand, thanking the God of Candles for giving her light this far. She would have to do without light now. There were steps to climb. She could do it. The Pink Pen

Detective could do it.

The pinpricks of light along the wall of the long rise of steps were still on. They had forgotten to switch them off in their hurry to leave. Perhaps they, whoever they were, had to get back to the dregs party before they were missed.

She hauled herself up out of the canal water, muck and dirt draining off her, frozen legs refusing to move. She had to move them by hand, like an old lady with severe arthritis. The pinprick lights beckoned her.

Fancy sat at the bottom of the steps, breathing hard, regaining a moment of strength. She was exhausted, black and blue, her clothes torn and bloodied. Everywhere hurt. But she refused to give up and die. She was going to get out.

She made herself crawl towards the steps and start climbing. It was a hundred or more steps, wasn't it? She couldn't remember. Each step was painful, dragged out, excruciating. She developed a pattern. She crawled on her hands and knees up five steps, and then she allowed herself to stop and rest.

Breathing deeply, she regularly allowed her muscles to relax and regain some normal strength, before forcing them again into this relentless climb. How many times five was it going to be? Mental arithmetic had never been a strong point.

'More, more,' she urged herself. 'Five, four, three, two, one. Well done, girl! Now we can rest. Rest, rest, rest . . . breathe deeply.'

There was no way of knowing how long it took Fancy to drag herself up to the top of the lead mine. Hours had diminished. Time was no longer relevant. Everything was divided into slots of five.

When she reached the top, finally feeling that there were no more steps ahead, she collapsed on the floor, spread eagled, her breath coming in short gasps. Every aching muscle protesting. Every painful joint crying for rest and sleep. Her brain acknowledging that somehow she had survived this hurdle, but knowing there were more ahead. She still had to get out, get away.

She did not know how long she lay on the floor of the lead mine office. It could have been hours, it could have been minutes. Eventually, she made herself grasp at something solid, a desk or a chair, and haul herself upright. She could see light through a small window, pale moonlight in a black sky, blinking stars.

There was nothing inside the office, anywhere. No ancient bottle of water. No forgotten ale or cider. Nothing to drink. No torch, no matches. It had been cleared out with relentless efficiency.

There was no trouble opening the door from the inside. The rush of night air was like nectar. Its sweetness flowed over her. Moorland, gorse, peat, heather. But outside the door was a bowl for thirsty dogs, full of rainwater.

Fancy drank it as eagerly as if she was a prize winner at Crufts.

★ ★ ★

Fancy felt sure she was on Mam Tor in the High Peak. It was a famous peak in the district, with a cairn of stones on the top. She understood why it was sometimes called the Shivering Mountain because she could hear the wind moving the shale on the slopes. Yes, it must be Mam Tor; she knew it had disused lead mines.

The wind was howling like a banshee. She couldn't see the vast, panoramic view but she could feel the space. After the terrors of the mine tunnel and the canal, the fresh air felt like freedom.

She remembered doing some research on the Tor for a book, years ago. All she could remember was that it was about 1,600 feet high and was the second oldest Iron Age fortress remains in England. A huge earthenware ditch surrounded it somewhere. She hoped she wouldn't fall down it in the dark. No idea of the time.

Carefully she checked that there was no parked car nearby, watching or waiting. There was no one there. They had gone.

The yard outside the mine office was the usual chaos of abandoned equipment and unwanted stuff. She needed a walking stick to help her down the path. Her shoes were sodden lumps of detritus but she dared not abandon them in favour of bare feet. She felt around until she found a gnarled piece of wood, broken from a tree, the right height and the right dimension. She tore off the unwanted branches till she had a reasonable stick and a protruding knob made a convenient handhold.

Before leaving the abandoned mine office she hunted round in case there was anything useful. She found a couple more plastic bags, a wodge of what looked like old receipts and a roll of Sellotape. She put her finds in the original plastic bag, which was wet now, and hung it from her jeans belt. She needed her hands free.

Now she had to walk to her freedom.

The path down from Mam Tor was a well-worn route for Peak walkers. There was starlight and occasionally the cloud drifted away from the moon's face so Fancy could see the path. It ran along a ridge with a steep fall either side, but she kept her eyes firmly on the path and nowhere else. No looking down.

'My trusty stick,' she said, planting it down with each step. It was a third leg. It took her weight, it upheld her tired body. She had taken to talking to herself.

She was no longer a writer, a published author. It all meant nothing. A million words scattered randomly across paper. Books on shelves were meaningless. Words on tapes echoed in the air. She was a woman fighting for survival, determined to beat whoever had left her down that mine to die.

At least she was not scrambling down the shifting side of the Shivering Mountain; she had a recognized walkers' path to follow. It would lead somewhere eventually. But there was a chill wind and her clothes were soaked. Soon she was also shivering.

Her walking took on a similar pattern as climbing the steps up from the mine: walk for twenty paces, then stop and lean on the stick for several deep breaths. Then start again, another twenty paces. Rest, pace. Rest, pace. Keep the circulation going.

She had several gates to go through and she took advantage of them to lean and stretch her aching back. Her spine was on fire with pain. The last gate led her into a car park. No cars. But the terrain was flat, tarmac, bliss for her torn feet. The sodden shoes had fallen off by degrees.

She sat down, back against a post, legs outstretched and gazed up at the stars in the dark night. It was so beautiful. She wondered if they were looking down at her, pitying her plight, wondering what on earth (her earth) this mortal was up to.

She brushed dried and caked debris off her feet, tried to massage some life back into them. Where was that expensive pedicure now, the soak in warm suds, the Russian Red varnish, the nourishing foot cream?

Iron Age men and women fashioned footwear from skins and fur. Catching and skinning a rabbit was not on Fancy's current agenda, though she thought she had seen dozens of tiny creatures hopping away from the path.

She divided the pile of receipts equally, smoothing out the paper. She put one pile into a plastic bag, placed her foot on top of the paper, then wrapped the bag round and round her foot, tying the handle ends on top.

As always, it was a struggle to find where the Sellotape roll began. It was a ploy on the part of the manufacturer so that you would throw the roll away in frustration. Organized people folded over the end. Fancy always marked it with a paperclip.

But she had patience and perseverance. She found the end eventually and peeled off several strips. The stickiness was not good — too ancient — but she wound it round and round her foot, pressing it down, hoping some of it would stick.

Then she did the same for the other foot, wedge of paper, plastic bag and Sellotape. She had shoes.

'Not exactly Jimmy Choo,' she said to her feet. 'But he would be proud of me.'

Her toes began to thaw inside the plastic bags. She got up and searched round the car park. She found another abandoned plastic bag, shook out the food container debris and wrapped her frozen hand in the bag. Not a perfect glove, but warm enough. She began changing hands with the plastic bag, to get warmth back into both of them. Plastic bags had a hundred uses. She would write a book on a hundred and one uses for plastic bags.

There was nothing else in the car park. No abandoned picnic basket with the remains of a game pie and an opened bottle of champagne. Only crumpled crisp packets and sweet wrappers. She found some broken crisps left in a bag and ate them, licked out the salt granules. The salt was euphoric.

It took determination to start walking again. She could have easily curled up in the car park and waited for dawn, for the first visitor to arrive with a car. That was if she survived the plunging temperature of the night, frozen and wet as she was.

It was straightforward to find the gate out of the car park and the walkers' path that led down to some small dale village. There was even a sign which kindly said *Footpath*. The narrow, gravel-shod path had to lead downwards.

Somewhere in the vast distance below she could see tiny, twinkling lights, mere blinks in the blanket of darkness. They spelled civilization, houses, roads, street lighting, water and pints and pints of hot coffee.

# 20

## Castleton

'Twenty paces, now rest for twenty.'

Fancy continued the same pattern, battling against a high wind that flattened her wet clothes. The Japanese platform shoes needed some getting used to. It was like walking on stilts but they protected her torn feet to some extent. The trusty stick took on magical properties. Harry Potter would have been proud of her.

She began to feel the shapes of other hillsides closing in and woodland looming, dry stone walls. It was not the desolate Mam Tor any more. She had left behind the hill fortress and was descending into husbandry, the farms and peasants. She wondered how many other wanderers had sought sanctuary in the village, stumbled into some rural cottage, exhausted and thirsty.

Fancy could feel the steep slope as she walked. She needed her trusty stick or she would have fallen. Clouds scudded across the flawed moon. The going down was endless, relentless, jolting. She lost all sense of time.

How many hours? Two, three, four? The path began to flatten out, become wider, meander, not straight.

She was not aware that she had reached the end of the path, or had gone through the signed opening, or felt the tarmac under her feet. She had been walking in a daze, on autopilot. There were lights ahead but she hardly saw them.

For a moment, she staggered about, hardly registering that it was no longer a path but a road. This was a flat surface. She could hardly believe it.

There was a bus stop. But she was not going to wait for a bus. No buses at this time of night.

The road into the village was up a slight incline, but she could manage that, though it was an effort. The village was almost dark, house lights were out, people had gone to bed. Hardly anyone was still awake. It must be very late.

But Fancy caught sight of some lights. It was a pub. Seventeenth century by the looks of it, very old timbers. She couldn't see the name. Cheese or something on the swinging sign but she could hardly read it. She moved herself towards the pub, praying that the lights would not go out before she got there.

She pushed open the door with the last of

her strength. The warmth hit her like an oven. It was like an unexpected blanket that enveloped her frozen body. She staggered, almost fell into the foyer. It was a cosy barroom, a fire dying down, heavy beams encompassing the heat. No jukeboxes, no gaming tables, no drinkers. They were about to close. If they weren't closed already.

She collapsed onto the floor, unable to move, breathing in the heat, feeling the smoothness of the timbered floor. She heard footsteps hurrying over the wood-boarded floor but could not open her eyes.

'Good heavens. Fred. Fred. Come here. Look at this poor woman.'

'Lord above. Is she dead?'

'No, she's breathing. But she's covered in blood and muck.'

'Don't move her, but get a rug or something. Cover her up. I'll ring for an ambulance. She's been in some sort of accident.'

Fancy heard the voices above her. They sounded kind, concerned. She felt the blanket being thrown over her and tucked in.

'Look at her poor feet. She must have walked miles.'

'See if she'd like a drink.'

'Brandy?'

'No, just plain water at first. Then perhaps some tea.'

The woman was peering over her. Fancy opened her eyes, saw nothing but dazzling light. 'Would you like a drink?'

Fancy nodded.

Then water arrived but Fancy could hardly drink it. Half of it went down her front. Still, it was something. Fresh water. She nodded her thanks. She was thankful just to be lying somewhere in the warm where no one was trying to kill her.

The woman came back with a cup of tea. 'Not too hot,' she said. 'And a bendy straw. I saw how difficult it was for you to drink. Let me prop you up. I don't think your back is injured. Say if it hurts too much to move, though. Now, is that better?'

Fancy sipped the warm, sweet tea. It was nectar. She could feel the strong support of the woman holding her up. The pub lady was a buxom woman with plump arms, a halo of grey curls. The liquid slid down Fancy's throat. It was sweet and invigorating. The best cup of tea in her entire life.

'Wonderful,' said Fancy, sucking up the last drop. 'Tea.'

'Are you feeling better?'

'A little, thank you.'

'Can you tell us what happened?'

Fancy thought about it. It was a long and complicated story. 'Someone tried to kill me, that's all you need to know. But please could you phone Jed Edwards, Derby CID. DSI Jed Edwards. Make sure you get through to him personally or ask for his mobile number. Can you do that for me? It's important.'

The woman scrambled to her feet. 'I'll do that straight away. My husband has phoned for an ambulance, but they'll take ages getting here. I think they have to come from Sheffield. Quite a way. Don't worry. We'll look after you.'

Fancy sank back, not caring too much any more.

By the time the ambulance arrived, Fancy was sitting in an armchair by the dying fire, still wrapped in a blanket. Her torn feet were in a bowl of warm salty water, being carefully washed by the landlady's wife, Betty.

'This young lady came into the bar in a really bad way,' said Betty as two yellow-coated paramedics arrived with their green bags. 'Lying on the floor, she was. She was covered in blood and could hardly move. Cold as stone.'

'So, miss? Can you tell me your name?'

'Francine Jones.'

'Where does it hurt?'

'Everywhere.'

'Can you move your fingers, toes . . . follow my finger?'

Fancy complied with the various tests. She knew nothing was broken. She could hardly have walked down from Mam Tor with a broken leg.

'How did this happen?'

'An accident.'

'Car accident? Was anyone else involved?'

He was looking at the blood on her front, the soaked and caked condition of her trousers, the torn feet in the bowl of water.

'I think you ought to come into Derby Hospital for a complete examination and get fixed up.'

'I'd like to wait for DSI Edwards from Derby CID first. He's on his way,' said Fancy, without much conviction. She was not sure if he was on his way.

'That's not sensible. Your feet need treatment. DSI Edwards can take a statement from you in hospital.'

Fancy didn't like the way he said that. She looked closely at his face. She didn't like the expression she saw. The woman medic had gone out to the ambulance to fetch a stretcher or a wheelchair, her face hidden. Fancy panicked. She was not going anywhere with these two strangers. They might strap her to the stretcher, wheel her away to anywhere, dump her in the River Derwent.

'No, I'm waiting for DSI Edwards,' said

Fancy firmly. 'I'm not moving. Some painkillers would help.'

'Are you sure that's wise?' said Betty, hiding a yawn. She had been up all day, working all evening in the pub. It was late. And she still had to lock up. 'They'll look after you in hospital.'

'I'm sure they will,' said Fancy, hugging the blanket closer. 'If I ever get there. Please believe me, there is more to this than me being a lost walker.'

'It wouldn't hurt to wait until the police arrive,' said Betty to her husband. 'This young lady seems to know what she's talking about. And that long, jolting ambulance ride wouldn't do her any good.'

'Are you refusing treatment?' the paramedic asked. He got out a pad of forms and started filling it in: time, date, location, condition of patient. 'You'll have to sign here.' Fancy scrawled *Jones*.

'Why don't you wait as well until the police arrive?' said Betty. 'It can't be long now. I'll make us all a nice cup of tea and some corned beef sandwiches.'

'Very kind,' said the medic, 'but we've got another call.' He began repacking his bag. The woman had already gone, reloading the stretcher.

The ambulance started up and drove off,

slowly at first, and then with more speed. It seemed to go faster than it came. Perhaps it did have another more urgent call.

Fancy was glad to hear them go. It might be irrational but she did not trust anyone.

'You're very kind,' said Fancy. 'And I know I'm putting you to a lot of trouble, when I can see you are both dead tired. Why don't you leave me here, in front of the fire? I'll be perfectly all right. I'm so comfortable and cosy. Just make sure that you lock up everywhere, please.'

'We always do. With this stock of alcohol around.'

'What about this detective you're expecting?'

'Leave some lights on. He'll knock. I'll open the door to him. I can still walk a few steps.'

'You should really get into some dry clothes and have a good night's sleep,' Betty said, bustling about. 'We've got a spare room upstairs. It's all clean and ready. Only take a moment to heat the bed. There's an electric blanket.'

'Oh, that would be lovely,' said Fancy, longing to lay down and sleep, to stretch out in warm clean sheets. She was sure they would smell of lavender. It would be bliss. 'But I've got to see the inspector first.'

'Are you sure you wouldn't like a sandwich?'

'No, thank you.'

'I'll leave you my mobile phone,' said Betty, pulling up a small table. She put her phone on it, with a bottle of orange juice and nuts and crisps from the bar. 'Help yourself.' She took away the bowl of bloodied water, returned with a towel to dry Fancy's feet. She left them wrapped in the towel.

'There, that's better.' She seemed reluctant to leave Fancy. 'This seems all wrong, leaving you here, after whatever you must have been through.'

'Please, you are both so tired. You can't stay up any longer. Your husband's almost asleep on his feet.'

'Running a pub is hard work,' said Betty.

'Her idea,' said Fred. 'It was Betty's idea.'

'Get some sleep, please. I shall be all right.'

Betty hovered in the doorway to the back kitchen. Fancy smiled at her. The cosy pub was a million miles away from the mine tunnel and the dark, dank canal. It could be another heaven. Nothing could happen to her here. She was safe and she knew it.

Betty and Fred would lock up. They were only upstairs. No one could get in. A pub would have a state of the art alarm system.

* * *

At that moment, the decision was made for them. There was a knock on the door; a tall figure stood outside. The porch light caught his dark and silvery hair. Fancy could not turn in the armchair, but she knew it was him.

'That's him,' she said. 'DSI Jed Edwards. Ask him to show you his warrant card.'

'Thank goodness,' said Betty, hurrying to the door. 'Is that you, Inspector Edwards? Warrant card, please.'

He was already holding his warrant card face against the glass pane. 'DSI Edwards. You phoned me. I came as fast as I could. Is Miss Jones all right?'

Betty unlocked the door, drawing back heavy bolts. They had not put on the alarm system yet. Jed stepped into the bar, his coat collar fastened, returning his warrant to his pocket. His face was drawn.

'How is she?' he repeated.

'A lot better,' said Betty. 'But she was in a pretty poor way when she stumbled into our bar and collapsed. Frozen stiff, covered in muck and blood, her feet tied up in bits of plastic and Sellotape.'

'Sounds like Fancy,' said Jed. 'She always goes for the dramatic.'

He hurried over to the armchair, momentarily taken aback by the figure swathed in blanket and towels. But her face was rosy from the heat of the fire, now stoked up, and her smile was radiant. Jed was the only person she wanted to see in the whole wide world.

'Jed. Oh, Jed. I'm so glad to see you.'

He pulled a chair up and found her hand. He saw its state, beautiful nails broken, cuts and scratches. 'They told me you'd gone home. I thought you'd left without saying goodbye to me.'

Betty heard the stifled, growling emotion in his voice and hurried Fred out to the kitchen. She did not return until she had made a pot of coffee and a plate of the promised corned beef sandwiches.

By then Fancy had told Jed all he needed to know. Shock never showed on his face. He had seen too many horrors in his time on the force. But this cold-blooded attempt at killing still shocked him. Fancy would have died, alone, in a cold black tunnel. Like being buried alive. Bound up, a prisoner.

Betty put the tray down on the table. 'Thought you might like a coffee, Inspector, and a bite. We're off to bed now, if you don't mind. Busy day tomorrow. Early beer delivery.'

'Thank you very much. You have both been very kind,' said Jed.

'And there's still that offer of a bed upstairs,' said Betty to Fancy. 'Don't worry about the alarm. We can reset it from upstairs.'

Jed poured himself a coffee and milk and a dash for Fancy. She took it gratefully. And managed a few bites of sandwich.

'I still think you should go to hospital to be checked over,' he said.

'I'm not moving,' she said. 'I feel safe here. And I feel doubly safe now that you're here. Remember, whoever put me down the mine thinks I'm still down there. They don't know that I got out, unless that paramedic tells them. I didn't trust him.'

'I can't see how the medics could be involved. Maybe they get a handout from some accident insurance broker, and you were slipping out of their hands. Don't worry about them, but I will check.'

'I hadn't thought of that. I'm getting paranoid.'

'They would have suggested you signed something on the way to the hospital, when you were at your most vulnerable. We have a lot to talk about, Fancy. I've been busy, found out a few interesting things. But this is not the time to tell you. You need a good night's sleep. Have you got any painkillers?'

'There's that bed upstairs,' suggested Fancy. 'Clean sheets, warm room, lavender-scented. Betty gave me two paracetamols.'

'Good, take them. Then I'll help you up. Can you walk?'

'I walked all the way down from Mam Tor. I think I could manage a few more steps. But where am I, Jed? It seems a lovely place.'

'This is Castleton, in the Hope Valley. A beautiful little village that keeps growing.'

'Hope Valley? I like that. It's giving me hope.'

'Hope for both of us.' His face broke into a smile. The first smile of the evening.

# 21

Castleton — Friday Morning

Fancy awoke in a strange bed, wondering where she was. The low ceiling was white plaster and sloping, with two corner beams. It was a double bed but she was alone. The pillows were soft and down-filled, the sheets clean and warm, a pink eiderdown hung over the edge. The curtains were pink, white and frilly. A feminine room.

The previous day's events came drifting back to her and she wondered how she had found the strength to get out of the mine, wade the canal, climb the hundreds of steps. She felt stiff and bruised, aching all over. She wondered about her poor feet but felt no inclination to investigate. They could wait.

Then she remembered Jed. Where was he? He had helped her upstairs, out of her sodden and ruined clothes and into a clean flannel nightdress provided by the thoughtful land-lady. He had cut off the duct tape and bagged it with the clothes.

She had fallen asleep almost immediately.

But where was he now? She wanted to

know. Surely he had not abandoned her?

She heard footsteps coming up the creaking stairs and stopping outside the door.

'Are you awake, Fancy?'

'Yes, but only just.'

'Betty's bringing up a pot of tea. I couldn't carry it.'

Jed opened the door. He was dressed, outdoor coat, carrying several carrier bags. Betty was following with a tray of tea. She smiled at Fancy.

'Well, I must say, you are looking a lot better. That's what a good night's sleep will do for you. There's a bathroom along the corridor. I'll put out some soap and towels and shampoo. You'll be wanting to wash your hair.'

'Thank you, I do indeed. I need a good wash. That canal water . . . '

Betty looked bemused. She knew nothing about the canal or the mine. No one had told her the full story. 'I'll leave you to it, then. Breakfast any time you want it. I do B&B, you know, so it's no trouble.'

Fancy looked stricken as Betty closed the door. 'B&B? This is a B&B? I must pay her.'

'Already taken care of, Fancy. I settled up this morning, before I went out.'

Fancy struggled to sit up, longing for that cup of tea, a luxury in bed. No one ever brought her tea in bed. She always had to get up and make it herself. There were two cups and she poured out both. It was pretty pink and white china. Jed nodded his thanks.

'Did you stay the night here?' she asked.

'I did. The whole night. Your virtue is now compromised. But you were dead to the world, reeking of canal water, hair like a haystack. Decent bed, though.'

'Always the perfect gentleman,' said Fancy, sipping her tea. More nectar. 'Never felt a thing.'

'Nothing happened, much to my regret.' Jed was grinning now, his glasses glinting in the sunlight from the window. 'And to show you my appreciation, I'm showering you with gifts.'

'I love being showered with gifts,' said Fancy, as he put the carrier bags on her bed. 'It's my favourite shower.'

'Castleton is not exactly a shopping Mecca, but you could hardly spend the day, pinned together in a blanket. Your clothes will be examined by forensics. They're more rags than clothes, anyway. You'll be amazed at what they can find. Traces from the boot of that car, for a start.'

'Clever stuff.'

Fancy looked at the label on the big carrier bag. It was from a walkers' equipment shop.

The small bag was from an unnamed boutique.

'Had to guess the sizes,' he apologized.

He'd bought her a packet of three white Sloggi pants and a soft white running bra, size medium. He had also bought a blue tracksuit with white flashes down the sides, again size medium, playing safe. No shoes, but a packet of ramblers' white double-strength thermal socks, size medium.

'I didn't think your feet were ready for shoes.'

Fancy burst out laughing. 'Is that how you see me, a medium girl?'

'Sorry, is that wrong? I can take them back.'

'No, they're perfect,' Fancy said quickly. 'I'm sure everything will fit and I'm very grateful. It was thoughtful of you.'

Jed finished his tea. 'I'll see you downstairs when you are ready. Then we can talk. Take your time. By the way, that mine is called Pennyroyal. It closed twenty years ago. A lot of history down there.'

★   ★   ★

The bath was a luxury too. She wallowed in the warmth, washing the scented water over her skin with a big sponge. There was only a

326

shower at Lakeside and only a shower at her converted church home. Both seemed a million miles away, a million years ago. It was if neither existed any more.

She washed her hair, rinsing out the reek of canal water. She must have smelt awful. Poor Jed. She dried herself and her hair with big towels, again blessing the generosity and kindness of her hosts. The underwear and tracksuit fitted, more or less. They were baggy and made for any shape of person. The sky-blue was a change after a week of wearing nothing but black and white.

No make-up. Her hair hung loose down her back, drying in the warm air. Socks on her poor feet. The cuts and scratches still hurt but the socks were big and comforting. She came down the stairs gingerly, hanging onto the hand rail, not wanting to slip on the polished treads.

'Good morning, everyone,' she said, tentatively, wary of her welcome.

'What a transformation,' said Fred. He was busy cleaning the bar. 'Did the early beer delivery wake you?'

'Never heard a thing.'

'We've laid a table over here for you in the corner. Privacy, if you've got things to talk about. Breakfast menu on the table. We can rustle up anything you want.' Betty was already busy, bustling about.

'What are you going to tell me?' Fancy asked Jed after ordering simple scrambled eggs and coffee. 'About last night?'

'There's an awful lot to tell you,' said Jed. 'You'll have to wait. We'll find a quiet spot. Then we'll go back to the centre and collect your things. They will have cleared your room out this morning. Room 425 is no longer yours. The girls will have done it for you.'

'Good heavens. Has everybody gone home now?'

He nodded. 'They're getting ready now for the next influx of students.'

'How awful. I never said goodbye to anyone.'

'They have a website — perhaps you could post a message on there.'

'That's a good idea. I don't want them to think I just walked out.'

'You were dragged out.'

'I had already packed everything except toiletries and night things. I don't know what I'm going to do. The drive back to London is out of the question at the moment; my feet are too sore.'

'Don't worry about that. If you definitely have to go back to London, I could drive you, any day. Then you could collect your car later.'

'There's no reason to go back just yet. I could stay here for a few days,' said Fancy, the idea taking hold. 'I like Castleton. It feels very safe.'

'There's Peveril Castle to look at on the edge of town. Henry II built it. A Norman church, big caverns open to the public. Then there's the Town Ditch, although you've probably had enough of caverns and mines.'

'No caverns. But a castle in the open sounds good. Yes, I'll ask Betty if I can stay for a few extra days. I could give her a hand, washing up or something.'

'Pubs have dishwashers.'

'Shows how ignorant I am.'

'But I'm sure she would enjoy your company.'

The toast arrived, hot and freshly crisp, no brown roof tiles. The butter melted on it quickly. Marmalade came in a lidded pot, not fiddly little packets.

'So, Mr Detective Man, aren't you going to tell me anything?' said Fancy, her mouth full of hot toast. 'I'm the victim here, remember?'

'It's all your own fault,' said Jed, pouring himself another black coffee. 'You brought it on yourself.'

Fancy gasped, then remembered to close her mouth. 'What? Me?'

'Yes, you, Miss Jones. I had a look through

a couple of back copies of *Macabre Mysteries* and I found the cold case of *The Missing Cover Girl* that I wrote for the magazine. You may remember it.'

'It was very well written,' said Fancy in a small voice.

'But someone, and maybe it was you, had added a footnote. It said: 'This cold case is getting warm. Perhaps there will be further developments in the case of *The Missing Cover Girl*. Watch this space.''

'Oh yes, that was me,' said Fancy, trying to remember why she had put the footnote. 'There was an empty space at the bottom of a page. It needed filling up. And I thought there might be more DNA evidence surfacing. You never know. And, of course, it was a plug to make people buy more copies of the magazine.'

'Well, you did more than that. You alerted someone that quite soon the case might be blown open. So they decided to either scare you off, or kill you off. They nearly managed to do both.'

'A sobering thought,' said Fancy. 'Do we know who it is?'

'We're getting close. But the DNA database came up with something interesting. They had a Jane Doe on ice. Jane Doe is an unidentified female body.'

'I know that.'

'She'd been in a road accident earlier in the year. No identification and no one came forward with a missing person. Eventually a Jane or John Doe will be disposed of, usually cremated, but a DNA record will be kept, or some small piece or organ, just in case.'

'No one claimed this accident victim?'

'No. But computers are wonderful. Her DNA print matched that of Thelma March-ant, the twin who disappeared all those many years ago, when Rupert Harlow was charged but acquitted of her murder.'

'So he hadn't murdered her.'

'No, he was innocent.'

'And then she was declared dead seven years later and Grace inherited her sister's half of the brewery millions. Grace had it all. Grace also married Rupert. She had the man and the money.'

'But Thelma wasn't dead at all. She was living out her own life. We don't know where or how, but she must have been furious. Firstly, she had wanted Rupert Harlow to be found guilty of her murder, and sentenced. I can't remember if the death penalty was around then. And she wanted her rightful share of the inheritance. Instead of which, she got neither. Which made for one very angry woman.'

'Why didn't she come forward and claim her share of the inheritance?'

'Perhaps she thought she would be charged with wasting police time by letting Rupert go to court on the murder trial. She may have thought she would go to prison or that Rupert would sue her for false evidence, the bloodstains.'

'Oh dear,' said Fancy, absorbing all these new facts. 'It sounds like the plot of one of my books.'

'Far too fanciful and far-fetched. Real life can be even more astonishing. Let's go back to the conference centre and fetch your things. You wouldn't want to lose your lecture notes. They might impound them. And I need you to make a statement of everything that happened last night, everything you can remember.'

The landlady, Betty, was delighted that Fancy wanted to stay on. 'Of course, we shall be pleased to have you around. Stay and recuperate. Castleton is a pretty place. When you feel better, you'll be able to explore. People walk for miles.'

'I could give you a hand. Make sandwiches or something.'

'Are you any good at bar work?' Fred asked.

Fancy looked blank.

'Pouring a pint?' Jed whispered.

'I could collect glasses, wipe tables, stack the dishwasher,' Fancy offered.

'Done,' said Fred. 'You're hired. When you're wearing shoes again.'

Fancy met Jed outside the pub. She had plaited her hair, having nothing to pin it up with. No combs or grips. All lost in the canal. She eased herself into his low-slung car. Jed had forgotten to buy a toothbrush. She wanted her things.

'I was glad it wasn't your car boot,' said Fancy.

'You thought it was me?' Jed hid his bewilderment.

'By then I didn't trust anyone. And you were always disappearing.'

'It's called work. Remember that funny word beginning with W?'

'You told me you were retired.'

'Semi-retired. There's a difference. I didn't want you to think I was watching you.' He put the car in gear and eased away from the roadside.

He drove slowly through Castleton, pointing out sights to Fancy. 'That's another good pub. That's a good café. That's where I bought your tracksuit.'

'I like this place,' said Fancy contentedly. 'I like it more and more. And all these great stretches of hills, rising everywhere, all around, so very green.'

'Spoken like a true townswoman. They're called dales.'

'Now you're making fun of me.'

'Not everyone is in awe of being with a famous crime writer, especially when she hasn't any shoes on and her plaited hair is coming undone.'

'Perhaps someone ought to have a look at my feet,' said Fancy, still feeling the soreness. And one felt swollen. Perhaps she had broken a metatarsal. They were such tiny, bird-like bones. 'And I'm covered in bruises.'

'I agree. A trip to A&E is on this morning's agenda.'

'Thank you. I don't want to be a nuisance.

'You're not a nuisance.' He was reading her reluctance. 'They don't do plaster these days for foot bones. They do strapping. The police surgeon should have a look at them, too. It's all evidence. I do have to get a statement from you, if you can cope with going through it all again.'

Fancy nodded. 'I'll try to remember everything.'

The journey back to the conference centre was nothing like her previous journey. She had Jed with her and she was overwhelmingly happy in his company. She had never felt so completely at home with a man before. She remembered the tender way he had looked after her last night, removing her sodden clothes with every thought for her modesty and comfort.

Again sponging her sore feet, wiping the blood off her face and crusted nose. He had helped her into Betty's voluminous flannelette nightdress, never a hand straying to the wrong place.

'Thank you,' she had said, touching his limp arm, forgetting he couldn't feel it.

'Thank you for trusting me again,' he said now, not taking his eyes off the road.

She began to recognize where they were. Soon they would be back at the conference centre. As they turned into the driveway, Jed crawled over the speed bumps, careful not to jolt her. The entrance was deserted. No cars, no people. Everyone had gone bar a few staff cars in the furthest area, some delivery vans unloading boxes.

'This feels very strange,' said Fancy. 'As if the life has gone from the place.'

'A different sort of activity. Cleaning. Preparing rooms. Getting ready for the next influx of people. Another conference about to start.'

There was a steady hum of vacuum cleaners and floor polishers. Trolleys of cleaning products stood about. Foyer flowers were being changed. Windows wiped down and polished. It was a mammoth spring clean.

They went through the entrance hall into the vinery, not expecting to see anyone they knew. A woman was perched on a stool by the noticeboards, taking down the dozens of notices, AGM minutes, instructions to do this and that, photos of speakers and details of the courses.

She almost fell off the stool when she saw Fancy, her mouth open.

'Good heavens, Fancy,' she said. 'We all thought you'd gone home.'

'No,' said Fancy. 'A slight delay. Call it technical research.'

The woman got off the stool and gathered the fallen papers and her wits. Drawing pins had scattered everywhere. She took her time collecting them. Fancy did not move to help. Jed seemed to be searching in his pockets with his good hand.

'Well, that's all right, then,' said Jessie, the conference secretary. 'We thought it funny, you not saying goodbye to anyone. Someone handed in a pearl necklace, by the way. They found it on the lawn at the dregs party. It might be yours. We all thought you had gone off to a private farewell party.'

'I don't know what you mean,' said Fancy.

'A private, fond goodbye,' said Jessie with a wink. 'Well, you know. You and the dishy detective. It wasn't exactly a state secret.'

# 22

## Still Friday Morning

'We've come to collect Fancy's case and her lecture notes. Her car is parked on the upper level, above Lakeside,' said Jed easily. 'Probably the last car left.'

'Oh, that's fine,' said Jessie, still flustered and red-faced from bending over. 'Take your time. The luggage may be in the manager's office. I don't really know. So much stuff gets left behind, especially hanging behind bathroom doors. You'd be surprised. I'm just clearing up all the odds and ends. The dining room is still open and the hot water heater's working. You can make yourself some coffee, if you don't mind a packet of instant Nescafé and those fiddly milk cartons.'

'Thanks,' said Fancy. 'That would be lovely.'

'That's fine. No need to hurry, is there?' Jed asked. 'Such a lovely morning. We can enjoy the gardens by ourselves.'

Jessie flashed a smile. 'Sorry, gotta go, folks, got a hundred things to do before I go home. I want to be leaving soon. Hope you can find everything you need. Like the tracksuit. Different,' she flashed at Fancy, as if she had just noticed.

It was indeed strange. All the vibrant life had been drained from the conference centre. Empty dining room, now cleared of breakfast debris and nothing set on the bare tables for lunch or dinner. The next conference would not start until the next day, Saturday. The bar was closed, shutters down. No one in the shop or foyer. In fact, no one around at all. Except the domestic staff.

The gardeners were busy mowing the lawns. Walking on the soft grass was bliss for her feet. Fancy and Jed had the gardens to themselves, sat on the bank of the sloping lawn, mugs of coffee in their hands, watching other people work. The local birds had returned, chirruping happily in their tall trees. They saw a squirrel hopping across the grass. The itinerant tabby looked forlorn and wandered over to them for company. He meowed hopefully for some breakfast sausage.

'What are we waiting for?' Fancy asked nervously. 'I want to get my things and be gone from this place. It's so creepy.'

'Not long now, Fancy. And it isn't creepy. That's your writer's imagination working overtime. Look at the sunshine and the lovely gardens. Be patient, Fancy. I'm with you. Nothing can happen to you while I'm here.'

'The place is deserted.'

'So is the Sahara desert. And Northcote is not deserted. You'd be surprised how many people are here, all working.'

Fancy tried not to think. The horrors of the previous evening were returning. The journey in the car boot, being dragged down the steps to darkness and nowhere. She knew it would be a long time before the nightmare receded. Castleton might help. It was a lovely place. She really liked the sprawling village.

Surprising thoughts were coming into her mind. She had never really enjoyed living in London, all the fumes and noise and traffic. The lodge seemed unnatural. Neither a proper church, nor a real home. A sort of halfway house, suitable for an eccentric London writer in limbo, but not forever. And the endless litter, mindless street furniture, rutted roads, the yobs trawling the streets looking for trouble.

On the drive through Castleton she had seen several House for Sale signs. No harm in looking around. She could write just as well in the depth of the Dales. What was email for? Snail mail still existed, too. Derbyshire was not exactly the other side of the world and the views were beautiful. And she fancied somewhere with a proper bath. She wanted to spend years soaking away the bad memories.

'Is there anything else you've forgotten to tell me?'

'Yes. We discovered there was an extra person at the conference. Someone who had no authority to be here, but nobody noticed, of course; who was wearing a white badge like a lot of other first-time delegates; who ate in the dining room, drank in the bar, but went to nothing. No talks, no lectures. Not a writer. It took a long time to track him down.'

'The invisible delegate. So who was it?'

'We think it was his car that was set on fire. And it had a French number plate. The plate has been traced through the vehicle licence records. Bless all those databases.'

'Who to?'

'A man called Leo Cousseau. Address: unknown.'

'But I thought it was Grace's husband's car that was set on fire? The farmer from Cornwall.'

'He was never contacted and has never been here. I've had it checked. He knew nothing about his wife's death and never drove up here. He's still in Cornwall, with his sheep.'

'Poor man. So he didn't know?'

'No, not till last night. Local CID had to go round to tell him.'

'Who was supposed to phone him?'

'The conference secretary, Jessie Whytely. Bad news is her unfortunate responsibility. She phoned from the conference office, or so she told everyone she had. Then a man, apparently from Cornwall, arrived, so everyone thought it was the husband, Rupert Harlow. But the farmer didn't arrive. It was instead a man called Leo Cousseau from France.'

'But I thought you interviewed Rupert Harlow.'

'So did I. But I actually talked to this Leo Cousseau. He's a consummate actor. I was taken in. But later, I thought, where's the remorse, the grief? His wife has been found dead and he shows no emotion. He knew all the facts and his story was word perfect.'

Fancy stood up, unsteadily, putting down the coffee mug. Her head ached. 'I want to collect my bags and notes and be gone from here. Everything freaks me out. I'm nothing, nobody, only a hard-working crime writer. I don't mean to harm anyone. None of this is anything to do with me.'

'Money never sleeps,' said Jed.

Fancy's wheelie suitcase, briefcase and lecture notes were found, safe and sound, stored upstairs in an admin office. She wanted to put them straight into her car but Jed stopped her. Not yet, he said. She was beyond arguing. She knew she couldn't drive till her feet felt they could use the pedals.

'We could take my things back to Castleton?' said Fancy.

'Sure,' said Jed. 'We'll put them in my car instead.'

They were standing at the window in the Lakeside room opposite 425. Somewhere in the distance, far beyond normal sight, was the North Sea. The room had been made up for the next occupant: hospitality tray refilled, fresh towels and soap laid on the bed. They did not touch anything.

Fancy could see an oblique view of her beloved vintage car in the higher car park, or from this distance what looked like her car. It was the only small brown car in an empty space and a long way off, so it must be hers. She clenched Jed's hand.

'Is this going to be all right?' she asked. 'Can we go now?'

'Of course. Everything is in hand.'

'I don't understand any of this, but I'm

343

trusting you,' she said.

'Trust me some more. Are you any good at acting?'

'Very good at acting. Oscar-nomination class. Do it all the time.'

'I want you to come down with me now and pretend to say goodbye to me in the car park.'

'Is that all? A fond goodbye?'

'A very fond goodbye would be acceptable. But don't get any ideas. Then I want you to go round to your car and pretend to get in it. The door will be unlocked. But don't actually get in. Don't in any circumstances get in it. Open the door, switch on the ignition, pretend to have dropped something, then immediately duck round the back and roll over the perimeter brick wall.'

'Roll over the wall? In my state? With my bruises? You're joking.'

'I'm not joking. Get over that wall and crouch down, flat on the ground if you can make it, hands over your head. Do exactly as I say, Fancy.'

'This is ridiculous,' said Fancy, irritated. 'I don't understand a word.'

'It may well be ridiculous in which case you can have a good laugh. We will both have a good laugh. And I'll help you back over the wall. Do you really want to be scared for the rest of your life, always looking over your shoulder, anxious to see who's following you?'

'No, I don't.'

'Then do this one last thing.'

They went downstairs in the lift and out of the back entrance to the top car park. It was a gloriously sunny day, one of the last of the summer, with a light, caressing breeze playing through the trees. The scent of the flowers, roses and lavender, wafted across from the garden and mingled with the sharp freshness of cut grass.

'Well, goodbye, Jed,' said Fancy, reaching up to give him the briefest kiss on the cheek. It felt a little rough, as if he had not had a good shave that morning. 'It's been nice meeting you.'

'If that's a fond goodbye, then I can't wait for the other kind,' said Jed dryly, patting her on the shoulder like a pet dog. 'Take care, sweetheart.'

'I'm nobody's sweetheart,' she said, turning away. It wouldn't rate as a scene from *Casablanca*.

★   ★   ★

Fancy walked across to her car, awkwardly in the thermal socks. The tarmac was hard. The

Vanden Plas looked a bit different but perhaps her eyesight had been affected by the darkness in the tunnel. It looked more polished than her old vintage, which had lost its shine. Same colour, same shape, even the same make.

She opened the unlocked door. It was different inside. The walnut facia and leather-covered steering wheel had gone, replaced by boring grey plastic. This was not right. She wanted to protest, to say something to Jed, but he had walked away and was going back into Lakeside. She turned the ignition key as told, and ducked down to pick up an imaginary handkerchief.

She hurried round the back, stumbling up a bank and rolling over the brick wall. As she hit the ground below, she heard a roar and an explosion. Flames shot into the air and Fancy hid her face from the heat and noise. The brick wall protected her from the explosion. She was shaking with fear and with indignation. Her car was on fire, a wreck, a smouldering mass of twisted metal.

How dare Jed expose her to this danger. She could have been killed. He must have known the car might be booby-trapped. Yet he let her go within yards of the car, her beautiful little vintage car, now wrecked and burning.

Jed leaped over the wall and crouched down beside her. His body protecting her. But from what? He was too bloody late.

'Are you all right?'

His arms were close round her but she was quivering, not from fright, but with fury. She fought him off with what strength she had left, mindful of what still hurt and was painful.

She turned on him fiercely, eyes blazing. 'No, I'm not all right. How dare you! How dare you put me through that! What a nerve. I could have been killed. You knew it was booby-trapped, yet you told me to go and turn on the ignition.'

'Calm down,' said Jed, holding her close. 'You're safe. I would have pulled you into Lakeside if you hadn't gone behind the wall. We weren't sure. We only guessed it might be booby-trapped and that they would use a mobile phone to detonate it remotely. But only if they saw you appearing to get into the car and turn on the ignition. We had to have proof. The bomb wouldn't go off instantly; there's usually a time lapse on these things. There were vital seconds that gave you time to take cover.'

'How could you? I'll never forgive you, you beast, you horror.' Her eyes were smarting with tears.

'Yes, you will, because now you're going to be safe.'

There seemed to be a lot of activity in the car park. Several police officers arrived, running, dousing the flames with fire extinguishers. Then she saw two more police officers coming out of Lakeside, holding a man between them. His hands were behind his back, handcuffed. He looked vaguely familiar. Late forties, short grey hair, tweedy clothes.

'That's Leo Cousseau, who blew up his own car in case anyone noticed the French number plates. This is the man who has been wandering round the conference all week, wearing a white badge that he was not entitled to wear. He's been eating with you, drinking with you, wandering about but not going to any lectures, planting nasty things to scare you.'

'I don't understand,' said Fancy. 'Who is he?'

'He kidnapped you yesterday, bound and gagged you and drove you to Pennyroyal, dragged you down all those steps and left you to die in the heart of a disused lead mine.'

'It was him? But why? There was a woman, too,' said Fancy, still trembling. 'I heard lighter footsteps.'

'We know. And here she is, in the custody

of Detective Inspector Morris Bradley. I'm sure he will have read her the Miranda rights.'

DI Bradley came out of Lakeside, a struggling, handcuffed woman in tow. WPC Richmond was escorting her, her hand firmly on the woman's arm. Dorothy craned her head and caught sight of Fancy. She nodded. A couple of police cars were screeching to a halt at the top of the car park. Cousseau was being down-headed into the back of one of the cars. It was like a scene from a film.

He was pale-faced, ashen, shaking.

The woman was also being taken to one of the police cars. She was in jeans and a T-shirt, her face wreathed in fury.

'How did you get out?' she shouted at Fancy, dragging back from her escort. 'We made sure you would never get out. You were supposed to die down there. Got a broomstick or something? Going to write a sequel to *Harry Potter* now, are you? You and your idiot Pink Pen Detective. You're nobody, you're nothing. My mother was worth a hundred of you. She deserved every penny. And she would have got it if it hadn't been for your stupid magazine, stirring up an old, dead story.'

She was bundled into the second police car, WPC Richmond getting in beside her.

The woman glared at Fancy through the window.

DSI Bradley had his mobile phone in his hand. He clicked it off. 'Recorded all that?' asked Jed. 'She always did talk too much.'

'You need no introduction to that woman,' Jed went on. 'You know her as Jessie Whytely, the writers' Conference Secretary, but she is also Jessica Cousseau, the only daughter of Thelma Marchant, one of the twin sisters, and now rightful heir to the brewery millions.'

Fancy felt faint. 'Jessie?'

'Nothing to be afraid of any more. Those two are going down on two counts of murder and attempted murder. Forensics will find evidence to link them with Grace's murder. Then there's counts of arson and administering a prohibited drug. We can prove the kidnap, the lead mine and the booby-trapped car. And guess what we found in the boot of their car? Some of the seed pearls from your top. They'd been torn off. We'll trace their mobile phone records, find evidence of journeys to London. The attempts in London will be more difficult to prove, but we'll get there.'

Jed helped Fancy to her feet and over the wall. She could not look at her car, still smouldering under mountains of foam. She couldn't speak.

'Time for more coffee, I think.'

He guided her through Lakeside and back into the garden as the two police cars sped towards Derby. And prison cells. For a very long time.

# 23

## Epilogue

'Jessie drowned her own aunt?' Fancy was incredulous. She was sitting on the grass, rubbing her feet. 'It's unbelievable. Grace was her aunt.'

'That's what people will do for money. A lot of money. They do horrible things.'

'But I don't understand. And then all those happenings to scare me in London and again here at Northcote. The hand in a biscuit tin, the scarves, the fire in a bucket, the date-rape drug, everything that has happened to me? Who did them? And why?'

'Mostly the invisible man. No one knew he was here or in London or took any notice of him. He's merely a middle-aged, grey man, wandering about. It's too easy to infiltrate a conference. There are no real checks. How many white badges can you read? The writing is usually so small and illegible, you'd need a magnifying glass. Did you ever check the identity of the person sitting next to you in the dining room or the bar or at a talk? It was too easy for him to mingle.'

'And I suppose he slept in Jessie's room.'

'She had a room in the oldest part of the house, lots of corridors to get there and a big bedroom with several beds. He could slip along late at night. The maids would never notice one more body. They don't do a bed count.'

They were sitting on the lawn again. There was still the same sunshine, but now it was a different air, more relaxed, a scent of freedom. Fancy could still smell the burning Vanden Plas. She grieved for her beautiful old car.

The admin office, alarmed by another fire in the car park and all the police activity, were thrown from their usual guest turnaround routine. Everyone was huddled in groups, gossiping. The housekeeper ordered a tray of coffee to be sent out to Jed and Fancy on the lawn. It arrived with a plate of chocolate cake, homemade oatmeal biscuits and a pot of coffee. A feast indeed. But they had no appetite for food. They were both high on adrenaline.

'So Leo Cousseau was smuggled in by Jessie,' Jed went on, 'arriving here as if he were Melody's farmer husband from Cornwall. But he arrived too early. That was their first mistake. I got road traffic to check the first possible arrival time, even if he had driven at sixty miles per hour the whole way, without a stop. He arrived at least an hour too early. At the time, it didn't mean that much.'

'We all thought, poor man. We were sympathetic.'

'Then the lack of grief. DI Bradley interviewed him first and it didn't seem natural, even if they hadn't been getting on as a couple. The man was a cold fish even when they took him into Derby to identify the body.'

'He never mixed. We didn't even realize he was Melody's 'husband' at first, then we thought he wanted to be left alone. But as you say, he wasn't the husband.' Fancy sipped more coffee. She was beginning to calm down.

'The next mistake was setting fire to Clousseau's car. They suddenly realized it had French number plates and someone might have noticed and queried it. But instead of removing them or changing them, they set the car alight. The fire officer said it was arson, a small incendiary bomb ignited from a mobile phone, he said. But he noted the plates and we checked them.'

'A bit like my lovely vintage car,' said Fancy, trying not to sound accusing. She was still angry about its destruction.

Jed leaned forward and took her hand with his good one. His skin was warm and smooth. His eyes behind his glasses were glinting with warmth. 'Don't fret, Fancy. I know vintage when I see it. I had your Vanden Plas towed away last night. It's safely locked in a staff garage. The car that was blown up today was some unidentified abandoned vehicle from our police pound, very similar, but no licence, no insurance. It would have gone to the scrap yard eventually.'

Fancy felt ashamed of her feelings. She could only nod her thanks and squeeze her gratitude. Her car was safe. 'Thank you, Jed, thank you.'

'Thelma had spent her whole life seething with indignation and fury that Grace had got both her husband and her share of the fortune, planning revenge. But she didn't know what to do without disclosing her own duplication. She had staged the blood spatters, the disappearance, in the hope that Rupert would be charged with her murder and found guilty.'

'But he wasn't. He was acquitted. She must have been gutted.'

'She was. She then spent years plotting and planning how to get the money. Somehow along the way, and we don't know with whom, she acquired a daughter, Jessica.

There's no record of a father or a marriage. Thelma went to live in France with Jessica, where she made a modest living acting in dubious French movies and television, using the name Melody Marchant. It seems to be a popular name in that family.'

'So Jessica was brought up in France. Once I heard her say, '*Bonne chance*' or something, and I thought how clever, she's bilingual.'

'I also once heard her use some French expression, and thought, like you, it was neat. But no, it was her native tongue. For years she was indoctrinated by her mother that the brewery fortune rightfully belonged to her. It was part of their life together. Jessie met and married Leo, and they also both believed that the money rightfully belonged to Thelma and that it would eventually pass to them. Quite a strong motive. Must be worth millions by now.'

'Then Thelma was killed in a road accident and all the DNA came to the surface. You told me about the unidentified Jane Doe.'

'Jessica and Leo panicked. Thelma was already declared dead. She could not die twice. They could not identify her. They let her stay in the morgue with a Jane Doe tag on her toe.'

'How horrid. Her own mother.'

Fancy's head was spinning. But she wanted

to know more. 'How did my magazine come into all this?'

'Thelma had been getting it for the last few years. She's on your subscription list. I checked. Slightly different name, but Jessie's French address. As long as *The Missing Cover Girl* stayed a mystery, she was safe. But when we started prodding around, she knew that she had to do something about it. And her solution was to get rid of you. With you out of the way, the magazine would flounder and die. No more cold cases to be solved.'

'But Thelma was killed in a road accident.'

'One of those things, stepping off a kerb in a busy street without looking. Could happen to anyone. And she carried no identification. But she had a daughter who took up the cause. Jessie vowed that no one would ever know the true story. And at the same time, she had her eye on the money. She would inherit if she came forward as Thelma's daughter.'

'Were there any more mistakes?'

'We found a roll of duct tape in the glove compartment of Jessica's car, which exactly matches the type of tape used to secure your wrists and ankles. And a white flower was found in the car park, which I'm told you were wearing in your hair at the dregs party. There will be forensic evidence in the boot as

357

well. The most minute fibres from your clothes, strands of hair, and the seed pearls from your top. They planned it, the two of them. They planned to leave you to die in Pennyroyal.'

'I might have died.'

'Yes, you could have died.'

'The Pink Pen Detective saved me. She told me what to do. How to get out and save my life.'

'Good for her. That reminds me, Fancy. Our next stop is the A&E department, to get them to look at your feet.'

'What will happen to the brewery millions?'

'I don't really know. It depends on what Grace put in her will. She may have left it all to her husband and his sheep, or perhaps left a trust for an annual writing prize. Children's stories, of course. She may even have left a legacy to the conference. They're always short of money.'

Fancy sat back on the lawn, the coffee growing cold in her hand. She had come to some sort of calming decision. 'I'm not going to write any more crime books,' she said. 'I've had it with crime. It's all too complicated. Who would ever think of a plot like that? Never. My Pink Pen Detective has gone to ground. She'll spend her retirement in the Bahamas, sunning herself, meeting wonderful men and drinking piña coladas.'

Jed watched her closely, for evidence of extreme shock or mental disturbance from the blow on her head. But there was none. It was reassuring. His clever and wonderful Fancy Jones was as right as rain, her eyes sparkling, ready to start writing again, to take up life, to live it to the full.

'So what are you going to do?'

'Maybe I'll move to Castleton, buy a cottage in the village or a small bungalow on the outskirts. I saw several this morning as we drove through. They looked really pleasant. Something with a bit of a garden to sit in with an iced drink. Get a dog and a cat. Maybe that tabby needs a home. I'll write funny, chick-lit romances. Always wanted to write funny books. Books that will make people laugh and feel happy, feel good.'

'We have several well-trained, retired police dogs wanting good homes.'

'Get me one of those, please.'

Jed let the moment hang in the air. He was not sure how she would take it.

'Will your new home in Castleton permit unexpected visitors? Visitors who are over-worked, usually dead-tired, who might arrive at unsocial hours?'

Fancy leaned across and looked at his dear face, the forward fringe of Roman-cut hair, the twinkling eyes. This was the only man she ever wanted to see, a moment she wanted to keep inside. He could come at any time of the day or night.

'That's the only kind of visitor I really want,' she said. 'I might even give you a key.'

# Acknowledgements

My grateful thanks to Dr David Thomas for putting me straight with medical queries.

More thanks to a retired Chief Superintendent Detective for meticulous police procedure.

To Simon Brett for his kind permission to name him as an evening speaker and star performer.

To the editorial team at Robert Hale for their endless patience.

All the delegates and officials at this Conference are entirely fictitious. If anyone thinks they spot a fleeting resemblance, then I am unaware of it. I'll buy you a drink next year.

We do hope that you have enjoyed reading this large print book.

Did you know that all of our titles are available for purchase?

We publish a wide range of high quality large print books including:
**Romances, Mysteries, Classics**
**General Fiction**
**Non Fiction and Westerns**

Special interest titles available in large print are:
**The Little Oxford Dictionary**
**Music Book**
**Song Book**
**Hymn Book**
**Service Book**

Also available from us courtesy of Oxford University Press:
**Young Readers' Dictionary**
**(large print edition)**
**Young Readers' Thesaurus**
**(large print edition)**

For further information or a free brochure, please contact us at:
**Ulverscroft Large Print Books Ltd.,**
**The Green, Bradgate Road, Anstey,**
**Leicester, LE7 7FU, England.**
**Tel:** (00 44) **0116 236 4325**
**Fax:** (00 44) **0116 234 0205**

# PORTRAIT OF A MURDER

## Stella Whitelaw

Harriet Dale is an insurance claims investigator and a talented, but out of work, actress. While untangling a stolen artwork claim, she comes across *The Frightenend Lady*, the portrait of Lady Eleanor Digby-Jones — victim of a two-hundred-year-old unsolved murder. The portrait also carries a curse. Anyone who moves it, dies. Axe Winston, an international art thief, and a lethally attractive man, spells danger. And for a moment, Harriet forgets the good advice given to her by DI Brice MacDonald — with dire consequences.

# MIDSUMMER MADNESS

## Stella Whitelaw

*Midsummer Madness* follows the fortunes of talented actress, Sophie Gresham, as she struggles with the secret she is desperate to hide from her theatre company. Sophie is shocked when she realises that Joe Harrison, their tough guest producer from New York, is in fact the penniless actor she once helped out in the days when she had more heart than sense. When Sophie is catapulted into a dazzling new television career, Joe Harrison proves himself useful, but not in the way that Sophie might have imagined . . .

# TO HONOUR THE DEAD

## John Dean

The unveiling of a new memorial stirs up deep emotions in a remote North Pennines village as the people honour their war dead. However, pride is in short supply at the ceremony as anger spills over and deep-rooted tensions rise to the surface. That night, the memorial is vandalized and an elderly war veteran is murdered, apparently by thieves after his Victoria Cross. Are the incidents connected? When Detective Chief Inspector Jack Harris is called on to investigate, he and his team discover a world of secrets and a conspiracy that stretches across the globe . . .

# THE ONE A MONTH MAN

## Michael Litchfield

Thirty years ago, Oxford was a city of fear for female students, terrorized by a killer dubbed 'The One-A-Month Man' due to the ritualistic regularity of his crimes. Advances in DNA profiling since the time of the murders has identified Richard Pope, son of a US senator and now a frontline CIA operative, as the killer — and survivor Tina Marlowe finds herself in danger once more ... The bad but brilliant detective Mike Lorenzo, exiled from Scotland Yard, is assigned to trace Tina before she is tracked down by her lethal enemy — just the challenge he needs to redeem himself ...

# AN INVISIBLE MURDER

## Joyce Cato

When travelling cook Jenny Starling starts her new job at Avonsleigh Castle, she is thrilled. She envisions nothing more arduous than days spent preparing her beloved recipes. But when a fabulous bejewelled dagger, one of the castle's many art treasures, is used to murder a member of staff, the Lady of the House insists that Jenny help the police with their enquiries. But how was it done? The murder was committed in front of several impeccable witnesses, none of whom saw a thing. It seems the reluctant sleuth must once again discover the identity of the killer in their midst . . .

# THE DOLL PRINCESS

## Tom Benn

Manchester, July 1996, the month after the IRA bomb. The *Evening News* reports two murders. On the front page is a photograph of an heiress to an oil fortune, her body discovered in the basement of a block of flats . . . Buried in the later pages there's a fifty-word piece on the murder of a young prostitute. For Bane, it's the latter that hits hardest. Determined to find out what happened to his childhood sweetheart, it soon becomes clear that the two stories belong on the same page, as Bane immerses himself in a world of drugs, gun arsenals, human trafficking and a Manchester in decay . . .